Series

Paranormal	Contemporary

Paranormal

Moons of Mystery
Sara's Moon (MF)
Charline's Solstice (MF)
Diana's Eclipse (MF)

War on Darkness
Darkness Defined (MM)
Order of Light (MM)
Knights of Nyx (MM)

Kisin Novels
Courting Death (MM)
Death, Love, & Tacos (MM)

True Mates
Truth in Exile (MM)
The Inescapable Truth (MM)
Truth in Lies (MM)

Lycan Detective Duet
Hart's Betrayal (MM)
Hart's Redemption (MM)

Contemporary

Ulwich Preparatory Academy
Our Last Fall (MM)
Our Secret Winter (MM)
Our Epic Spring (MM)

Oak Haven Romance
One Brave Thing (Enby/M)
All the Hype (MM)
The Bright Side (MM)

the *Brighter* SIDE

Oak Haven Romance

S Bolanos

Contents

Chapter 1

MOVIE NIGHT WAS SACRED. It had been since Jasper and I had started the tradition in our teens. Being in our thirties—barely—wasn't about to change it, though it'd be nice if my so-called bestie could pick up the takeout once in a while. What was so wrong with my place that *I* couldn't host? Not that any of that mattered now, since I was already at Jasper's apartment complex.

I made my way down the hall, painfully aware that the paper takeout bag I was cradling like it was a temperamental cat was in jeopardy of becoming a paste. My careful hold couldn't save the soaked bag for long, given how dramatically the opening was soggily listing to the side. And honestly, I felt that. I too was soaked through and eager to flop down.

I persevered until I reached Jasper's door, where I ran into a new quandary—no hands. No way could I risk changing my grip on the sodden paper that was definitely now within microseconds of disintegrating. Shrugging, I bumped the door with the toe of my sneaker. When nothing happened, I did it again with more conviction.

"I'm coming!" the shout came from within. A second later, the door opened and a shorter man with dark hair and teasing brown eyes stared grumpily. "Geesh, Mace, you act like you don't have a key. Or that it was locked," Jasper added belatedly.

"And I would have used said key if I'd had hands to spare." Something decidedly wet hit the laminate flooring with a disturbing *plop*. Belatedly, I realized my battle with the paper bag was in serious danger of coming to an abrupt conclusion. "Give me a hand?"

Jasper's eyes nearly bugged out of his head. "Good grief, how much did you get?" he exclaimed, taking some containers from the now fully exposed top.

"Thanks," I said as I followed him into the open kitchen. Most of Jasper's apartment was open—the living room, breakfast table, and kitchen basically all shared the same space—and only a door separated the single bedroom and en suite from the rest of the place. Even then, it was a decent-sized apartment, though you'd never know it by all the knick-knacks cluttering every "reasonable" surface. "You ready for movie night?" I asked, tossing the soggy remnants of the paper bag into the trash.

"Darn right I am. I've been looking forward to this all week."

I paused mid-pulling down plates and cast him a concerned look. "Is everything okay? I thought things were going well with your photography business."

He shrugged. "I suppose. But doing staged shoots and professional headshots isn't exactly art, you know?"

I set the plates down so he could start loading them with food and leaned against the counter. "Yeah, but those things *enable you* to pursue more artistic photos."

He made a characteristically sour face at the unwelcome reality check. Jasper was what you would call a free spirit. Not surprising, given that both of his parents were honest-to-goodness hippies.

"You just wait," I added with a beaming smile. "You'll snag the perfect shot and break out. Then you'll have to scramble to get enough photos ready for a gallery."

"Have I ever told you how nauseating your persistent optimism is?"

I laughed. "Only about every other time we hang out. Which, now that I think of it, makes it at least a dozen times a month. Besides, *someone* has to balance your moody ass."

"I don't tell you *that* much," he replied with a grin. "Now stop dripping water all over the floor before one of us ends up slipping, and the night turns into an ER marathon instead of a rom-com one."

"Yeah, yeah. Towels in the hall closet?"

Jasper straightened, his face screwed up in concentration. "Uh..."

"Right, they're still in the hamper waiting to be folded."

"I was getting to it!" he argued as I walked toward his bedroom.

A minute later, I was back, wearing some spare clothes I kept here for those nights that I ended up staying over and toweling my hair. "That's better. Hopefully, the rain lets up before I head out tonight."

Jasper paused on his way to the couch, holding both our plates, and looked at me with surprise clear on his face. "You're not staying?"

"Can't." I plucked my plate from his grip before he could forget he was holding it. "I have to be at the shop to accept a book delivery. The shipment is already late, and I'm not leaving anything to chance."

"Well, you know the offer always stands if you change your mind."

"I know." We plopped down on the comfy couch and pulled up our watchlist of movies for the night. While he was selecting the perfect one to kick off the marathon, I noticed a small, discolored bronze statue chilling on the end table. "I see you've been raiding the antique shop again. Please tell me you're going to clean it before taking pictures."

"Absolutely not!" he replied indignantly, tossing the remote onto the coffee table. "The patina is the whole point. Besides, it's on loan. I can't very well return it in a different condition than when I borrowed it."

"You say that like you actually plan to take it back," I teased.

"Shut your face," he replied with a smile that negated any potential sting.

Once we'd finished eating, we leveraged the pause between queued movies to clean up the plates and grab some dessert—aka wine—before curling back up on the couch. I should have expected that after two glasses Jasper would want to talk instead of keep watching the tragedy of miscommunication happening on screen.

"So I was chatting with the crew," he began without any sort of preamble, leaning forward to refill his wineglass and topping mine off while he was at it. Since staying the night and waking up even more ass-crack of dawn than I already had to wasn't an option I wanted to entertain, it seemed a ride share would be in my future.

"You talked with the crew about something before *me*?" I asked in mock horror. The group of artists he collectively referred to as "The crew" rarely, if ever, got information before I did. Perks of being the bestie, even if I didn't have an artistic bone in my body.

"Only because they wouldn't be here tonight." Of course they wouldn't. Movie night had been *our* thing since we were fifteen, when my family had kicked me out and Jasper's had taken me in.

"*Anyway*, like I was saying, I was talking with the crew about the new neighbor."

"Oh no! Not sweet old Mary Ann. I hope she's okay."

Jasper waved his hands. "No, no. Not *that* neighbor. The one across the hall."

I thought hard about who had lived there. "The mean mechanic?"

"That's the one. He moved out last week, and a new tenant has already moved in."

I snorted. "Good riddance. That guy was like a rain cloud ruining a perfect day, no matter how nice we were to him."

"Oh, I don't think he was all that bad. At least he was hot."

I side-eyed my best friend. "You're only saying that because you had a crush on him."

He rolled his eyes dramatically. "Only for like a couple of weeks. Then, even I couldn't deal with his rotten personality."

"So what's the new tenant like? Have you had a chance to meet them?"

Jasper turned shy and fidgeted with the fringe of the pillow he'd been holding. Oh no, I already knew where this was going. "Sort of. We bumped into each other the other day, and I swear, Mace, it was freaking electric."

I barely bit back a groan. Yep, another crush. I couldn't help wondering how long *this* one would last. "Really, Jasper? I thought we talked about this. You promised that when you turned thirty you'd give them up." While I didn't expect that to happen magically overnight, it had been months, and he didn't appear to be making any effort at all.

"Okay, I did. And I will!" he added quickly. "But hear me out. This guy is beyond hot, like makes-mean-mechanic-look-drab smoke show hot." I arched my eyebrows at him, and he huffed. "Stop looking at me like I'm shallow!" I raised them higher. "Ugh, you're the worst."

"And I seriously need to look into a rehabilitation program for chronic crushers."

Jasper snickered. "I don't think that came out the way you meant it to. Besides, you're not even letting me finish. This guy is *totally* crush-worthy. Killer looks aside, he's unbelievably nice. He holds doors open for people and offers to help Mary Ann with her groceries. He even sounds like he means it when he says good morning."

"Uh-huh. So does this outrageously attractive, decent human being have a name?"

"Atticus," he sighed dreamily, then took another sip of wine. Oh, this was bad. We'd blown right past "maybe" a crush straight into "dancing heart eyes" crush territory... and it had only been a week. Suddenly, Jasper's smooth face dipped into a frown. "There's only one problem. He doesn't seem to know I exist at all."

"I thought you said you ran into each other? A little hard not to know you exist then."

"Okay, maybe 'bumped into each other' was a bit of a stretch. We rode the elevator together." He didn't have to add that he hadn't spoken one word to the new guy; I already knew from experience. I bit back another frustrated sigh. We'd had so many conversations over the past fifteen years about this that it wasn't even worth digging into it again. And yet, I already knew I would.

"You could always just knock on his door and introduce your-self," I suggested.

He looked at me as if I'd said he should vacation on the moon. "I can't do that!"

"I assure you, you can. It's not hard. Here, I'll do it now." I set aside the remnants of my wine and went to push off the couch.

Jasper latched onto my arm and dragged me back down. "Quit playing around. I'll get to it." I gave him a dubious expression. "I will!"

The sigh I'd been fighting finally slipped out. "When? This isn't high school. You can't just wait around for someone to magically fall in your lap. You've gotta put yourself out there. There's nothing wrong with making the first move."

"I know that," he replied defensively. "And I will put myself out there. Soon. I just want to... feel him out first."

I snorted in my effort to hold back a laugh, but the laugh won. "I don't think 'feeling' him is in question."

"For goodness' sake, now who's the one behaving like they're in high school?" he asked with a quirked eyebrow.

"In my defense, you walked right into it," I replied with a smile. "Now, are you going to keep waxing poetic about your latest crush, or are we actually going to watch these movies?"

Two more movies later, the wine was gone and both of us were nodding off. We dutifully cleaned up, or cleaned as much as our half-asleep, inebriated brains could manage. Why we drank wine when neither of us could really handle it, I'd never understand.

"Love you," I said with a goofy grin, ruffling Jasper's dark hair, once we'd wrapped up and made it to the door.

"Love you too," he replied, wrapping me in a tight hug that I happily returned. We made quite the pair—damn near polar opposites in every way—but he'd been my best friend since I was fifteen and he always would be. "You sure you're good?" he asked for the third—or was it the fifth?—time. "Come on, Mace, just stay the night. You can get up early for the delivery."

I scrunched my nose in distaste, though was a little impressed he remembered after all the wine. "I'll be fine. Besides, I can always crash again after I'm done since I don't have to work-work until the afternoon."

"Always the optimist," he said with a grin.

"You know it." I booped his nose, and he swatted my hand away. "I'll let you know when I get home," I said, unlocking the door. When it refused to budge despite turning the handle in every direction, I pulled harder and nearly pitched backward when it abruptly swung open."

Jasper cackled like the unhelpful fiend he was. "You really make it too easy sometimes."

"I see how it is. Taking advantage of poor old tipsy me to play pranks. Just for that, *you* can get the takeout next time."

"But you always pick the best stuff," he countered, holding the door as I marched into the hallway.

"Liar."

He winked, and we shared another laugh, then bid each other good night–again.

I rested my back against the wall beside his door and took a moment to bask in the warm, floaty feeling. Drinking during movie nights was one of the few times I let myself indulge. Though maybe I needed to have a chat with Jasper about checking the ABV content of the wines he chose. We'd only split a bottle, and I felt like I was swimming. I was tipsy enough to be happy about it, but still.

I pushed off the wall and laughed when I nearly fell on my face. Oh yeah, *definitely* needed to chat with Jasper. Ooh, or maybe I could start picking out the wine. I shook my head and chuckled to myself as I regained my balance. He'd never go for it. Snorting to myself, I fished out my keys only to remember after I yanked them out of my pocket and sent them sailing, that a rideshare was picking me up. Shaking my head and mentally swearing to be the one to pick out next week's wine, I bent to retrieve the errant keys and naturally ended up on my hands and knees because my balance was *shot*.

"You're not honestly driving home like that, are you?" a rough voice asked as I not so steadily got back to my feet.

I glanced over to see who Mr. Judgy McJudgerson was and found a man roughly my age frozen in the process of unlocking the door across the hall, a displeased scowl pulling the corners of his mouth down. I snorted a laugh at the irony of bumping into the very guy I'd just spent the last four hours trying *not* to hear about. Funny, Jasper hadn't mentioned that his neighbor kept weird hours. Oof, I was getting old if I thought midnight was a weird hour to get home on a Friday night.

"Is that funny to you?" he asked.

Instead of responding right away, I ran my gaze over him. He was tall like me, wore his rich brown hair in a shaggy cut, and had the most startlingly gray eyes I'd ever seen. He also had biceps for days, and though it didn't look like he was rocking a six-pack, he clearly took care of himself.

"I guess you *are* as hot as Jasper said," I said with a wide grin, leaning back against the wall and crossing my arms. And exactly like every other guy Jasper crushed on.

Confusion momentarily lightened his features, then the storm clouds rolled back in. "What? Nevermind. Forget I asked. Just tell me you're not about to stupidly get into a car drunk," he demanded.

I raised my eyebrows at the unwarranted hostility and decided it was time he got called out. Sadly, Tipsy Brain was still in charge, and it had different ideas of how to accomplish that.

"Oh, I'm getting in a car," I said in defiance, grinning wickedly. He opened his mouth, no doubt to lecture me on safe driving, and I held up my cell. Thankfully, it stayed in my hand and didn't decide to take up flying like my keys had. "Scheduled a ride share thirty minutes ago. Not that it's any of your business." Right on cue, my phone chimed with a notification of my driver's arrival. I gave Mr. Judgy a mock salute. "See you around."

Somehow, his scowl actually deepened. He rolled his eyes and pushed his way into his apartment. I laughed to myself as I made my way out to the front of the building. Atticus may *look* like Jasper's type, but his personality was about as far away from it as possible.

Chapter 2

I CLOSED THE ANNEALER so the glasswork I'd been working on for the better part of the afternoon could slowly cool down while my apprentice, Maria, put away the punty the glass had been attached to. Sweat threatened to drip into my eyes despite the cloth headband tied around my temple to prevent it. I grabbed a damp towel from the cooler and smiled at Maria as I tossed her one as well.

"Great job today," I said, scanning the hot shop and making a mental inventory of things that still needed to be put away.

She smiled brightly, her lip piercing glinting in the light emanating from the furnace not far away. "Thanks, boss." On the other side of the shared hot shop space, Barry chuckled, prompting Maria to wink at me.

"Don't encourage her," I grumbled at him, then turned to remind Maria, "We're a team. I'm not your 'boss'."

She finger-combed her bright pink hair, repositioning her sagging ponytail. "Okay, *not-boss*, how do you want to divvy up cleaning?"

"I've got it. You go enjoy your evening."

She scowled at me, hands on her hips, sass radiating off of her like heat radiated out of the glory hole. "That's the third time this week, Atticus. You know I'm perfectly capable of putting this place back in order."

"I know. I also know it's Saturday and of the two of us, you're more likely to have plans."

"You could have plans if you wanted to," she fired back.

"Could I?" I asked playfully, mentally crossing my fingers that she wouldn't go there. Should have known better.

Her sigh could have formed a sizable glass bubble. "One of these days, you *have* to let me set you up."

"But not tonight," I replied with forced cheer. Dating and I didn't really get along. I kept weird hours, was a sweaty disaster more often than I wasn't, and basically sucked at all things social. And if I didn't know that for myself, I'd had enough boyfriends nail the observations home.

"It's never the night," she scoffed, not backing down.

I glanced at Barry for support, hoping he'd recognize the silent plea on my face as his cue to intervene. Except he had his head down, dutifully pretending he couldn't hear our conversation. I floundered to come up with an adequate defense to put her off as I returned my focus to my persistent apprentice. Clearly my desire to avoid this conversation was written on my face, because she held up a hand and shook her head.

"I'll let it lie. *This* time," she added with an intense finger point at me. Somehow her concession felt like more of a threat than her offer to set me up. "For once, you're right. I do have plans tonight. You remember my sister, Sofia?"

"Of course! When did she get into town?" I asked with genuine enthusiasm.

She squinted at the clock on the far wall. "She should be rolling into town in an hour, assuming she didn't hit traffic."

"Be sure to tell her I said hi," I said, as I gathered the tools we'd used for today's piece. "And remind her she owes me a new set of cork paddles!"

"Will do!" Maria called back before slipping through the metal barn door that separated our workspace from the other "cooler" workspaces of the Oak Haven Artists' Co-Op."

I resumed organizing the tools, then grabbed the stiff-bristled broom to remove any lingering remnants of glass from our breakage earlier.

"You really should let her set you up," Barry said from beside the kiln he used to fire his pottery.

"Not you too," I groaned, banging the dustpan on the inside of the trash bin. We'd salvaged what glass shards we could earlier, but some pieces were too small to save.

"I'm just saying it couldn't hurt," he countered. I grunted, but that didn't dissuade him. "It's been, what, three years since Tom? Longer since your last date?"

There was nothing internal about my wince, though it was a toss-up whether it was at hearing my ex's name or realizing just how long it had been since I'd bothered to try. "Maybe," I conceded after a minute. "But I don't need anyone setting me up. I'm perfectly capable of getting a date on my own."

Barry held up his hands in surrender. "Not disputing it. On another note, I thought you were taking a hiatus from commission work to create some original pieces."

"If only." I flopped onto the bench I'd sat on most of the day as Maria and I put the finishing touches on a custom set of wine glasses. Mercifully, the water I guzzled from the water bottle I kept beside the bench was still bitterly cold. Staying hydrated in the hot shop was always a challenge.

"What's going on?" Barry asked, sealing up the kiln, then mirroring me on his bench. "Is it about needing the cash up front?"

I shook my head. "No, nothing like that. Just experiencing a crippling case of the horror vacuum."

He sucked his teeth. "That blows, man." He chuckled. "Get it? Because you're a glassblower?"

"Har har. Anyway, that's why I picked up a couple of commissions. Better to fill the time than dwell on my creative ineptitude," I finished sullenly.

Barry's bushy gray brows pinched together, and he rested his arms on his thighs as he stared intently at me. Finally, when I didn't think I could take another second of his scrutiny, he straightened. "Nah. That's not it. Don't get me wrong, I'm sure that's part of it, but it's not all of it. Something has got you worked up. You normally wouldn't have dropped that catch earlier."

"Noticed that, did you?" I rubbed the back of my neck and gave him a self-deprecating grin.

"Dude, across the street noticed. So what gives? What really has you distracted?"

I released a defeated sigh. Barry's attention to detail was great... until it was turned on you.

"Ha! I knew it. Did something happen?"

"You could say that. I was kind of... a jerk to a guy last night," I admitted, though saying it out loud didn't really capture how shitty I'd been.

"Wait, did you hook up last night? No wonder you don't want Maria setting you up with someone," Barry said with far too much excitement.

"Uh, no. It was a guy in my new apartment complex."

He smacked his knee. "That's right! You finally told your old landlord to shove it."

"All I said was that if he couldn't be bothered to fulfill his end of the rental agreement and fix the washer, then I didn't have to hold up my end and pay rent." I rolled my shoulders, the discomfort of the whole situation making me anxious all over again. I avoided confrontation whenever possible, but even I had to draw the line when the washer flooded the building for the third time and I was expected to cover damages.

"Isn't that what I said?" Barry asked.

I shook my head. "Anyway, it had to be close to one in the morning. The guy was leaving the apartment across the hall and was totally drunk. I could have been nicer about it, or better yet, minded my own damn business..." I trailed off and looked at him meaningfully.

"Oh." His eyes widened as understanding dawned. "*Ohhh*... I get why the idea that he might be getting into a car like that would upset you."

"But he *didn't*. I was just a complete ass to him out of nowhere. Turns out he was taking a rideshare, so it was a moot thing, anyway."

Barry's mouth twisted to the side, the way it usually did when he was ruminating on an idea. "This has got you really twisted up, huh?"

"I guess. I didn't think so, but then I spent the rest of the night tossing and turning and beating myself up." In a huff of frustration, I ripped off the soggy headband, letting sweaty strands of hair fall into my face.

"Sounds like you should try to make it up to the guy. Is he attractive?"

"What does that have to do with anything?" I asked a tad aggressively. What did it matter that the stranger had dancing blue eyes, or blond hair that softly fanned across his forehead, or that the smirk he'd given me had woken up a lust I'd feared had abandoned me?

"Because there's more than one way to be a dick," he replied with a conspiratorial wink.

I flung the gross headband at him. "Dirty old man."

"Ack!" Barry squawked, trying and failing to fend off the sweaty fabric that had landed smack dab on his equally sweaty shirt. "Glass sweat stays on *that* side of the shop."

I laughed, the sound filling the room and further lifting my dreary mood. "You might have a point," I said once I'd sobered up and retrieved the offending headband. "Now I just have to hope to bump into him again so I can do that. And figure out *how* to do that," I tagged on belatedly.

Barry snorted. "Being right is cheapened when I'm covered in your work nastiness." He scrunched his face in distaste, and I couldn't help but laugh again. "As for 'how', I hear an apology goes a long way. Beyond that, I'm sure you'll figure something out."

"Yeah, I'm sure I will." The real question was how long it would take to offer said apology and if that would be *before* my anxiety stole what little sleep I managed.

Chapter 3

I GENTLY CLOSED THE door to Jasper's bedroom. He was still passed out, curled around a pillow like he was worried it might try to escape while he slept. While I didn't have to be at Literary Lighthouse until ten, I couldn't pretend to be asleep any longer, no matter how comfy Jasper's bed was. The curse of training yourself to wake early. No such thing as sleeping in on weekends.

Once I'd gathered my things, I did a final sweep to see if there was anything else. Finding nothing, I let myself out and locked the door behind me. I was checking my phone for any urgent messages from the morning staff when someone cleared their throat. I looked up and started.

"Oh, it's you," I deadpanned, narrowing my eyes at Atticus, who also appeared to be leaving for the day.

He gave me a guilty smile and an awkward wave that I refused to label as cute. "Hey."

I pocketed my phone, reassured that the new hire hadn't burned the bookstore down, and straightened. "You'll no doubt be relieved to discover that I'm sober."

He winced. "Okay, I totally deserved that. For what it's worth, I'm sorry I behaved so poorly last week. It's, uh, really been bothering me. You didn't deserve that, and I was way out of line."

"Oh," I said again, because I was a regular wordsmith first thing in the morning. Maybe Jasper's judgment *hadn't* completely plummeted and Atticus *was* a nice guy. More research would be required before a definitive ruling could be made. "Apology accepted, I guess."

His smile became more genuine as relief seemed to blanket him. I was getting a better idea of how the man had caught my bestie's attention. "I was just on my way out. Was planning to hit up Kaleidoscope for some fresh coffee. Would you be interested in joining?"

My eyebrows shot straight up. From rude to apology to... whatever this was.

Atticus cringed. "I didn't mean it like that. Not a date. Definitely not a date." He threw his hands out in front of him, panic spreading like a rash on his face. "Not that you're not dateable. Just that I wouldn't... wasn't... I mean, I date you. Men! I date men," he clarified in a rush, his face turning an impressive shade of pink. "Oh, for fuck's sake." He facepalmed, bringing the rambling to a merciful end.

My lips twitched as I fought not to smile. "Thank you. It's been a while, but it's nice to know I still have a chance on the market."

"Let me try this again." He dropped his hand and gave me a sheepish smile. "I'd like to make up for my dreadful behavior by buying you a coffee."

I considered him for a minute. Unlike many of the men Jasper set his heart-eyes on, Atticus had a higher chance of making it past the crush phase, if only by virtue of living across the hall. "Now that you mention it, I haven't had coffee today." I pretended to check my watch. "And I have some time before I need to be at the shop. Throw in a pastry and you've got a deal." And I'd get to run some reconnaissance without looking like a creep.

"I could do that. Meet you there in a few?"

"It's a date," I said, just to watch his eyes widen in mild panic. "I'm Mason."

He held out his hand. "Atticus."

"I know." I winked and turned to go, waving a hand over my head as I walked to the elevator. "See you there." It probably would have made more sense to wait for him to regather his wits and take the elevator together, but I'd never been one to pass up a good mic-drop moment. Jasper and I had that in common.

Exactly five minutes later, I pulled into a spot in front of Kaleidoscope. That was one benefit of being awake far too early for a Saturday—plenty of rock star parking. I went inside and began perusing the ever-changing, thematically quirky menu, though I was pretty positive I already knew what I was getting.

"Look what wiggled out from between the pages!" Jace, my favorite barista, shouted in greeting as he emerged from the back room. He set down the box of recyclable to-go cups and straightened the "he/him" tag on his apron. "Did they let you off your leash or did you escape?" he asked with a wide smile.

"His drink is on me," Atticus inserted from behind me, his rough voice causing goosebumps to erupt on the back of my neck. I shrugged, and Atticus stepped up beside me, presumably to ensure that I didn't buy my own apology drink.

Jace glanced from me to him, his eyes getting wider with each pass. "Oh. My. Sweet caramel heaven. I am *so* here for this. Well, don't keep me in suspense. When, where, how. I need details. All of them."

A laugh burst out of me at Jace's over-the-top antics, while Atticus looked like he was hoping the floor would open up and swallow him whole. I got myself under control and placed a reassuring hand on Atticus's arm—and *holy shit*, the man was jacked. "Sorry to disappoint you, but he's simply buying me a coffee to make up for being a Class A jerk the last time we ran into each other. And a cheese danish," I added with a smirk.

"Okay, now I *know* you're having a go at me. Atty has to be the nicest, sweetest, least jerkiest person I've ever known," Jace said with a scowl, crossing his arms for good measure.

I reconsidered the awkward man at my side. That was two people now convinced whole-heartedly of Atticus's saintly demeanor. Maybe I'd just caught him on an off day. First impressions were important, but they weren't everything. Abruptly, I realized I was still touching Atticus in a way that directly contradicted what I'd just told Jace about our non-date status. I quickly released him and smiled brightly at Jace.

"So... I know it's not on the menu right now, but do you think—"

Jace held up a hand. "One Silver Lining. Got it. And what about you, handsome? What are you feeling today?" Jace asked, turning his attention to Atticus.

"Hmm," Atticus mused, leaning against the counter while he scanned the eclectic menu behind the barista. "What would you suggest?"

"Depends. Are you still on a frozen frappe kick?"

Atticus smiled warmly, revealing faint laugh lines around his mouth and eyes. "I'm going into the shop later, so yeah."

"In that case, how about a Forgotten Secret? It has that dark roast I know you love, but a splash of fun with blue spirulina."

"Uh, do I want to know what spirulina is?" Atticus asked, shooting me an anxious look.

"Just think of it like extra good for you stuff that just happens to dye the milk blue. You'll love it." When Atticus still looked dubious about the recommendation, Jace unpacked the sass. "Excuse me, when have I ever steered you wrong?"

Atticus chuckled, and I found myself smiling at how relaxed he looked when he did that. "I don't know why I ever doubt you. Okay, we'll take a Silver Lining and a Forgotten Secret as well as a cheese danish and one of those English muffin egg sandwiches."

Order placed and paid for, we scooted down to wait. A few minutes later, we had our orders in hand.

"You, uh, don't have to stay if you have somewhere to be or you know, you just don't want to," Atticus said as he placed the plate holding his breakfast sandwich on top of the glass holding his frozen drink, which did in fact have a solidly blue layer. "I probably should have specified the drinks to go. That was inconsiderate of me. I'll just let Jace know."

I threw out a hand to stop him, surprising both of us. "No. It's fine. I enjoy eating here. I also wouldn't mind joining you. If that's alright?" Not to mention, my recon mission for Jasper was already bearing so much fruit. I couldn't walk away *now*.

"That'd be nice. You sure you don't mind eating with a Class A jerk?" he asked with a small smile.

A laugh burst out of me at the unexpected playfulness. "I *may* have misjudged you. Just a little," I said, pinching my index finger and thumb together.

"That makes two of us," he said as we took a seat at a table by a window. "I really am sorry for how I acted last week. I swear that's not like me. People drinking and driving is just a big trigger for me." He rolled his frosty glass between his palms, his gaze firmly on the light dusting of cinnamon decorating the top. "But I shouldn't have assumed or been so rude."

The last of the frostiness I felt toward him thawed. It seemed we'd both made assumptions. "How about a do-over?"

His head jerked up, his gray eyes wide with surprise.

I smiled and held out my hand. "Hi, I'm Mason Albright."

"Atticus Garner." His warm hand wrapped around mine, and my pulse spiked. I was acutely aware of the rough calluses on his hand and how his grip was firm yet soft, much like the man himself.

Suddenly feeling awkward, I withdrew my hand and hid behind taking a sip of Kaleidoscope's take on a London Fog. "In the interest of new beginnings, we both know why *I* was out so late—"

"Do we?" Atticus asked, the laugh lines around his eyes crinkling.

I nearly choked on my drink at the unexpected playfulness, and I had to remind myself I was only here for reconnaissance. For Jasper. "Touché," I replied, and if it sounded a bit strained, that was nobody's business but mine. "My bestie and I have a standing movie night."

"Really? On a Friday? Not that I'm ever doing anything interesting beyond working up a sweat on a Friday night, but I imagine other people have legitimate plans."

Okay, now I was beyond curious. "Working up a sweat" could mean *a lot* of things. It would be so like Jasper to develop a crush on a guy who only did hookups.

"Not that there's anything wrong with hanging with your bestie on Friday," Atticus quickly added when I didn't fill the void with a response.

"It hasn't always been on Fridays," I said, circling the rim of my cup and trying not to think about why we'd started movie night all those years ago. "There were even times when it was only once a month instead of every week. We adjust as needed. Normally, I'd have stayed the night, especially when we've been drinking, but I had to be up early for a delivery."

Atticus sipped his drink and waited a breath before asking, "Delivery of what?"

"Oh, books. I'm the manager of Literary Lighthouse Bookshop."

"That's pretty cool. Maybe you can en*lighten* me why it's called that and why there's a miniature lighthouse on top of the store." There was that smile again. And the playfully teasing.

I cleared my throat and continued to chant in the back of my mind, *reconnaissance, reconnaissance.* "The town stories are definitely more interesting than the reality. The owner, Marcus Forester, is obsessed with them. When his wife told him she'd always dreamed of having a bookstore, he made it happen. With lighthouses. There's one inside as well, though it's hard to see under all the books."

"I don't know. Supporting your partner's dreams sounds pretty interesting to me, and sweet." His gray eyes sparkled, much like the edible silver glitter that topped my drink.

"I suppose it is. Though I've always been a fan of the story that says Mr. Forester was convinced the shores of Lake Erie would expand and wanted to be prepared."

Atticus let out a rich laugh that did a better job of warming me than the hot drink I'd ordered. "By building a lighthouse in the middle of Oak Haven?"

"To be fair, Oak Haven was much smaller then. The bookstore's been around for ages."

"I know," he replied with a wink.

Reconnaissance. Reconnaissance. Reconnaissance.

"That so?" I fired back, or would have if my voice hadn't betrayed me.

"Yeah. I grew up in Oak Haven. Went away to study my craft, but came back. There's no other place I'd rather be. This little town is special," he added wistfully.

I was on the verge of asking what "craft" he'd studied when my phone rang. A quick glance at the caller ID said it was the store calling. "I knew it was too good to last," I muttered and held up a finger to put a metaphorical pin in the conversation as I swiped to answer. "Just tell me nothing is on fire."

"There're no literal flames," Casey, the assistant manager who opened on Saturdays, said dubiously.

"But…" I prompted.

"The register is on the fritz again. I'm telling you that thing is possessed! Please come work your magic. I'll owe you one."

"You already owe me one from the last time," I grumbled half-heartedly. "I know it's an antique, but you can't be afraid of it."

"Yeah, well, Mr. Forester needs to move into this century. An updated system would do wonders for the shop, not to mention keeping track of the inventory," Casey replied. He had a point. But I wouldn't tell him I'd been trying to get the owner to update the point of sale system since I'd started five years prior.

Across the table, Atticus mouthed, "Everything okay?"

I nodded and told Casey, "You're in luck. I'm already awake, dressed, and caffeinated. I'll be there shortly." He made some more promises of owing me—not that I'd ever collect—then hung up. I pocketed my phone with a sigh. "Seems like I'm desperately needed at work."

"Sounds like it."

"Thank you for breakfast," I said, already gathering my mostly empty cup and totally forgotten danish.

"Thank you for accepting my apology." To my surprise, he stood as well. "It was a pleasure to get to know you better."

"Yeah," I replied absently, equally surprised to discover I was sad at having to leave so soon. I blamed it on not getting around to eating the danish, and not at all because I was disappointed about leaving the good company.

"So, uh, at the risk of being awkward—again—would you like to maybe do this again? Have breakfast together? It's... nice having someone to talk to over breakfast," he confessed.

"That would be... nice." Maybe not the best idea I'd ever had, because, yeah, Atticus was certainly nice to look at and not at all the grump I'd thought he was. But he was Jasper's crush and thus off-limits. Then again, I hadn't really gotten a chance to learn much about him before being summoned.

"It's a date," he teased with a knowing grin.

I laughed at how he'd successfully turned my own words back on me once more. With a farewell wave, I made my way to the exit, carefully wrapped danish in my pocket, and determined to gain more insight into the mysterious new neighbor next time.

Chapter 4

THE SCREEN DOOR BANGED shut behind me as I stepped into my parents' house. "Mom! Dad! I come bearing sustenance!" I hollered.

"Be there in a moment!" Dad shouted from deeper in the house.

I set the food down on the breakfast table, then walked to the far wall of the kitchen where a picture of Jessica, my younger sister, hung. It's a moment frozen in time. Her blue eyes, so like my father's, are brimming with laughter. Her hair is a wild halo of brown caught in the wind. The usual mix of happiness at the memory and bottomless sorrow swirled in my stomach as I pressed my index and middle fingers first to my lips, then to the photo.

"Miss you, Jess," I whispered, then returned to the table to unpack the food.

"Oh, sweetie, you spoil us," Mom said, entering the room. "You don't have to bring food *every* time you visit. I'm perfectly capable of cooking. Your father is too, for that matter."

I gave her a hug that seemed to swallow her. "I enjoy spoiling you. Besides, as your only offspring in town, I'm pretty sure it's my job. Speaking of which, any word from Carmen?"

"You know your older sister. Busy as always," Dad answered as he joined us beside the table. He squeezed me tightly in a side hug while picking up a container. "Ooh, my favorite."

"Which you'll be sharing," Mom added with a meaningful scowl that held zero heat.

"No need." I pulled out a duplicate container and passed it to her.

"Atta boy," Dad said, slapping me on the back. "Sit, sit. I'll get the plates and utensils."

I knew better than to try arguing with him, so I pulled out the same chair I'd sat in for almost every family meal over the last thirty-odd years. Many of my friends in my school days thought it was weird that I was such good friends with my parents. As I got older, though, that judgement turned to envy. I talked to them about everything, and I didn't foresee that changing anytime soon.

"Thank you, dear," Mom said, accepting her plate from Dad along with a kiss on the cheek. Married for forty years and they were still every bit as in love as when they'd first met. If they weren't relationship goals, I didn't know who was. Mason's smiling face flashed unbidden in my mind. I mentally shook my head. We'd had coffee and cleared the air. There was nothing to say we were headed toward anything remotely resembling a relationship.

"So what's big sis up to these days?" I asked, heaping food onto the plate Dad set down in front of me. "Still pretending she loves corporate life?"

Mom leaned over to smack my arm. "Hush, you. Your sister works hard, and we're very proud of her."

"Though it'd be nice if she visited once in a while," Dad grumbled under his breath. Mom either didn't catch it or didn't think it was worth commenting on.

"I suppose one of us had to have a conventional job," I teased. "Would anyone like some water?" I pushed away from the table and wandered to the cabinet where I began taking down glasses.

"Oh! There's lemonade in the refrigerator," Mom chimed.

I gave her a mock-serious look. "But is it the good stuff?"

She huffed while Dad guffawed. "I don't know why you like that powdered stuff so much. It's not even real lemonade. No matter what the container says."

"Is that a no?" I paused, fingers inches from the pitcher handle, the cold of the fridge washing over me.

"Who do you take me for? Of course, it's that awful sugary concoction."

I laughed and finished pouring the glasses—lemonade for me and Dad, water for Mom—and brought them to the table along with some napkins. "You're the best," I said, bending down to kiss her cheek before resuming my seat. "Anything new with you two?"

"Your mother has taken up gardening... again. She's convinced she can turn that black thumb of hers green," Dad said, giving Mom an endearing if slightly indulgent smile.

"I *will* be triumphant! Turns out I'd been planting things in the wrong season. Poor dears never stood a chance." She looked down at her plate sullenly, as if giving a moment of silence for all the plants that had met an untimely end at her hands.

I chuckled and gently patted her shoulder. "I have faith in you. You'll get it... eventually." I shared a look with Dad, who was doing his best to appear supportive.

"You're sweet to say so, Atticus." She gave herself a good shake and smiled. "What about you, dear? How are the new anxiety meds treating you? I know it's always a struggle to get the balance right."

"They seem to be doing well. Dr. Mary is pleased with how I've taken to them. I'm just glad we were able to find something non-stimulant that doesn't zone me out." Everyone nodded in commiseration. Sometimes stimulants were called for, but with the work I did, I couldn't afford some of the iffier side effects. "And you, Dad? Has the hardware store convinced you to retire yet?" I poked.

He snorted. "Never. They'll have to drag my wrinkled gray ass out by the ankles first."

"That was more of a picture than I needed," I said, but I also got it. My dad was a damn institution when it came to Walter Hardware. He'd been there for as long as I could remember, and there was no better man to go to for advice on how to fix things. The only reason he wasn't running the place was that he preferred to work with people directly instead of getting bogged down by "administrative nonsense," as he called it.

"Enough about us," Mom butted in before Dad could go into yet another lengthy speech about how the hardware store would crumble to the ground without him there to keep everyone on their toes. "Tell me more about what's been going on in your world. A little birdie told me you've become a bit of a workaholic." That would undoubtedly be Maria.

"I'm not a workaholic," I scoffed, rising to gather the dishes and taking them to the sink.

"Then what has you at the hot shop until all hours?" she countered.

I stiffened. Not for the first time in my life, I wondered how my mom managed to know everything. It had to be spies. Finally, I shrugged. "Just bored, I guess. Don't have much going on these days." I could practically *feel* my parents sharing a concerned look. "I'm fine, really," I added as I finished rinsing the dishes and turned the water off.

"Mmm hmm," Mom hummed, unconvinced.

"You gotta put yourself out there, son. We want you to be happy. That's all we've ever wanted. But you can't wait around for the perfect man to waltz into your life," Dad said emphatically.

I snickered. "I don't know about *waltz*." Maybe throw his keys at me. Okay, now I was really putting the break before the scoring. Though now that Dad mentioned it, I couldn't help but wonder if Mason *did* like to dance. Not waltzing, but maybe a chill club vibe. I quickly snuffed out that line of thinking. I did not need to be thinking about what Mason Albright's body would feel like pressed against mine. When I turned to resume my seat at the table, I was surprised to find them both wearing eager looks. "What?"

"You've met someone," Mom declared, damn near blooming with giddy joy.

"No, I haven't," I argued. The image of the morning sun shining through the coffee shop's large windows to illuminate Mason's face flashed through my mind. "Not really..." I hemmed. His rich laugh filled my ears, and I fought not to shrink or blush beneath my mom's knowing look. "Okay, maybe. Sort of," I quickly added when her gray eyes widened with excitement.

"Well, don't just keep it to yourself," Dad grumbled, clearly every bit as invested in my love life—or lack thereof—as Mom.

I sank into my chair with a put-upon sigh, but couldn't stop the grin twitching at the corners of my lips. "His name is Mason Albright. Have you heard of him?"

They both shook their heads, but it was Mom who said, "I don't think so. He doesn't sound like a local. A transplant maybe? Any idea how long he's been in Oak Haven?"

"No, we didn't get that far. We—"

Dad cleared his throat, pairing it with a warning look.

"Good grief, Harve. He's a grown man. Hearing that he's having sex won't put me in a fit of vapors. Why, just this morning you–"

"Whoa!" I interjected before she could get into details. "That's not something I ever need to hear. Besides, it wasn't like that. We were having breakfast at Kaleidoscope, but he got called away for an emergency at work before he could even eat."

"Oh. Well, I suppose that *does* make more sense. You've never been one for those 'hookup' apps," Mom said, her face pinched with obvious disapproval of said "apps." Meanwhile, Dad just looked plain relieved. "Where does he work?"

"He's the manager at Literary Lighthouse," I supplied excitedly, though I wasn't entirely sure where all of this enthusiasm had come from. Hadn't I just been telling Maria and Barry that I was perfectly fine without a man in my life?

Dad brightened, leaning forward. "I think I know the fella. He comes into Walter's periodically to get things to repair shelves. About yay-high," he held his hand up just above his head, apparently forgetting he was still sitting, "light hair, easy attitude?"

"That sounds like him."

"You'd like him, Betty. Good kid, though I don't think he's been here all that long. Few years, maybe?" He scratched at the scruff on his chin as he pondered the time. Knowing him, "a few years" could easily be a decade, possibly more.

Mom rolled her eyes. "You act like I never leave the house. I've been to the bookstore."

"Shame it wasn't to get gardening books," Dad mumbled.

"Harvey Garner, what did you say to me?"

Dad cleared his throat and sat straighter in his chair. "So, when are you going to see him again?"

"Uh, I'm not sure. We agreed that it'd be nice to have coffee again," I replied, my anxiety swirling.

Mom placed a hand on Dad's forearm to stop him from saying whatever it was he'd opened his mouth to say. "Then I guess it's a good thing you know where he works. You can visit him at the bookstore and schedule a time."

The sudden spike of anxiety eased as I realized I hadn't completely missed my chance. "Yeah, I could do that."

"And maybe get a phone number while you're at it," Dad tacked on. Mom immediately smacked him on the arm. "What?" he protested. "We all know he didn't get it the first go-around."

I chuckled at their antics while mentally kicking myself. Why had it never occurred to me to get his number? His agreement to get coffee again hadn't *felt* like a brush-off. But maybe it was. I wasn't always the best at picking up cues like that. Or noticing when things were off—like your long-term boyfriend having a whole secret ass family.

"Now see what you've done," Mom scolded. I glanced up in alarm, worried about what I might have unintentionally done, to find her glaring at Dad. To his credit, Dad looked abashed at the rebuke.

"Sorry, son. Like I said, we just want you to be happy." He placed his hand over Mom's and they shared another loving look. "Would it be pushing things too far to get you to agree to at least try to get his number the next time you see him?"

I smiled, though the gray cloud of anxiety continued to lurk at the back of my mind. This was nothing new, and I loved them all the more for it. And maybe... maybe Mason and I could make each other happy. There was only one way to find out. "I'll try."

Chapter 5

SOME DAYS, IT REALLY felt like we had way too many books. Everywhere I looked, books crowded the shelves, many of which bowed beneath the collective weight. I sighed inwardly as I hefted the recently inventoried shipment off the counter. The register wasn't the only thing that could stand to be updated. There was vintage character that added an air of charm, and then there was woefully outdated to the point it actually made our jobs harder.

"What would you like me to do now, Mr. Albright?" Denise, our newest hire, asked, her light blue eyes wide with earnestness.

I set the box on the floor with a grunt. Thirty-one wasn't old, but it damn sure felt like it some days, and a seventeen-year-old calling me "Mr. Albright" wasn't helping. "I've told you to call me Mason, Denise," I said, knuckling my back. What I wouldn't give for a deep tissue massage.

Her fair cheeks stained pink. "Sorry, Mister Al-Mason. Did you want some help stocking those?"

I glanced around the tight space where I'd be working. Shelves of books bracketed me on three sides, leaving a narrow walkway about three feet across. The aisle was barely wide enough to fit me and the box. I couldn't imagine adding another person. We really needed to reorganize the store... again. Having the new arrivals by the door made sense at the time, but it was proving to be more than impractical. Especially when it meant using the pass-through shelving. Yeah, definitely needed to reconsider the layout.

"Mr. Mason?" Denise prodded.

I barely bit back a sigh. Something told me that was the most compromise I was going to get from the overeager teen. "Uh…"

I scanned what I could see of the shop. On the other side of the shelves I was facing was the front door, miraculously uncluttered for a change. Mickey was tackling the restoration of the children's section after the latest whirlwind of kiddos. I was handling the restock. Which really only left… My gaze fell on the front counter and the notoriously temperamental register.

"Can you mind the floor until I finish with these?" The other boxes could wait for now.

"Are you sure?" she squeaked.

I stepped around the box to give her a reassuring pat on the shoulder. "You'll do great. And don't worry about having to ring anyone up. Just help as much as you can, and when someone is ready to check out, grab either Mickey or me."

"Okay. I think… I think I can do that."

"I *know* you can. You've been doing great learning the store," I said with a smile. It was a slight exaggeration. There was still plenty for her to learn, but it wasn't a lie. Luckily, the vote of confidence did the trick. She squared her shoulders, and with a fierce glint of determination in her eyes, spun on her heel to take up a post in front of the counter.

I returned my attention to figuring how I was going to get the box of books to fit on shelves that were already overstuffed. It didn't take long to get lost in the work. Even my frustration at the books constantly getting pushed off of the shelf one way or the other took a backseat to my single-minded focus on accomplishing the task at hand. I barely registered the tinkling of the bell over the door as the latest customer came in.

"Welcome to Literary Lighthouse," Denise greeted. "What can we help you find today?"

I smiled at her cheery tone. She really had come a long way from being too terrified to even look at customers, let alone *talk* to them. It was a shame I didn't catch the customer's response, even though they were just on the other side of the shelves where I was working.

"Oh! Sir, I'm sorry. We ask people not to touch the suncatcher. It's very delicate and cherished by the owner," Denise said, anxiety edging her voice.

I was already prepared to step around the shelves to intervene when a familiar chuckle froze me in place.

"I know," a rough but pleasant voice replied. "I'm the one who made it."

I bent down to peer through the gaps above the books to get a look at the customer and nearly swallowed my tongue at having my suspicions confirmed. Oh shit. What was Atticus doing here? I could have smacked myself. It was a bookstore. There was no reason he *shouldn't* be here. That I'd never seen him here before didn't mean he was here for me. Right?

My brain was still a whirling storm of possibilities dismissed almost as fast as they presented, when yet another book sprang free of the shelf. It landed with a solid thump into the box I'd nearly finished emptying. "Stupid damn book," I muttered to myself. "You either stay where I put you or I swear I'm gluing your pages together." I took vindictive joy in squeezing the paperback between two of its brethren, hopefully tight enough this time that it would stay. Or maybe the tightness *was* the problem?

"Do you always threaten the books?"

I glanced up and met Atticus's gray eyes peering at me through the same gap I'd used. A yelp escaped me, and only years of tripping over Jasper's clutter saved me from falling on my ass and taking the shelves down with me. I was still attempting to regain my footing when Atticus appeared in the opening of the narrow aisle.

"Sorry about that," he said with a sheepish smile. He pulled the treacherous box out of the way. "I didn't mean to spook you."

"Oh no, it's fine. I'm fine. Not spooked at all." I dusted my hands on my khakis and cleared my throat. Way to be chill, Mason. "What brings you into the store?" I asked, stepping out of the crowded alcove so I wouldn't feel quite so caged.

"Would..." he began, then seemed to change his mind. He stuffed his hands in the pockets of his jeans—that I was *not* going to think about how well they hugged his thighs—and dropped his gaze to the floor. "After we talked the other day, I wanted to see this lighthouse bookshelf you mentioned. But only if it's no trouble," he added in a rush, his head popping up to reveal eyes sharp with anxiety.

I couldn't help but smile. Partly to put him at ease and partly because he was just that damn adorable. Maybe Jasper really was onto something with this one. "It's no trouble at all."

He visibly relaxed, his shoulders dropping from where they'd bunched around his ears, and he stood straighter, reminding me again that he was just as tall as I was. "As long as you're sure."

"Perfectly positive," I said, scooting the nearly empty box with my foot so that it slid closer to the counter. "Denise, are you still okay to watch the front? Mickey should be about done tidying the kid's section, then he'll take your place so you can go on break."

"I can handle it, Mr. Mason," Denise replied, tightening her ponytail and looking a bit like she expected to go into battle.

Mentally shaking my head, I waved for Atticus to follow me. "It's right this way." We wove around packed shelves I couldn't help but straighten. "You'll have to forgive the mess. I'm desperate to reorganize this place, but the owner is having none of it. He's convinced that *every* book in stock has to be on the floor. Doesn't help that he insists on keeping everything exactly the way his late wife left it, even though our inventory has tripled. Hence why there are books literally everywhere."

"Better than broken glass," he mused.

"Where would *that* be an issue?" I asked with a laugh as we continued to work our way to the back wall of the store. "Know of some rampaging bull taking out the local china shops?"

"Where I work, actually," he replied with a grin.

I paused and looked back at him over my shoulder, confusion undoubtedly all over my face. "In a china shop?"

A rich laugh that sounded like it had come straight from his core burst out of him. I nearly clutched my middle to quell the sudden riot of butterflies. Oh. Oh no. A good laugh was my kryptonite. Which would be perfectly fine any other time, but Atticus wasn't for me; he was Jasper's crush. Any interaction I had with Atticus needed to be solely for gaining intel for my bestie.

"Not quite, though I certainly feel like a clumsy bull at times. I work in the hot shop at the Artists' Co-Op. I'm a glass blower." Unlike his uncertainty from before, Atticus was pure confidence now.

"No shit?" He shook his head, a smile still playing around his lips. I glanced back toward the entrance, not that I could see it past the haphazard arrangement of shelving. "Wait, so when you said... You really *did* make old man Forester's suncatcher?"

"Yep. One of my first ever commissions." Though his smile was on the shy side, there was no missing the pride he took in his work.

"Wow. It's... it's beautiful. No wonder Mr. Forester won't part with it."

A sudden frown creased his forehead. "Is there something wrong with it? I'm sure I can fix it." He moved as if he was going to double back to the front of the store.

"Nothing like that," I said, coming to a stop at our destination. "I've just been trying to buy it off him since I started working here." Maybe should have kept that part to myself. At least I didn't gush about how I used to stare transfixed at the delicate pieces of glass as they swayed in the light.

"I'm glad it's appreciated. Now, about this lighthouse book-case," he said, blatantly changing the topic. Was he uncomfortable with praise? I was so busy trying to figure him out it took me a moment to register what he was referring to.

"Oh! It's right here." He frowned again, clearly not seeing the unique shelving despite my grand ta-da gesture. Vanna White would be proud. "I did warn you that it could be hard to see sometimes."

"Okay, but there's hard to see and then there's," he waved his hand in a circle at the chaos of books, "whatever is happening here."

I laughed and rubbed the back of my neck. "Yeah, I think the book situation has gotten a little out of control."

"Normally, I'd say 'it's a bookstore, that's kinda the point,' but I'm inclined to agree."

"If you look closely, you can see how the shelves start wide at the base and get progressively narrower the higher they go." I pointed to the very top, where I could just make out the faint outline of the supposed lantern room. "The top piece is solid flat wood that could stand a fresh coat of paint. Though I always thought it'd be cool if there was an actual light at the top to tie it all together."

Atticus squinted at the old, crowded shelves with their subtle curve. "If you say so." He reached for a stack of books that someone had left sitting flat atop a row of shelved books.

"You'd never know that this was supposed to be a featured display. I hate that it's just as cluttered as everything else. It *should* be visible from the moment you step inside, drawing you in," I commented as I removed another pile of mis-shelved books. Like a scene straight from one of my nightmares, a rickety shelf wobbled beneath the shifting weight. In slow motion, a couple of books tumbled free. No sooner did I clock what was about to happen than it was too late to do a damn thing to stop it.

The entire shelf tipped precariously, sending all of its books crashing to the floor. But it didn't stop there. The domino effect was in full swing now. Books from that shelf hit others on their way down, which unbalanced another shelf, causing *more* books to careen free, and another shelf and another.

Atticus and I stood frozen, helpless, as the avalanche of books landed in a heap at our feet.

"Everything alright over there?" Mickey shouted from somewhere nearby. Sadly, books tumbling to the floor was not an uncommon occurrence.

"All good!" I shouted back, continuing to stare at the disaster. "Well," I said with every ounce of enthusiasm I could muster, "I was wanting to rearrange."

He gave me a look that said he was more than a little surprised that I wasn't going completely bananas. Wasn't the first time someone had looked at me like that, and I doubted it would be the last. Slowly, he turned to look at the now empty shelves. "Hey, I can see the lighthouse."

I'd like to say I laughed because if I didn't, I'd cry. There was no telling how much damage the books had sustained or what it would take to get the shelves back in working order. But I ended up laughing so hard, I cried anyway. It was a bit of a relief when Atticus laughed with me. Once we sobered up, we started picking up the mess. I didn't dare risk the shelving again, so I began stacking the books in towers on the floor.

"You really don't have to help," I said, accepting another stack of books from Atticus. "This is my job, not yours."

He shrugged. "I feel a little responsible since I'm the reason we were looking at the shelves in the first place."

"Suit yourself." I wasn't about to turn down an extra pair of hands.

We continued to make little towers of books at the base of the lighthouse in companionable silence. Between the two of us, it didn't take long before we could see the original hardwood flooring again in all its worn, stained glory.

"So what really brought you to the shop?" I asked as Atticus started inspecting the shelves, wiggling some back into position and testing others. They were looser than I remembered.

He jerked, his hand bumping the shelf he'd been messing with so hard it nearly bounced free to land on the floor. "Not all that slick, am I?" he asked with a self-deprecating grin.

"I mean... you *could* have come in just to see the lighthouse shelves. They are pretty cool. You could have come in for a book, which would make sense, and I'd be happy to help you find whatever you're looking for. But I don't buy it." I crossed my arms and leaned against the wall after checking that it wasn't more unstable shelving.

"You got me. I, uh, realized we hadn't set a day for our next breakfast meetup. And I don't have your number, so I couldn't call and ask."

I blinked at Atticus, my brain on the verge of going offline. Holy fucking Jesus, Mary, and Joseph. He *was* here for me. "Uh..."

He took a deep breath and talked over the words I couldn't seem to find. "I was also thinking it didn't have to be breakfast. Maybe dinner? And maybe not so casual?" By the time he'd finished, his cheeks were flushed, and he was breathing like he'd just finished a decathlon.

Forget my brain going offline. I blue-screened. The only coherent thought I could form floated unattached through my mind. *Atticus is asking me out.*

"So... what do you say? Dinner tomorrow night?" he asked, grey eyes uncertain yet bright with hope.

"Yeah. That would be nice. That popular restaurant in Deer Rose?" Who was talking? Was *I* saying those words?

Crinkles formed around his eyes as he grinned brightly enough to put the suncatcher to shame. "I'll meet you there at eight." He turned to go, faltered, then turned back with a sheepish smile. "Should probably get your number this time."

"Of course." A hand that couldn't possibly be mine—no matter if it did have the same scar running across the back of it—pulled out my cell phone, unlocked it, and casually passed it to Atticus. He quickly typed in his information. There was a ding. Then he passed the device back.

"There. Now I finally have your number, and you have mine too. I'll see you tomorrow, Mason," he said. And who the fuck let the butterflies back in here!

"Looking forward to it."

He grinned and carefully extricated himself from the clustered towers of books. Then, with several glances over his shoulder, still wearing that beaming smile, he made his way to the exit.

I blinked and shook my head. At that moment, Mickey emerged from an adjacent aisle. "Way to go, boss."

I slowly turned to look at him, my brain taking its sweet ass time to reboot. "What just happened?"

Mickey snickered. "You got a date. Looks like the dry spell you've been denying is officially over. Props, he's hot."

Brain finally back in full gear, I switched to manager mode. "Good grief, Mickey. You sound like you're in high school. Go grab some boxes so we can sort this mess while we fix the shelves. I have a date. It's not a big deal."

Mickey rolled his eyes, likely to lean into the teenager act, gave me an ironic salute, and disappeared back into the aisle he'd emerged from.

I continued to stand there, still baffled by what had just happened. Not the shelves collapsing. That was par for the course. But getting asked out. It had been... a while. And damn Mickey, I was *not* having a dry spell. And now I had a date. With Atticus.

An error message flashed large in my mind.

Fuck. I had a date with Atticus.

Chapter 6

I TURNED THE BLOWPIPE in a steady roll, while the nearly two thousand degrees in the glory hole worked their magic. Slowly but surely, the glass at the end of the pipe turned white with the heat.

"Door," I said, rocking my weight back on my heel to smoothly extract the glob of molten glass. In perfect synchronicity, Maria opened the door that kept the heat mostly confined to the glory hole and shut it again as soon as I was clear. Still rolling the pipe, I took a seat on the bench, letting the pipe rest against the metal stand while Maria grabbed the cork paddles.

Sparks flared with each firm pass she made using the thick paddles, gradually shaping the malleable glass into the desired form. We repeated the process several times: roll and shape, roll and shape.

"Flash?" Maria asked.

I nodded, pleased at how good she was getting at judging how much the glass could afford to cool before risking a break. I'd just stood to put the glass to reheat back in the glory hole when the sound of chimes and birds whistling filled our corner of the hot shop.

"What is that?" Maria asked, glancing around for the source and nearly clipping the piece we were working on with the door.

"Shit," I hissed. "Thank goodness for alarms." I tilted my head for Maria to take my place, spinning the punty. "Are you okay to finish up on your own? I need to head out."

"No problem, boss." We seamlessly—or as near as possible—switched places, though I didn't let go of the pipe until I was positive she had a good balance on the weight. "Got a doctor's appointment or something?"

"Actually, I have a date," I replied, feeling smug.

She stopped moving to stare at me.

"Maria! You have to keep it moving." While it wouldn't be the end of the world if we had to start the piece over, I didn't want to if we didn't have to.

"Sorry!" she exclaimed and awkwardly resumed the slow spin. Once she had it back under control, she glanced at me. "I think I need to get my ears checked. It sounded like you said you have a date."

"That's because I did. We're meeting up in Deer Rose at eight."

Her eyes widened comically. "What the hell are you still doing here? Go, go! I can handle this."

"Thanks," I said, a grin cracking my cheeks. I grabbed my things and headed toward the exit with a spring in my step.

"And come back with details!" she shouted after me. Chuckling, I quickened my pace. Surely there was enough time to take a quick shower before hitting the road.

There was in fact *not* enough time for a shower and everything else I wanted to do to prepare, but there was no help for it now. I shot off a quick text to let Mason know I was running behind.

Atticus

> Lost track of time. Will be a few min late.

Mason

> LOL

> Glad it's not just me

Atticus

> I'll let the restaurant know in case they need to alter the reservation.

He sent back a "thumbs up," and I tossed the phone on the counter so I could finish getting ready. The bad news was that "a few minutes" became half an hour. The good news was that the restaurant didn't tell us to pound sand. That was one perk of going out on a weeknight.

"Sorry again," I said as I jogged up to the entrance to The Tinted Rose. "Sadly, time management isn't something I've completely mastered." Mason's warm laughter pulled me out of my head, and I finally got my first good look at him for the evening. "Whoa," I whispered under my breath.

Mason was already a good-looking man, but much in the way adding cane work elevated glass to a whole other level, so too did

Mason's outfit. Features that I'd admired about him before were now accentuated to the point they nearly took my breath away. At first glance he appeared perfectly casual with his hands in his pockets, but a closer look revealed an understated sex appeal.

He'd styled his blond hair to give it that messy-on-purpose look, and I'd be lying if it didn't make me want to run my fingers through it. The way he was standing said he was perfectly comfortable in the dark navy trousers that looked obscenely soft and seemed to flow over his legs, somehow making them appear even longer. He'd rolled the sleeves of his cream-colored button-down to expose his forearms and make the otherwise fancy as fuck ensemble more relaxed. Didn't hurt the way it hugged his chest either.

As I got closer, I nearly did a double take at discovering the shimmer of copper lining his blue eyes and making them pop. I was so busy drinking him in that I nearly missed that he was doing the same to me.

Suddenly, he ducked his head and seemed to chuckle to himself. "Why am I not surprised you clean up so nice?" he asked, lifting his head to reveal a twinkle of mirth in his glorious eyes. The color was so pure, I instantly wanted to replicate it in glass.

"I hope I didn't keep you waiting," I said. "So much for only a few minutes." I shrugged, but the cavalier attitude didn't quell the anxiety building in my chest. Mason was gorgeous and smart and witty. I wasn't even sure how I'd gotten him to agree to go out, especially after our less-than-congenial first impression of each other.

"If anything, I should be thanking you for running late. Now would probably be a good time to confess that the only thing I ever manage to be on time for is work." He gave me an abashed smile as he rubbed the back of his neck. "But now that we're both here," he gestured to the entrance, "shall we?"

We walked inside, where the host greeted us. He politely took our names, then led us to a small round booth where the lighting was somehow softer than anywhere else in the restaurant. There was even a votive candle casting flickering light over the petals of the small assortment of roses that made up the rest of the centerpiece.

The host set down our menus and asked if we'd like to see the wine selection.

"None for me," we both said at the same time. The host made his departure, and I glanced askance at Mason. To my surprise, a red glow tinted his tan cheeks.

"Contrary to how we met, I actually don't drink that often. Really only at home or when I don't have to go anywhere afterward. If I'm going to drink, I want to enjoy it and preferably not spend a fortune." He cleared his throat and fussed with unraveling his silverware.

I fought a smile. Mason didn't owe me an explanation or even the hint of a justification, but it was really sweet that he offered one. Suppose that meant I should offer at least a little something in return. "It's good to know you're safe when you drink. And again, I'm really sorry for my behavior that night. I was way out of line. Normally I'm better at keeping internal thoughts internal." My suppressed smile slipped free.

"I'm guessing drinking and driving touches on a trigger point?" he asked tentatively.

My grin faltered, and it was an effort to keep it from turning into a grimace. I used the time it took for the waiter to set our waters down to choose my words. "You could say that. It's not that I don't drink ever, just… not often."

"Good to know," he replied with a nod and an understanding smile. "Okay, no more heavy stuff. A night out is supposed to be fun." He held up his glass of water, and I couldn't help but chuckle as I mirrored him. "To a fun evening in good company."

I echoed the toast. We clinked our glasses together and took a sip before setting our glasses down. "Now," I began, picking up the menu, "I don't know about you, but it has been *a while* since I was here." Oops. Did I just accidentally admit to not having been on a date in recent history? Shit. Mason ducked his head, and it took me a moment to realize he was laughing to himself. "What?"

"I promise I'm not laughing at you," he said, lifting his head. "I'm just so relieved it's not just me. The way this town talks, you'd think everyone was either dating or already paired up. No room for bachelors in the gossip column."

The conversation remained light as we discussed nonsensical things. We placed our orders, and I marveled at how natural talking with him was. Not long later, the waiter returned with our entrees.

"So, you're not originally from Oak Haven. Are you?" I asked, loading my fork with potatoes.

"What gave it away?" His broad grin lit his face so much that for a second, I forgot what we were talking about. I frantically scrambled for the thread of conversation and a reasonable reply.

"Well, for starters, it's not called the gossip column. It's just news."

He tilted his head back to release a rich laugh. "I feel like I walked right into that."

"You said it, not me," I replied cheekily, earning myself another laugh that warmed me every bit as much as the furnace back at the hot shop.

"I mostly grew up in Colorado, but travelled a bit in my late teens. Sometime during college, my bestie's family rolled through here. Jasper and I liked it so much that when we finished school, we settled here. It's nice to be somewhere where being gay isn't treated like a crime," he added so quietly, I was sure it was really for himself.

I could worry about why that extra bit sounded so significant later. Right now, I had a far more pressing issue. "So, Jasper. You and he..." I left the question unfinished as I stared way too intently at the piece of pork I was cutting. When Mason didn't immediately respond, I risked a peek at his face. To my surprise, a confused frown pinched his face. I could see the moment he understood what I was asking.

He laughed. "Goodness no. Don't get me wrong, I love Jasper, I do. But we'd kill each other if we ever tried dating. We may get on great as friends, but as prospective lovers we couldn't be more opposite." I barely checked a relieved sigh, but something in Mason's expression told me he clocked the relief just the same. "Full disclosure, it's been a while. Like longer than I care to admit," he added sheepishly, his cheeks turning a light pink.

"Then I guess that's another thing we have in common." I grinned, hoping it would alleviate any lingering embarrassment. "I'd like to say—and have said to my apprentice—that I don't have time to date. But... yeah." I pushed around a lonely green bean on my plate with my fork. Okay, maybe it wasn't just Mason's possible embarrassment I was worried about so much as my very *real* embarrassment.

"I hope you're not opposed to talking about your work, because being a glass artist has to be one of the coolest occupations I've ever heard, and I'm going to need to know everything," he playfully demanded. I wasn't ashamed to admit how grateful I was for the blatant change of topic. The last thing I wanted to get into was my ex, *why* he was my ex, and why I'd avoided dating for so long.

"I don't mind at all. I'll tell you anything you want to know about glassblowing. And probably a bunch you don't," I added as an afterthought with a grin. "Though honestly, it'd be a hell of a lot easier to show you."

He sat up straighter, his eyes visibly shining with excitement. "Wait, that's a thing I can do?"

"Of course. Not like there's some strict rule about who's allowed in the hot shop and who's not. You should totally stop by sometime."

He bit his bottom lip, his teeth pulling lightly at the soft flesh. "I might have to take you up on that."

Chapter 7

THERE WAS SOMETHING SERIOUSLY wrong with me. Absolutely no part of last night's date with Atticus had anything to do with reconnaissance. Not the place—which I'd picked. Not the sexiest outfit in my closet—okay, second sexiest. And certainly not the bronze eyeliner—even if it did make my eyes bluer.

I was two seconds away from calling up Jasper and spilling the whole sordid truth; I was so appalled with myself. Then, my phone dinged with a notification. Fully expecting it to be Jasper, I opened the messenger app by rote.

Atticus

I had a really great time last night.

Guilt warred with excited butterflies. I'd be lying if I said the conversation hadn't flowed effortlessly. We'd laughed, shared details about ourselves—nothing too drastic, very first-date level stuff. But even admitting that much forced me to admit that I wanted there to be a second, and a third, and maybe more. I'd always struggled to connect with the guys I dated. A therapist probably would say it was a fear of abandonment that held me back. But I *connected* with Atticus. And it had felt like the most natural thing in the world.

While I was lost in my labyrinth of conflicting emotions, several more texts came through.

Atticus

> Also probably should have said last night, you looked absolutely incredible.

> I can't stop thinking about your eyes

> WOW that was *way* too much

> Why don't these apps have a delete function? Or at least an edit.

> Oh look, it does. Don't suppose it will do any good now though since you've definitely already read the message. Someone should really take my phone away from me. I didn't even know it was possible to ramble in a text. Shutting up now *facepalm*

I bit my lip, but it did nothing to stop my grin. Excitement buzzed in my chest like all the butterflies had synced their flapping. Or maybe they were bees. Either way, Atticus's adorable series of messages effectively side-tabled my uncomfortable guilt.

Mason

crying laugh emoji

For the record, I think the rambling is cute. I had a great time too.

Atticus

You're sweet to say so. But then you're sweet all the time.

Heat rushed through me at the innuendo that I might *taste* sweet as well. I was probably reading too much into it, but then I was also pretty sure the train I was on had abandoned the rails a while ago.

Mason

You only think I'm sweet because you don't really know me

Atticus

I'd like to

Also, now I'm thinking of you like one of those sour candies where the outside is super sweet, then the inside is tart. I've always loved those.

I read the messages, then read them again. If I bit my lip any harder to keep from smiling like a clown, I'd put a hole in it.

Mason

Is this your roundabout way of asking me out again?

Atticus

pouty face What if I was hoping you'd ask *me* out?

A laugh—okay, a giggle—burst out of me. I was typing my response and hitting send faster than I could think about what I was doing.

Mason

I really did have a great time. What would you say to a repeat this Saturday?

Atticus

> *smiling blush face* I'd say it's my turn to pick the place. Let me noodle, and I'll let you know tomorrow morning. Just be sure to keep your afternoon open.

Normally, that'd be a problem on a Saturday since I came in late and typically stayed 'til close. But for a change, I was actually opening so Casey could go to an event out of town.

Mason

> Done. Already looking forward to it.

As if the universe knew I was signing up for something I definitely shouldn't be, my phone rang with a hard dose of reality. I quickly swiped to answer and prayed my voice wouldn't give me away.

"Jasper, hey. What's up?" I asked in what I hoped sounded casual and not at all fifty shades of guilty.

"Where are you? You were supposed to be at the apartment an hour ago," Jasper said, sounding more than a little exasperated.

I glanced at the time and frowned. "We have hours yet before Movie Night. Though I guess while I have you, any preference for takeout?"

"Did you forget it's dinner with the fam tonight? You'll have to meet us at Brickyard Oven. We're heading that way now. But next week you're totally picking up Mexican," he added, taking most of the sting out of the rebuke.

"Yeah, see you there." I ended the call and squeezed my eyes shut as I tapped my forehead with my phone—hard. *Stupid, stupid, stupid.* I'd gotten so wrapped up in that date—dates—with Atticus that I wasn't supposed to be enjoying or even wanting, that I'd completely spaced about Jasper's parents coming to town. It was one of the rare occasions we'd "cancel" our usual Movie Night.

I scrambled to pull myself together and raced out the door of my rental house. Fortunately, I didn't live far from the restaurant, so I arrived shortly after everyone was seated.

"Hey, sorry I'm late," I apologized as I pulled out a chair to sit.

"Oh, no you don't, mister," Cathay, Jasper's mom—or as I called her, Mama C—said, her face serious as she stood. Then a smile cracked her rosy cheeks, and she opened her arms wide. "Not without giving Mama a hug first."

I chuckled and grinned back at her, then stepped into her warm embrace. She might look like she'd blow over in a stiff wind with her wiry frame, but she was deceptively strong. Like spider silk, she appeared delicate and even fragile, but she could give steel a run for its money.

"I swear you're taller. Doesn't he look taller, Ed?" she asked, stepping back and glancing at an equally older man.

"He's the same height he's always been. Now, come here, son." Mama C tsked at her husband, but stepped aside so he could claim his own hug. Edmond Rivers had hair every bit as dark as his son's, though his was liberally peppered with gray. He also was a big fan of the hearty backslap-hug. He squeezed tight and then smacked my back hard enough to make me wheeze before letting me go so we could all take our seats.

I stole a glance at Jasper, who was unsurprisingly snickering to himself. "I'm telling you, they like you more than me. Always have. No sooner do they get to my place than it starts. 'Where's Mason? Did you tell him when we were coming? He's not stuck at work, is he?'" He shook his head and smiled ruefully. "Sometimes I don't think they're here for me at all."

"You know that's not true," I said, giving him a good shove. A sentiment that was echoed by his parents. "They only like me more because I actually remember to *call* more than once a month," I teased.

"That reminds me," Mama C interjected. "I saw the latest photos on your website. Whatever happened to letting dear old mom see them before the rest of the world?"

Ed gave her a scandalized look. "But he always sends them to me." Mama C looked about ready to explode at the unfairness when Jasper intervened.

"He's messing with you, Mama. Hell, not even Mason sees most of my pictures until they're posted."

I nodded to add credibility to the truth, though I might have said "half" instead of "most". Per usual whenever Jasper's family visited, we spent a good amount of time catching up on each other's latest goings on in between ordering and receiving our meal.

As we settled into eating the massive pizza pie, the conversation gradually shifted focus away from me. Not that I begrudged it in the least. I loved Jasper's family. They'd taken me in when they barely even knew me, had provided and nurtured without constraint. But they weren't *my* family. It felt wrong to still long for the people who had initially raised me, then tossed me aside like I was nothing.

Maybe I should have known how they would react to finding out I wasn't straight. But we lived in Colorado, which was damn liberal most of the time. And they'd always been okay with the queer community. But apparently, that acceptance didn't extend to "one of their own." I could still hear my father saying, "No son of mine is gonna be a fag." Since they couldn't change my sexuality—at least that much they understood—they fixed the part about me being their son.

Something Ed said caught my attention, drawing my mind away from dark memories. "What was that?" I asked, glancing between Jasper's parents.

Mama C chuckled. "Ed and I were just saying that the day Jasper doesn't have some new crush he's obsessing over will be the day we know he's been abducted by aliens."

I couldn't help but join Ed in a loud burst of laughter while Jasper watched on with a scowl.

"We don't have to worry about anything like that from you," Mama C said, reaching across the table to place her hand over mine, and gave me that motherly smile that simultaneously made me miss my mother fiercely and wish that Cathay really was my mom. She patted my hand, then settled back in her seat. "Right, let's hear it, Jasper. What handsome man has captured your attention?"

"Geesh, you two are worse than Mace," Jasper griped, tossing me a look that clearly read "traitor." I winked at him, and he rolled his eyes, but not even his so-called irritation could quell the smile twitching on his lips. "Okay, fine, there *may* be someone. He recently moved in across the hall. And while I haven't *really* introduced myself, every time we bump into each other, he is *so* nice. He might just be the nicest, sweetest man I've ever met."

My heart sank deeper and deeper into my stomach as Jasper continued to regale them with all the awesomeness that was Atticus Garner. At some point, he'd discovered not only the man's last name, but that he worked at the Artist Co-Op. I was a little surprised, considering everything else he'd picked up, that he hadn't gleaned *what* Atticus did at the Co-Op.

"Mason, honey, are you all right?" Mama C asked, worry tinging her voice and creating wrinkles on her face. "You look a little green, dear."

I choked on my drink of water, prompting several very firm back slaps from Ed. "I'm fine. Really. Just distracted. Work stuff," I added vaguely, still coughing.

Ed frowned and crossed his arms. "That darn bookshop. You're such a capable young man. I don't know why you put up with any of the nonsense at that place." He shook his head in a familiar show of frustration and disappointment.

"I like it there. And I'll get my way with the store, eventually. For now, I like the people I work with and have a schedule flexible enough to let me do just about whatever I want. It pays to be the manager." I smiled and hoped it didn't look as forced as it felt.

"Well, I still think you work too hard," Mama C said with a sniff. Abruptly, a gleam entered her eye, and she gave me a sidelong look. "I don't suppose *you've* been dating anyone?"

Jasper's loud snort spared me from coming up with a response. "Mace? He hasn't even had a passing interest in anyone since…" His gaze darted to me almost too fast to catch. "In years. Certainly no one he's liked enough to tell me about."

While I appreciated that he'd not brought my last failed relationship into the mix, he was wrong. I'd liked plenty of guys that I wouldn't have minded getting to know better. But they'd all been objects of Jasper's relentless crushes and thus off-limits. Except for his former neighbor, the mechanic. That guy really was an asshole.

"Chin up, Mason," Ed said. "The right one is out there somewhere."

"Just look at the bright side. At least you'll always have each other," Mama C chimed in.

I ducked my head to hide the flare of heat in my cheeks and made a noncommittal noise of agreement. With any luck, they'd take my reaction as embarrassment instead of the stomach-curdling guilt it really was. Like the amazing friend he'd always been, Jasper immediately pulled the conversation away from me and my pathetic lack of a love life. Except, it wasn't lacking so much anymore, because I *was* a traitor. A better man—a better friend—would cancel the date, or better yet, come clean. But no matter how I hated myself for it, I knew I wouldn't.

Chapter 8

EXCITEMENT THRUMMED THROUGH MY veins even as I tackled the mundane chore of laundry. That same excitement was also the reason I'd woken up at the ass crack of "you've got to be kidding me". Days that I could sleep in were rare, thanks to a busy workload of commissions. It would figure that when I finally had one, I'd squander it. And yet, I couldn't find it within myself to care.

I glanced at the time on the stove as I carried the stack of freshly folded clothes through the open living space into the bedroom. Only six more hours until my next date with Mason. Admittedly, it felt a little ridiculous to be this eager for what was technically only a second date, but no amount of telling myself to relax was going to make it happen.

I paused in the doorway to the bedroom and leaned back to look at the peninsula where I kept my meds. For a second I was worried that because my schedule was different today that I'd forgotten to take them and that was the source of my over-the-top enthusiasm. It wouldn't be the first time it had happened, and it wouldn't be the last. As I continued to stare intently at the small collection of bottles, a vague memory of knocking something into the sink when I was taking them while attempting to make coffee surfaced.

Relieved and at least ninety percent confident I *had* taken them, I continued on my way. I was halfway through putting shirts into the dresser when my phone dinged in the other room. Hoping it was Mason, I dropped what I still had into the open drawer and zipped back into the living room.

I snatched up my cell as I flopped onto the couch, a smile already on my face. A smile that slid right off to plop on the floor as I read the text notification.

Maria

911 CALL ME

The call didn't even complete its first ring before she picked up.

"Atticus, oh my goodness, I'm so sorry. I don't know what happened. I know you were taking the day off, and I totally love that for you," she said, the words coming out in a flood.

"Take a breath," I said as calmly as I could, though my anxiety was spiking something fierce. Was I *sure* I'd taken my meds? "What happened?"

Maria audibly took a deep breath on the other end. "The annealer didn't close all the way last night."

"Fuck." I dropped my head back on the couch. "How bad?"

"We might be able to salvage some pieces, but the main body of the pitcher is beyond repair. I really am sorry, Atticus. I could have sworn I checked it." She sounded on the verge of tears.

I took my own bracing breath and sat up straighter, my mind already whirling with what we would need to do in order to have everything ready for pickup this evening. "It's okay. Glass breaks," I said, reciting the mantra of glassblowers everywhere.

"But this is supposed to be your day off. You haven't had one of those in… I don't even know when." She sniffled, and I willed my heart not to sink too much.

"Hey, everything will be fine. I'm going to change and head over. Do what you can to get things organized. The pitcher itself doesn't take that long, and the glass isn't thick. With some luck, we should be able to get it ready and cooled down in time. We've got this."

She mumbled some sort of agreement and ended the call.

I took a moment to wallow in self-pity and to come to terms with what I had to do next. I didn't recall pulling up Mason's information. It didn't bode well that my work was already getting in the way and we hadn't even had our first kiss. Probably wouldn't be having one ever now.

With each ring, disappointment tightened my chest, and I had to fight to keep my spirits up. After more rings than I cared to count, the voicemail clicked on, and my heart might as well have fallen through the cushions. Rather than leave a message, I looked up the number for the bookshop.

A bright, feminine voice answered after only one ring. "Literary Lighthouse, this is Shanae. What can I help you discover today?"

"Hi, this is Atticus Garner. Is Mason available? I tried his personal phone, but he didn't pick up." I snapped my mouth shut. Nothing like an extra dose of anxiety to have me over-sharing.

"Yep. Give me a moment and I'll get him for you." There was an odd click and then silence.

I was beginning to wonder if the store didn't have any hold music when background noise filtered out of the speaker. Just barely, I made out someone who could have been Mason asking who was on the phone and what they wanted. Shanae's response was too faint to catch, but suddenly there was a louder thump that sounded suspiciously like someone had stumbled over some-thing.

"Atticus?" Mason asked, sounding out of breath. "Sorry I missed your call. I forgot to plug in my phone last night, and it's charging in the office. What's up? You decide you don't want to catch the screening of *You've Got Mail* in the park after all?" he asked with an undeniable hint of teasing.

"Um, actually..."

"Oh shit, you did." Mason's response was understandably sur-prised. Not only did I fucking love all movies Meg Ryan, but I'd made no secret that *You've Got Mail* was one of my favorites, and I was looking forward to watching it with him.

"Not quite." Good grief. Why couldn't I just spit it out? At the rate I was going, I'd never get to the hot shop in time to bust out a new glass piece.

There was some shifting around on the other end, then quiet. "I'm in the office. What's going on? You sound really bummed. Are you sick?"

I almost barked out a bitter laugh. If only. "I'm fine. Well, not *fine*, but not sick. Something's come up at work and... and..." To my surprise, Mason laughed, the warm sound flooding through the speaker.

"I'm a big boy, Atticus. It's okay if you have to cancel. Life happens." It even sounded as if he was smiling. I found it hard to believe he could be so chill about it—I certainly wasn't. Then again, it *was* only our second date, even if we had been texting like teenagers.

"I'm really sorry. I promise I'll make it up to you." With my luck, that wouldn't be a promise I'd be able to keep.

"Seriously, Atticus, it's fine. We can reschedule. You could even say the universe is doing me a solid. While you may not be sick, Mickey is, and I was floundering for how I was going to cover his shift. Now it's easy. I will."

"We'll have to catch the next Movie in the Park," I said, picking up what remained of my optimism off the floor.

"And have a Meg Ryan marathon," he replied, the smile still in his voice.

There was nothing forced about my responding grin, even though he couldn't see it. "Absolutely."

"Oh, hey. Sounds like the kids are here for 'Story time with Shanae'. I need to get back out there." He paused, and I figured that was the end of it. I should have known he'd surprise me. "Atticus, please don't stress about this. We'll get together another time, and it will be just as great. I just hope your work thing isn't too dire."

My heart melted a little. When was the last time I hadn't had a guy blow up at me for having to cancel because of work? Had I ever? Certainly not with an added expression of concern for *why* I had to cancel. "It'll be a stretch, but I think we can pull it out." Mason gave a snort, and I had to laugh when I put together why. "No puns intended," I added.

"*Sure* they weren't. Anyway, I really gotta go before the tiny terrors tear Shanae apart. Talk to you later?"

"Absolutely." I ended the call feeling more rejuvenated and notably less depressed. Still sad, because I wouldn't get to see him today, but hopeful that I would get to another day. Ideally soon. Determined to conquer the day, I launched off the couch and raced to change into hot shop-appropriate clothes.

A scant three minutes later, I was in the hall locking up the apartment. Still in crisis management mode, I took a step back and bumped into something solid that let out an "Oof."

"Well, fudge," a masculine voice said as I spun around to see folders scattered across the floor.

"I'm so sorry!" I immediately bent to retrieve the papers, well, photos.

The guy waved my apology away. "They're not even that good. I really only printed them so I could figure out *why*."

I passed him the last folder, carefully sliding the large print to sit more securely. "Best of luck with that. And sorry again. I swear I'm not normally so oblivious to my surroundings." I shook my head and ran a hand through my hair. I seemed to be apologizing a lot lately for things I didn't normally do.

"It's okay," the guy replied.

"You sure you're alright?" I asked, already glancing down the hall toward the elevator and mentally debating if the stairs might be faster.

He chuckled. "I'll live."

"Okay. Sorry again!" I shouted over my shoulder, already several steps down at his assurance.

Six hours later, not only was I not with Mason, but salvaging the decorative pieces proved to be nigh impossible. When I'd arrived at the hot shop, red rimmed Maria's eyes and her nose was swollen. It took getting her to repeat the glass artists' mantra "Glass breaks" several times before she pulled together enough to do more than open the gate to the glory hole and pull cane.

In the end, we had no choice but to push back the pickup two hours. Fortunately, the client, much like Mason earlier, chose to see the delay as fortuitous instead of inconvenient and unprofessional. I'd just finished wiping off my face with a cool cloth when Maria caught my eye.

"You know, the bookstore closes at eight. I bet if you hurry, you could make it." Maria glanced across the hot shop to the large digital clock mounted on the wall.

I let out a sigh and shook my head. "It is what it is. Plus, we still have to clean up." Because of course, blowing a pitcher couldn't be *easy*. We'd had two crack at the last stage, and one plain fell off the punty and shattered.

"Nope. I can clean up. It's my fault you lost your day off."

"It happens to all of us, and you don't know that it was your fault. It could just as easily have been me." She frowned, and I plowed ahead before she could interject. "Besides, I'm gross." I plucked at my sweaty shirt, which likely had slivers of glass embedded in the fibers.

There was a sharp snap of fabric, and I looked up from examining my sweat-stained shirt. "Then I guess it's a good thing you have a few backup shirts here. Re-wet that cloth and wipe down your arms," she ordered. "Then you can put this on and spritz some of this." She sniffed at a bottle of cologne that sure as hell wasn't mine. I generally didn't bother with the stuff.

"Do I want to know whose that is?" I asked dubiously.

"It's yours. Consider it an early birthday gift. Because it is."

"My birthday already passed."

She narrowed her eyes at me. "Christmas, then. Now quit stalling. Oh! If you can swing it, wouldn't hurt to pick up a peace offering."

I shook my head again, but this time in laughter instead of defeat. There was no point in fighting. One way or another, Maria was pushing my ass out of here. And was I really complaining about the chance to see Mason? I snorted to myself as I tossed aside the towel and pulled on the fresh shirt. The cologne wasn't too bad either—earthy with the slightest hint of citrus.

Before I knew it, I was standing outside Literary Lighthouse with a bag of all of Kaleidoscope Coffee's remaining pastries. Five minutes after close. They had already locked the door, and the lights inside were off. Then a couple of lights at the back flickered on, and I glimpsed blond hair over the shorter shelves toward the back. Taking my life in my hands, I rapped my knuckles on the glass door.

Chapter 9

WHEN MY DAY WANTED to go sideways, it really didn't fuck around. First, I'd overslept because I hadn't charged my phone. Then, I'd dropped my fresh cup of coffee from Kaleidoscope while attempting to unlock the bookstore and waiting patrons watched on. Amid that, a fucking squirrel had stolen my pastry, and I was out of the snacks I kept in the office. Atticus calling to cancel our date without suggesting an alternative day had felt like the cherry on top of a shit-tastic morning. But did I really deserve any better?

Clearly, the universe was telling me in no uncertain terms that continuing anything with Atticus was a mistake. A point emphasized by my current punishment for daring to dream. Not only had Story time with Shanae been twice the nightmare it normally was, but one of the little monsters had knocked into the children's books display, forcing us to cut the event short and cordon of that section of the store until we could deal with it.

Except there hadn't been a moment's reprieve all day. Which was why I was still at the store, despite aching feet, hunger gnawing at my belly, and a shitty attitude only sleep could fix. I barely even thought about Atticus after the call. Okay, that was a lie. He'd hovered at the back of my thoughts, getting more distracting with each hour that passed without so much as a passive text.

I ambled out of my office after obsessively checking my phone for the hundredth time. Jasper had messaged about finding the answer to his latest photography dilemma, accompanied by a slew of pictures I hadn't a prayer of understanding. After typing and deleting several responses, I threw in the towel and settled for a "thumbs up" and slipped the device into my back pocket.

A rap on the locked glass door made my irritation surge. I was hellbent on ignoring it as I debated how best to take care of the children's section disaster, when the rap came again, more insistent.

"What part of fucking closed is so hard to understand?" I grumbled to myself as I wound my way to the front of the shop. Even if the sign hadn't been flipped from "Open", most of the lights were off and the door was locked, not to mention the hours were printed on the damn door. Taking a deep breath and reminding myself not to yell at a potential customer, I lifted my head and finally caught sight of who was so determined to get my attention. "Atticus?"

He gave me a tentative smile and held up a stuffed bag with the Kaleidoscope Coffee logo on it. When I continued to stand there like a cardboard display, he pointed at the lock. "Any chance of you opening this?" he asked, his voice slightly muted through the glass.

I grabbed the keys out of my pocket and scrambled to unlock the door. "What are you doing here?" I asked as I held it open for him.

"Sorry, I know it's late and you probably want to get home. If you were leaving, I won't hold you up," he said, the words coming out in a nervous rush that perfectly echoed his abashed expression.

"I wasn't. Leaving. I'm not leaving," I replied with all the eloquence one would expect from a bookstore manager. Resisting the urge to smack my face, I gestured to the bag. "What's that?"

The question seemed to perk him up. He squared his impressive shoulders and offered a shy smile. "I felt really bad about having to cancel and wanted to make it up to you. I really hope you like Kaleidoscope's pastries, because I bought everything they had left before racing over here."

"I..." I needed to tell him to go, that this wasn't working out, wasn't a good time for me and never would be. Not with my best friend pining after him like a God-forsaken tween instead of a fully grown man with bills and a business. Only the disconnect between my brain and my mouth that seemed to emerge whenever Atticus was around was in full force. "I love their pastries. Did they have any of those lavender honey sticky buns left?" I asked, locking the door behind him.

His grin widened. "Just one and your name's on it."

"Is that so?" I teased, raising an eyebrow at him.

"Well, not literally, but it's yours just the same." He set the paper bag on the register counter and ducked his head, his earlier anxiety returning in full force. "Look, I really am sorry about cancelling. I'd love to promise it won't happen again, but I'd be lying. Work stuff comes up *a lot*. Part of the trouble with running your own business-of-one is that there's no one to replace you if something goes wrong. So more often than not, I have to drop whatever I'm doing to put out fires, usually to the detriment of other parts of my life. Anyway—"

I quickly stepped up to him, unable to bear another moment of watching him spiral, and placed a hand on his arm. "Hey, don't beat yourself up. Like I said earlier, life happens. It's okay."

"But it's not," he countered. "This always happens when I like a guy. Work gets in the way and ruins any chance I might have had."

Despite my earlier conviction about the universe telling me dating Atticus was not a good idea, a smile tugged at my lips. "So you like me, huh?"

"Should think it's pretty obvious by now," he replied with a smirk. "Anyway, yeah. I just wanted to swing by to apologize in person and bring a peace offering."

I reached for the bag and peered inside. "Hmm. Seems like a lot of pastries for one man." An idea came to me. "What would you say to giving me a hand with fixing up the children's section? I come armed with pastries that an incredibly handsome man gave me. Don't worry, I promise not to tell him I'm sharing." I gave him a playful grin and held up the bag for emphasis.

He chuckled and ducked his head. It was too dark where we were standing to tell, but I'd bet my favorite book he was blushing. "You really want me to stay?" he asked softly. The finest threads of nerves wove through the question like an intricate braid.

"Yeah, I really would," I said. I was a little surprised at how much I meant it. Normally when I had a shitty day, I just wanted to be left alone, but now that Atticus was physically here, being alone was the furthest thing from my mind.

Atticus followed my lead and pulled a pastry from the bag. "So what's wrong with the children's section?"

"Honestly? A better question would be what's *not* wrong with the children's section." I guided us through rows of overstuffed shelves to get to the far corner of the store.

He let out a low whistle when we emerged onto the chaotic scene. "Oh my."

"Yeah," I sighed. "This area is really too cramped to allow kids to move around. It's a miracle something like this doesn't happen every week. Oh wait, it does." My subsequent laugh was more forced than I would have liked.

"What if…" He paused, glancing around the tight space littered with children's books and knick knacks then back the way we'd come. "Never mind. It's not my place."

I stepped toward him, my skin buzzing with awareness of his proximity. "No. Please tell me. I want to know." The buzzing in my fingers intensified. I wasn't aware I'd reached for him, let alone touched him.

"I was thinking how cool it would be if people walking by could look inside and see the children's story time."

"I'm liking this so far. But how would I accomplish that? Not sure if you've noticed, but the entire store is kind of like this." I held out my arms to encompass the surrounding chaos. It was easier to ignore how much that bothered me with Atticus here.

"Move the section over to the lighthouse shelves. You could decorate the display with things that coincide with that week's reading. It would help those shelves not to be so cluttered, and you wouldn't have to worry about kids knocking anything over because there'd be more room to move around.

I could have smacked myself. The solution seemed so obvious when he said it out loud. "I love that idea. But it could take a while to do."

"That's okay. I don't need to be anywhere tonight. Besides, even if I did, this is where I *want* to be." I didn't know whether to laugh at the cheesiness of the statement or swoon. Either way, it was a damn good, *effective* line.

We lost track of time as we worked together to relocate everything in the children's section. By the time we were finished, it was a toss-up what hurt more: my face from smiling so much, my ribs from all the laughing as we shared silly stories, or my back, because, fuck, I was getting old. I stood back from the lighthouse shelves, which finally looked like a proper display. Pride in what we'd accomplished filled my chest. Then, I absentmindedly checked my phone and saw what time it was.

"Oh shit. When did it get so late?" I looked at Atticus, who hadn't uttered so much as a syllable of complaint even though I knew he'd had a long, trying day of his own. "I'm sorry."

He shrugged. "I'm not. This looks great."

I admired our work once again. "That it does. Come on. We should get out of here before I pass out on the floor."

"Walk you to your car?" Warmth suffused my chest at his earnest offer.

I nodded, not trusting my voice. We stepped outside together, and I locked up the store. For possibly the first time, I was actually sad about scoring great parking on the street. It meant that all too soon we were at my car, and I... I wasn't ready to say goodbye. Considering how most of the day felt like it would never end, that was more than a little surprising, especially given how it was past midnight now. We stepped up to the side of my car, and I laughed as I suddenly realized that both times Atticus had been to the store, I'd put him to work.

"What's funny?" he asked, looking at me, his features partially shadowed despite the abundant streetlights.

"It just occurred to me that this is twice now I've enlisted you to help me fix things in the store."

"I'm happy to help," he replied with what I was coming to recognize as his usual affable grin. Before I could say anything, his gaze flicked toward my mouth. My heart raced, and my breathing became shallower when his gaze continued to linger. "You have..."

Out of the corner of my eye, I saw his hand raise, but I couldn't bring myself to look away from his intense focus. An electric shock jolted through me when his thumb glided along my cheek.

"Just a bit of powdered sugar," he said, almost absently, his gaze slowly rising to meet mine.

"Oh." Normally I'd be embarrassed, but that required more brain cells than I was currently operating with. We continued to stare at each other, the quiet of Oak Haven wrapping around us.

"Mason."

"Yeah?" I replied, breathless with anticipation.

His voice dropped low, each word feeling like a caress. "I would really like to kiss you."

"I would really like that."

There was no room for panic or doubt as he seemed to close the distance in slow motion. Then his lips were against mine, firm and warm and so, so soft. The kiss was gentle and unhurried, and I felt myself falling into it, into him. When was the last time I'd had a first kiss that didn't feel like the guy was trying to prove something? Atticus held my face, the pads of his fingers rough on my skin, as he continued to massage my lips with a kiss that was quickly rocketing to my top three all-time best first kisses.

Abruptly, I realized that the falling sensation I was experiencing wasn't entirely abstract. I was actually sliding down the side of the car. While potentially embarrassing, this was fine. All I had to do was get my feet back under me. Unfortunately, Atticus chose that moment to end the kiss and pull away, leaving me to my fate.

"Shit," I hissed as gravity exerted itself with a vengeance.

He scrambled to catch me, and I fought to ignore my blossoming mortification. He laughed good-naturedly once he was confident that I had my footing and wasn't hurt. "Think it'd be safe to say you're falling for me?"

"I'm never going to live this down, am I?" I groaned.

A smile that filled me with a warmth I hadn't felt in ages stretched his lips. "Not a chance."

Chapter 10

TO SAY I WAS enjoying my time with Mason would put it mildly. We'd had several dates now, all wonderfully low key—grabbing coffee, meeting up for lunch, walking in the park. And kisses. Wonderfully sweet kisses that warmed me from the inside and world-defining kisses that made me painfully aware of how long it had been since I'd been with someone.

"What's got you all smiley today?" Maria asked from where she was busy color matching for a replacement glassware set.

I rested the punty on the cradle and kept idly spinning it as I turned an even bigger smile on her. While I enjoyed my work, I was typically too focused to smile about it.

She walked over with a color bar in hand, waving it like a wand. "Wait. Wait. Let me guess. The dating is going well."

"You could definitely say the dating is going well." More surprisingly—at least to me—was that the dating was still happening. The more time I spent with Mason, the more time I *wanted* to spend with Mason.

He had a quick wit, a passion for literature that was inspiring, and a penchant for always finding the silver lining. While I'd had a few close calls of having to cancel again, we'd navigated them with surprising ease. Hell, I'd almost managed the ever-elusive work-life balance. Which forced me to confront an ugly truth: I had time to spend with Mason because I *made* time. And what did that say about all of my past relationships? I'd always believed I was putting in the work, but maybe I hadn't.

"So... is it official?" Maria prodded, mercifully dragging me out of the increasingly depressive thoughts.

My smile returned almost as fast as it had fled. I appreciated she didn't ask if I'd been seeing the same guy. Hookup culture was great for some people, but it had never been my vibe. "Not too sure about the official aspect, but you could say I'm tentatively optimistic that's where it's headed."

Thank goodness we didn't have any finished pieces sitting out, because Maria's squeal of joy could have shattered glass. "Ah! I love that for you so much."

I chuckled and returned my focus to my arguably now too hot blob of molten glass. "I kind of love that for me too."

She leaned down to get a better look at what I'd pulled from the annealer. "What are you working on? Did we get another commission?" It had taken what felt like forever for Maria to refer to it as "our" work, and pride at my blossoming apprentice glowed in my chest.

"I actually have no idea. Kind of going where the glass takes me." I glanced back at her and did a double take at the color bar she was holding. "When did we get that?" I asked, positive I would have noticed the exact shade of Mason's eyes sitting on the shelves.

"Oh, it's new. Came in with the last shipment. It's Sky Blue Opal. Isn't it pretty?" She waved it in the light to emphasize the dramatic color. Then, before I could respond, lurched to a stop. "Is it okay that I added it to the order? Last time, you said—"

"That if there's a color you want to play with to add it to the order sheet," I finished for her. "Yes, that still applies. I know you're technically my apprentice, but I think of you more as a partner in glass."

She beamed. "Then you *do* think the color is pretty?"

Suddenly, I knew exactly what I wanted to make. "It's more than pretty. It's perfect." I jolted to my feet and immediately encountered a problem. "Uh, would you mind keeping this spinning while I grab some colors?"

"No problem. Did you want to take this one with you?" she asked as she handed over the color bar and took over spinning the punty. "It doesn't really match the way I'd hoped it would."

I took about two steps before I turned back to her. "And could you add some more gather from the furnace? That bit won't be enough for what I have in mind."

"Sure thing, boss," she replied with a little salute and a wink.

I rolled my eyes, but let the teasing stand as I went to secure a few more color bars for what I now had in mind. With Maria's help to get started, I had a solid foundation to build from by the time she left to meet up with some friends for an early lunch. From there, time slipped by in a haze of creativity.

"Wow."

I glanced toward the entrance of the hot shop at the whispered exclamation. Where I expected to find Barry ready to give me a hard time, I found a much more welcome sight. Mason grinned and walked closer.

"I'd say you look hot, but I feel like that's a given, considering you're in front of a big-ass fire." He chuckled and set the bag he'd been holding down on the worktable by the color bars.

"Well, it is around two thousand degrees Fahrenheit." He let out a low whistle, and I waved him over with my free hand. "Sorry, I'd get up, but I can't let this stop moving."

He nodded, his fascinated gaze fixed on what I was doing as he stepped closer. "Two thousand degrees? That's insane. And what are you doing now?"

"Now, I'm about to flash it, add some color, and put it back in the glory hole."

He turned a completely deadpan expression on me. "Shut your face. It is *not* called that."

I laughed so hard it was a wonder I didn't jostle the punty right off the cradle. "Yeah, not sure who was in charge of naming that, but I assure you, it is." I worried my lip, not sure if what I was about to do was a good idea or not. Then, decided to go for it. "Would you like to help?"

The way he lit up banished any doubts I harbored. "Really? You would let me?"

"Of course. Think of it as a brief lesson in glass blowing."

He chuckled. "Suppose it's only fair, since I always seem to put you to work anytime you're within a ten-foot radius of Lighthouse. Okay, what do you want me to do?"

That question had a whole lot of answers. Some I believed we might be ready for, others not quite. "First, why don't you tell me what brought you by?"

"Oh, um, I unexpectedly found myself with the day off and thought I'd bring lunch on the off chance you hadn't eaten yet. I hope that's okay."

"I'd be glad of the company. And lunch," I added once I realized how the morning had gotten away from me. "First, put on one of the spare set of gloves and see if you can find an apron. Wouldn't want to burn any of that pretty skin."

He flushed and quickly did as I said, then returned to my side. "Now what?"

Mason looked fucking adorable in Maria's apron, which barely covered the essentials on him, and it took me a moment to figure out where I was in the glassblowing process. "Okay, I want you to stand right by the glory hole doors and be ready to open them when I say."

He snickered, but moved into position. "Holy fuck, it's hot over here."

"Two thousand degrees, baby." I spun the punty slowly a couple more times, then got a good handle on the metal pole. "And... open." I backed the molten gather out and stood where I had plenty of room to move. "Close and be prepared to open again on my say."

"Got it," he said with intense focus.

Holding off the laughter I desperately wanted to set loose, I swung the punty like a pendulum, careful to keep it turning often enough. It wasn't until I was ready to go back into the glory hole that I realized Mason was staring at me slack-jawed.

"Open." I got the shape into the heat and glanced at him, still staring at me in amazement. "What?" I asked with a chuckle.

"No wonder your arms and shoulders are so jacked. I mean, gym muscles are one thing. But muscles you actually work for? That's sexy as hell."

I tried, and probably failed, to keep my embarrassment at the praise to myself. "You think I'm sexy, huh?"

"I have eyes and am reasonably confident you own a mirror. Besides, you think I'm pretty," he fired back with a playful gleam in his eyes.

"I think you're more than pretty, Mason," I said, my voice becoming husky.

Deep pink radiated across his face. It could have been the heat, but I didn't think so. Especially not when he cleared his throat and blatantly changed the subject. "So, how much does that thing weigh, anyway?"

"Come over here and find out."

He took a nervous step away from the doors and shook his head. "I couldn't. What if I break it? You've already put so much work into it."

His concern just made me smile wider. "You won't break anything. I'll be right here." He cautiously came closer, and I maneuvered to the side so he could see my hand placement. Then, I had us switch places, keeping close behind him in case he needed me to step in. "Slowly keep it turning. That's it. Just like that." I placed a hand at the small of his back as I leaned forward to ensure everything was level. "You're doing great. First thing every glassblower learns is 'glass breaks'."

"Would have thought for sure it'd be 'don't put your dick in the glory hole'."

Laughter burst out of me. "Okay, we'll call it a close second." He smiled at me, and if I had thought for a second that I could kiss him without him dropping the glass, I'd have done it in a heartbeat. "Now, gently lift the punty off the cradle."

"The what?"

"The long metal pole you're holding," I replied with a note of teasing.

"Right. That makes sense. Are you sure I won't hit anything inside?"

I rubbed my thumb in a circle on his lower back, where I'd apparently never removed my hand. "Certain. You're not going anywhere, just getting an idea of the heft. Take your time and don't over-anticipate. Better to start with not enough lift than too much." I thought for sure he'd make another quip, but his face became serious once more.

"Okay." He started small, the muscles in his arms tightening briefly. Then he applied more force and continued to add until the punty hovered maybe an inch above the cradle. "Wow, that's... every bit as heavy as it looked when you were swinging it around."

Picking up on his nerves, I reached around him to help steadily lower the metal pole back onto the cradle. He slipped from between my arms, letting me take back over. I was sad to lose the proximity, but it was probably for the best. "Technically, the punty itself hardly weighs anything. It's the counterweight and the gather—the molten glass—that have the actual weight."

"It's really amazing what you do," he said, with wonder once more in his eyes and in his voice. Pride had me puffing out my chest at the praise. "What are you making?"

I smiled at him. "You'll have to wait to see until it's finished." No way was I about to tell him that my first creative piece in what felt like ages was for him.

Chapter 11

 and see.

The words played over and over in my head. They played when Atticus asked for a pair of massive metal tweezers, which he used to *literally* pull the glass into sinuous shapes. They played as he explained the importance of flashing to prevent the glass from cooling and cracking while he was still working. When he absently mentioned the stack of newspapers and what it was for, the words might as well have been a printed headline.

Somewhere amidst everything, we ate lunch, taking turns to grab a couple of bites before switching back to rotating the punty-pole. Then he was using the pair of scary-ass tweezers—a jack—to narrow the point where the glass attached to the punty-pole. My heart damn near lurched up my throat when he tapped the steel pipe and detached the glass piece.

"What's that face for?" Atticus asked as he finished putting the strangely amorphous piece into what he called "an annealer" to keep the piece hot enough to continue working on later. Though apparently it was more often used to gradually cool pieces down.

"I can't figure out what it's supposed to be. Not knocking the creative process or anything, but it's kind of driving me nuts." I huffed and followed him to the worktable to help him clean up. "You really won't tell me what it is?"

He grinned broadly. "You'll have to wait and see." He paused, seemed to consider something, then added, "I will tell you that what we worked on today is only one part of the larger piece."

I groaned dramatically. "You. Are. Killing. Me. What, in all of our interactions so far, tells you I'm a patient man?"

"I promise your patience will be rewarded."

"That's a bold promise, especially since I didn't notice a timeframe attached to it. Do I at least get a consolation prize?" I batted my eyelashes at him for good measure.

His rich laugh filled the hot shop and set my insides buzzing. "And what sort of prize did you have in mind?" My dick twitched at the undercurrent of promise in his voice. I glanced around for inspiration, then it hit me.

"Do you have everything taken care of that needs to be? Got your things?"

"Yes. Why?"

Instead of answering, I grabbed his hand. "Come with me."

I didn't realize how late it had gotten until we stepped outside of the Artist Co-Op into a deepening twilight. On the upside, not only had I spent most of the day with Atticus and learned about glassblowing, but the darkness served my purposes perfectly. I dragged him over to where I'd parked at the back of the lot. You'd never know it had been the last available spot, given my car was now one of only three left.

"Get in," I ordered, opening the backdoor and gesturing.

"Why do I suddenly get the feeling I'm being kidnapped?"

Without so much as a pause, I gave him my keys and shoved him inside, forcing him to scoot all the way to the other side as I ducked in after him instead of walking around to the other door like a sane person.

"What's going on?" he asked as I slammed the door shut behind me.

"This." I surged forward, mashing our mouths together.

He released a muffled sound of surprise, then his fingers were sliding through my hair as he pulled me close and kissed me back. His mouth moved against mine in a dance that both grounded me and elevated the buzzing in my veins. Fuck, I wanted Atticus so bad it felt like I was going to crawl out of my skin.

I ran my hands shamelessly over his shoulders and arms, getting lost in the defined muscles I'd just spent the last several hours appreciating. When his tongue teased my lips, I gladly opened for him and nearly came in my fucking pants when he grabbed my thigh and pulled me closer. He untangled his fingers from my hair to run the flat of his palm down my torso. I gasped when his fingers tipped the button of my trousers.

"Is this okay?" he asked, his face barely visible in the rapidly darkening night.

I mindlessly nodded. "Uh-huh," I added aloud when I realized he couldn't see me any better than I could see him.

Done with words or sounds that didn't involve his mouth on mine, I dove into another heated kiss. I curled my fingers around the back of his neck as our tongues continued to glide over each other. I didn't even realize he'd undone the button of my pants and drawn down the zipper until he palmed my erection through my briefs. A groan of unexpected pleasure filled the car.

Atticus pushed down the band of my briefs, freeing my cock. He rubbed his thumb over my slit, gathering the copious precum that I should probably be embarrassed about. But how could I possibly be anything other than ecstatic when he had his hands on me? He spread the liquid around my cockhead, then down my shaft before wrapping a firm hand around me and giving a decisive stroke.

"Fuck. Atticus," I gasped loudly, falling back against the closed door.

He continued to stroke me like we had all the time in the world, periodically swiping over the sensitive tip, which was now definitely leaking like a faucet. I moaned at the incredible buildup of sensation, bracing myself on the back window and the headrest of the front seat. He liberally peppered kisses along the flushed skin of my neck. He tried to seal our mouths together once more, but I was panting so hard it was a lost cause. His motions sped up, and my imminent orgasm raced toward me.

I reflexively thrust into his perfect grip, increasingly desperate for release. My hand slipped on the window, and only sheer force of will kept me in place. The intense pleasure continued to compound, driving me to the brink.

"Damn, sunshine, you feel so fucking good in my hand. Like you belong there," he rumbled in a low voice right by my ear that sounded like pure sex.

A cry ripped free of my throat. My head fell back against the now condensation-slick window. And I came so hard I thought for sure I'd pass out. He gentled his grip as he milked every ounce of cum I had in me. By the time he released me, I was a quivering mess of sated bliss.

He placed a tender kiss on the side of my mouth and leaned back, giving me room to breathe in the humid car. "How's that for a consolation prize?" He probably intended to sound teasing, but he still sounded like sex.

The only response I could manage was a small grunt that was closer to a whimper. Once I corralled enough of my brain cells, I put myself away and sat up straighter. "I really only intended to make out. A lot," I finally said, still slightly out of breath. Abruptly, the rest of my deliriously content brain came back online. "Wait. You... I didn't..."

"Don't worry about it. There's always next time," he added with a grin before pressing his lips to mine in a chaste kiss. Then he finished cleaning my spend off his hand with the tissues from the box I kept in the back and chuckled. "Hooking up in a car. Haven't done that since I was a teenager."

I didn't even think before I replied, "I've never done this." There was an awkward pause, and I wished like hell I could take the words back, lie, say something else that wasn't quite so pathetic.

"I'm honored I get to be your first." He leaned forward to press the sweetest kiss against my lips. I shuddered, both overwhelmed and grateful he didn't dig into what I'd said.

"I swear I'm not a selfish lover. You have to let me make it up to you."

"Okay. You can make it up to me by letting me take you out to dinner." Though I couldn't really see his smile, I could hear it. My doomed heart fluttered wildly. It was a miracle my response was even intelligible.

"When were you thinking?"

Another tender kiss. "Now sounds good."

Rather than answer with words, I flung myself at him and kissed him with every ounce of feeling I had.

"I'll take that as a yes," he said with a chuckle when I gave him a chance to breathe. "Oh, and you're driving."

My burst of laughter took me completely by surprise. I couldn't recall the last time I'd been this relaxed and happy. "Deal." I was now extra grateful for the dark as we relocated to the front seat. "Where to?" I asked as I backed out of the space.

"How about the diner?" he suggested.

I hesitated. Jasper and I went there together often. It was also a nexus of gossip. Hence, the hesitation. I already counted it as a bona fide miracle that no one at Lighthouse had said anything to Jasper about me and Atticus. Going to the diner with Atticus felt a little like pushing my luck with the universe.

"Or... not the diner."

"Huh?" I asked, suddenly realizing that I'd stopped halfway out of the space. "Um, the diner, yeah." *Think think think.*

Atticus placed a hand on my leg, and warmth suffused my thigh. "If you don't want to go to the diner, that's okay, Mason. We could sit on the ground, eating off paper plates, and it wouldn't matter. All I care about is getting to spend time with you."

I finally took a stuttering breath and let the tension go when I released it. "How do you always know exactly what to say?"

"I would argue that I *rarely* know what to say." He gave me a cheeky grin that had a warm glow to it thanks to the streetlight we'd pulled up by. "Okay, not the diner. Is there a particular type of food you're in the mood for?"

It was oh so tempting to ask if he was on the menu, but I felt bad about how I'd reacted to his first suggestion. "It's not that I don't like the diner. I do. I just tend to eat there a lot because it's—"

"Close to the bookshop." He smacked his palm against his forehead. "Of course. I should have thought of that. So, what are you in the mood for?" The twinkle in his eyes could have been due to the streetlight making them shine silver, but his voice had taken on a similar huskiness as it had earlier.

I swallowed thickly. "Actually, that paper plates thing sounds kinda perfect. There's a food truck on Elm that I've been wanting to try. It's a kind of Asian fusion."

"That does sound good. Well, what are you waiting for? Drive on, good sir." His theatrical delivery undoubtedly had the desired result, and I was still laughing when we reached the stoplight at the end of Main.

I glanced at him, and a question that had been niggling at the back of my mind pushed forward. "I've been meaning to ask. Is there a reason you don't drive?"

"Easy. I don't have a car. Never wanted or really needed one." He paused, and I could feel his anxiety ballooning to fill the confines of the vehicle. "Does it bother you? That I don't drive? I never meant for you to feel like you always had to."

I reached over the console to give him the same reassurance he'd given me and gently squeezed his thigh. "I don't and it doesn't," I said, answering his questions in reverse. "More curious than anything. Trust me, I have no problem holding you captive in my car. I mean, driving us wherever we want to go."

He lifted my hand and placed a kiss on the back, waking my stupid rabble of butterflies and sending them into overdrive. "And you say I always know the right thing to say."

Chapter 12

I HUMMED TO MYSELF while I got the hot shop ready for the day. Normally, Maria would have done this, but I'd been so excited about my new original piece I hadn't been able to sleep. Today I planned to refine the base I'd begun with Mason and hopefully start on the blown top piece. Which meant I needed to select an array of yellows to evoke the sunlight Mason brought to my day whenever I saw or heard from him.

I was up to seven colors that I would absolutely need to whittle down to a more reasonable number when my phone rang. Surprised that I'd left the ringer on, I set the color bars on the worktable and pulled it from my pocket to see who else was awake at this hour. My stomach swooped unpleasantly when I saw it was my mom.

"Hey Mom. You're up awful early."

"Hello Atticus," my dad said in a tone that immediately made my chest tighten. "You might want to sit down."

I floundered for a chair and nearly landed on the floor in my rush to sit. "Dad? Why are you calling on Mom's phone? Is she okay?"

"Your mother is fine, Son. She's driving." At that moment I heard the woman in question cursing up a storm at someone apparently incapable of driving in their own lane. "But something has happened. To Carmen," he said, his voice strained.

"What do you mean? Does it have to do with her work? She promised she'd visit soon." I'd been looking forward to introducing her to Mason, assuming he was up for it.

"She was in a wreck. A bad one."

My world narrowed down to a pinpoint. "No," I whispered in disbelief. This wasn't happening. Not again.

"We're on our way to the hospital in Mist Wood Springs now. She's pretty banged up. Last we heard, they were taking her into surgery. From what we can tell, the other driver..." My dad's words got swallowed by white noise as my anxiety merged with dread.

First Jess, now Carmen. My throat constricted. I gasped for air, but couldn't get enough to fill my lungs. Black crowded in on the edges of my vision. All I could see was metal twisted around Jess's body, her normally bright eyes staring up at a gray sky. Except it wasn't Jess, it was Carmen.

I swayed and tried to grip the table, but my hands were so numb I couldn't feel anything. The sound of glass shattering was muffled, as was the shout that followed. Then I was moving, turning. And there was Mason. Tears leaked from my eyes as I struggled to catch even the smallest breath. My lungs burned.

"Can you hear me?" Mason asked in a voice that sounded far away, like he was underwater.

"She... she..." I tried to say with the tiny amount of air I'd gathered.

"Atticus, I need you to take a deep breath for me. Can you do that?"

It was almost impossible to hear him over the roaring in my ears. I shook my head, still fighting for air.

"Yes, you can, baby. Come on, breathe with me." He placed my hand that I hadn't realized he was holding on his chest and took a long breath.

I violently shook my head again, my panic compounding the longer I went without air. He looked away for a moment. His lips moved, but I couldn't hear anything. Just the steady roar settling into a disturbing muffled buzz. Something cool and wet touched the back of my neck, and I nearly launched into him.

"It's okay. You're safe. I'm right here."

My chest convulsed as I took three rapid breaths that gave no oxygen. "It... It..."

"Shh, don't talk yet. Focus on breathing."

I tightened my grip on his hand, though I could barely feel it. "It... It's... h-happening ag-gain," I pushed out, my voice so strained I doubted he could hear me.

"Easy. I want you to look at me, baby. Just keep your eyes on me. We're going to breathe together." He took his hand from my vice-like grip, and I frantically reached for it. "Okay, okay. You can keep holding my hand, but I'm going to place it on your chest. Okay?"

I nodded as he did exactly as he said and used his other hand to keep my palm flat on his chest. "Sh-she d-dying ag-gain."

Fear flashed in his blue eyes, launching me into another series of desperate gasps. "What did I say? Breathe with me. Breathe in. One. Two. Three. And out. One. Two. Three. Just like that. In, one, two, three. And out, one, two, three. Focus here. Feel the breath." He tapped my hand held over his chest as he slowly modeled the breath again. "Now feel it here." His fingers tightened briefly on my chest.

I mimicked the move, digging my slowly warming fingers into his firm chest.

"That's it. I'm right here. I'm not going anywhere. Breathe in. One. Two. Three. And out. One. Two. Three."

I desperately wanted to do as he said. Suddenly, my throat opened just enough for me to gasp. Sharp pain sliced across my chest as more than a trickle of air made it into my lungs.

"There you go. You're doing great. Try to go a little slower next time. We'll do it together. Are you ready?"

I nodded, and he went back through the breathing exercise, keeping his voice calm and even. We continued on like that—in, one, two, three, and out, one, two, three. Gradually, my breaths got deeper, and the world no longer sounded like it was swaddled in cotton. When he added a hold for three in between breaths, though, I started gasping again, and we started all over.

Mason never moved his hand from my chest, and he didn't let me remove mine from his. The tenor of his voice remained steady as we repeated the breaths together again and again. All the while he offered words of encouragement and praise as my breathing gradually got deeper. The black receded from the edges of my vision, and my heartbeat slowed to something resembling normal.

When I could finally hold the air without hiccuping, I slumped forward. Every part of my body ached, especially my chest. He maneuvered closer—or maybe he'd always been that close—and rested my head where I could hear the steady beat of his heart and the measured whoosh of air filling his lungs.

"That's it. Just breathe," he whispered while he combed his fingers lightly through my hair.

I wasn't sure if the move broke me or put me back together. Either way, a sob ripped out of me. I clung to him like a child, soaking his shirt as I ugly-cried into him. He still didn't pull away. He continued to hold me while sobs strained my already sore chest and gently rubbed my back. I had absolutely no idea how long it took for me to come down or how long we sat like that. Eventually though, I sniffled and pulled away.

To my amazement, he passed me some tissues as well as a damp cloth and offered me a sweet smile. "There you are. How are you feeling?"

"B-b…" I paused to take a deep breath, mindful to hold it, before slowly letting it back out. "Better."

"Do you want to talk about it?"

I grimaced. "This is not how I wanted you to find out I had severe anxiety." As if the mere mention of the word was enough to send me back into a spiral, my adrenaline spiked and I looked around frantically for my phone. "My parents—"

"Are at the hospital now. Carmen is in surgery. They promise to call as soon as they know more." I looked up at the sound of Maria's voice. She stood nearby, clutching my phone, several paper towels, and looking paler than a ghost. I turned my gaze back to Mason. While his eyes appeared a little tight around the edges, he was in a much better state. I didn't want to think about what I looked like.

"How did you know what to do?" I asked Mason as I accepted the towels to clean my face from an obviously rattled Maria.

He looked at me for a moment before sitting back and shrugging a shoulder. "I kind of suspected you might have anxiety. So, I looked into it. I wanted to be prepared in case, you know, you needed me to be." He glanced away, his cheeks turning a faint shade of pink.

I took his hand and gave it a gentle squeeze, causing him to look at me once more. "Thank you. Thank you too," I added to Maria.

She held up her hands defensively. "I just did what he said. Your boyfriend is a champ."

A cold that had nothing to do with my panic attack slithered through me. We hadn't had "the talk," and while we'd been dating for a few weeks, I had no clue where Mason stood as far as exclusivity and labels.

"Mason Albright," he said with a smile, holding out a hand to shake. "And I don't know if I'd go so far as 'champ'. Adequate, maybe."

"Maria Rodriguez," she replied, accepting it.

He turned his beautiful grin on me, and it faltered slightly. "I'm serious, though. If you want to talk about it, I'd like to listen."

I took a deep breath that strained my taxed lungs. "When I was thirteen, my little sister was killed in a car crash." Mason didn't interject or pepper me with questions. He squeezed my hand and nodded encouragingly. "She was only eleven. She'd been playing at a friend's house. I was supposed to walk home with her, but I wanted to stay out with my buddies." Tears welled in my eyes as I recalled how selfish I'd been.

"Her friend's mom was going through a rough divorce. She'd been drinking. It wouldn't have been a big issue if I'd done what I was supposed to." I appreciated that Mason didn't offer platitudes. I'd been to enough therapy over the years to recognize that I'd been a kid and done a kid thing. Or that the mom never should have gotten behind the wheel. But that didn't magically erase the fact that Jessica was gone now.

"All three of them—Jess, her friend, and her friend's mom—died in a head-on collision with a delivery truck. My friends and I had been playing nearby, and we heard the crash. We immediately ran over. The truck driver was pretty banged up, but because of the height of the truck, he was able to walk away." My breathing stuttered, and I fought to get it back under control.

"You don't have to keep talking about it," Mason said softly, giving my hand another reassuring squeeze.

"I think... I think I need to. I want you to know. Jess and I were really close growing up. We did nearly everything together. Until I hit puberty. Suddenly, I thought I was too cool to hang out with my baby sister." I shook my head. "Now Carmen, my older sister by seven years, has been in a wreck."

"Fuck, Atticus," he exclaimed. Then I was surrounded by his arms in a fierce hug. I squeezed him back just as tightly and let myself sink into the comfort he was offering.

"And it's not just the wreck. I'm terrified she won't get the care she deserves. If she were in Oak Haven, it would be one thing. But she's not. I think it happened on her way here."

Mason pulled back slightly, and I saw the concern and confusion in his eyes. "Why would it matter where it happened?"

"Because Carmen is trans."

Understanding lit his eyes, and he pulled me back in. "Your parents are there now, and something tells me they'll do whatever it takes to make sure she's taken care of. After all, they raised you," he added in a whisper.

I knew I liked Mason—*a lot*—but I was starting to feel like it could be a whole lot more.

Chapter 13

TRY AS I MIGHT to remain present, my thoughts kept straying to Atticus. Right now he was on his way with his dad to Mercer County Hospital, where his sister had been moved to undergo a specialized surgery. I'd considered offering to take him so his dad wouldn't have to drive all the way here and back, and had even taken the day off.

In the end, I'd chickened out, fearing that might be over-stepping even if we were "official" now. I couldn't even appreciate that I was in a relationship for the first time in *years*, because I was so worried about Atticus and his sister, whom I hadn't even met.

So now, instead of working at the bookstore or providing moral support for my boyfriend, I was window shopping with Jasper along Main Street. Keeping up with my best friend was difficult on most days—I'd never been much for window shopping—but it was proving especially challenging today.

"Ooh, let's go in here. Looks like they've gotten some new items," Jasper exclaimed. He grabbed my arm and dragged me into the local antique shop before I could formulate a response.

I begrudgingly let him pull me along. "Don't you practically live here?" I grumbled, though apparently not quietly enough. He shot me a dramatic glare.

"Shut your face. I'm an artist, and this place is the best in town for inspiration." He huffed and walked deeper into the deceptively large store, leaving me to follow in his wake.

I was tempted to add that he clearly wasn't looking in the right places then. The day I'd spent with Atticus in the hot shop had been incredible. Watching him work and seeing the different stages of glassmaking was mesmerizing.

"Welcome to Memento on Main, Oak Haven's premiere antique shoppe. How can I—Oh. Hey, Jasper." I glanced up to see one of the shop's three full-time employees positively beaming at Jasper.

"Darling, angel, sweetheart, light of my life." Jasper approached the petite man with brown curly hair and solid rimmed glasses, likely in his mid twenties. He gave him an air kiss on each cheek and then held the clerk at arm's length. "Do my eyes deceive me, or are there some new treasures to discover?"

"Oh. Uh, yeah. We've got some new inventory. You'll probably want to look at the heirloom brooches first. Some really beautiful pieces came in yesterday. True treasure." The clerk pointed in the appropriate direction, not that Jasper needed any help navigating the store. Hell, he practically worked here.

"Excellent! But, however magnificent they are, we all know that you're the true treasure here. Don't we, Dusty?" Jasper winked at the increasingly flustered young man and sauntered off to explore.

I mentally shook my head. I wanted to grab Jasper and shake him. Tell him to stop flirting so over the top with the poor guy. It bordered on cruel. Not because Dustin wasn't ridiculously adorable in his cardigan that most likely had come from the store. But because Jasper was so wrapped up in his own crushes, he couldn't notice when someone was crushing on him. And Dusty was crushing *hard* if the pink cheeks and look of adoration were anything to go by.

Dustin finally spotted me and did a little hop of surprise. "Hello. Welcome to—"

I held up a hand before he could get into full swing. "I'm with the over-the-top dumbass." The poor clerk's cheeks darkened. "Not like that. We're best friends. Thus, the dumbass crack," I added hastily.

"Oh. Right. Um. I'm just going to go... straighten some things. Over there." He all but scurried off to straighten the fictional "things".

With a sigh, I wandered after Jasper, my gaze conveniently finding every single decorative glass item along the way. When I finally found my best friend, he was elbow deep in antique jewelry and fasteners, crooning with delight.

"You weren't kidding, Dusty. These are magnificent." He glanced up, and his wide grin went flat. "Oh, it's you."

"Gee thanks. Not like *you* dragged *me* in here."

He waved a dismissive hand and went right back to ogling the intricate pieces. I rolled my eyes and got comfortable. We would be here awhile. Implying that he could come back later wouldn't work. What if the piece he was thinking about was gone? Suggesting that he dial back the flirting would be a waste of breath. And I'd long since given up pointing out when guys were blatantly crushing on him. Experience had taught me that if they weren't the object of his current crush, he barely even saw them.

I wasn't sure exactly how much time had gone by while I scrolled on my phone and resisted the persistent desire to text Atticus. Jasper moved from the brooches—once he'd collected a "borrow" collection—onto the bronze pieces. Dissatisfied with what he found there, he meandered his way to the ceramic figurines, which apparently were "new". I was beginning to think we'd never leave when he finally declared he was finished.

While he was haggling with who I assumed was the shop owner—a gruff, portly man—who insisted that while Jasper could "borrow" a few items for his photography, he would need to buy the rest, I caved and texted Atticus.

Mason

> Hope everything is going well.

I debated adding a "Miss you *kiss emoji*", but decided against it. He was understandably preoccupied, and I didn't want to be a bother. So imagine my surprise when my text immediately showed *read*, and three little bubbles danced at the bottom of the screen.

Atticus

> The surgery went great. Carmen now officially has a metal plate in her head, several pins and other things the doctor mentioned in her arm, and a metal hip. She keeps calling herself the Bionic Woman. I don't think it's because of the drugs.

I responded with a laughing emoji and replied

Mason

> I mean, technically she is?

Atticus

> No! Not you too. I forbid it. You're not allowed to gang up on me with my sister *pouty face* It's bad enough my dad is helping her come up with a superhero slogan.

I bit my lip to keep from laughing.

Mason

> Any winners?

Atticus

> So far "Steel-arming crime" is in the lead, though I'm partial to "The hard head of justice."

"Alright, *now* we can go," Jasper said with an exaggerated sigh, like he wasn't the reason we'd been here for damn near two hours.

I quickly locked my phone and slipped it into my back pocket. I'd have to tell Atticus what I thought of the slogans later. "Where to next, fearless leader?" I asked as we stepped out onto the sunny sidewalk. Thankfully, a steady breeze kept the day from being too hot, but it was a close thing.

"Okay, spill," he demanded with crossed arms.

"W-what?" The sudden flare of panic had me second-guessing everything. Had I been too noticeable texting Atticus? Was I smiling at my phone too much?

He released the most dramatic of dramatic sighs and rolled his eyes before dropping his arms and stomping over. "You've been distracted all day. I get that antiquing isn't really your thing, but you usually put at least *a little* effort into faking enthusiasm."

Well shit. "Sorry, I'm just stressed about a new release delivery that's running behind." The lie came far too easily, which disturbed me more than the lie itself.

"Geesh, Mason. I love you, but you need a dang life. You act like work is your whole identity outside of the time we spend together. When's the last time you had a date?" Jasper demanded to know in his holier-than-thou tone.

I snorted. "You're one to talk. I don't see you traipsing off on any dates lately *or* asking any of your crushes out. If anything, you should march right back into Memento and ask that cute clerk out."

"Dustin? He's not interested in me like that. And if you think he's so cute, then why don't *you* ask him out?" he challenged.

It was on the tip of my tongue to say I was already dating someone, but this wasn't the time. And at the corner of Main Street wasn't the place. "What about *you* using work as an identity? When's the last time you went out just for fun?" He opened his mouth and I immediately tacked on, "With*out* your camera."

He sniffed imperiously and squared his shoulders. "As a matter of fact, I'm going out with some people to an art exhibit in Erie,

Friday after next. I'd have told you about it sooner, but you've been a Denny downer all day." Despite his high horse, he looked a touch abashed.

"You're cancelling movie night?" I had no idea why that hurt so much. It wasn't like it was the end of the world.

"Please don't be mad," he said, walking toward me. "I'd already agreed to go to the event when I realized on what day it would be."

I forced myself to smile, but the sting was still in my heart. "It's not like we haven't rescheduled before."

"Yeah, but normally it's because we're *both* doing something. I feel bad leaving you in town all by yourself. All I can picture is you mopily eating takeout and watching depressing movies," he said with an exaggerated frown.

He was cancelling movie night to go out with other people. Which meant I had a Friday all to my lonesome. Except, I wasn't on my lonesome anymore. I had a boyfriend. A boyfriend I could spend a Friday night with.

"Uh… Earth to Mason. You okay there, buddy? Oh goodness, I've broken you. That's it, I'm calling and saying I can't go." He was already endeavoring to pull out his phone while juggling his bag of borrowed and purchased antiques when I threw out my hands.

"No!" I said way too forcefully. He looked at me askance, pausing with his phone halfway out of his back pocket. "There's actually an exhibition I wanted to check out, but I knew you'd hate it."

"Oh heck, it's not another exhibition on bookbinding again, is it?"

I shrugged, more inclined to let him make his own assumptions than to fabricate yet another lie. Besides, now I had an entire evening I could safely spend with Atticus, and I had plenty of ideas on how I wanted to spend it.

Chapter 14

My dad pulled his truck up the drive, parking closer to the house than he normally would have. I turned a beaming smile on Carmen and fought like hell not to wince at all the bruising on her face and arms. Or what was visible of them. It was a close call which shade of bruising was more disturbing—the nearly black purple bruises she'd had two weeks ago or the greenish-yellow ones they'd morphed into.

I thought for sure she'd be in better spirits once she was free of "too damn many wires and tubes" and somewhere more familiar. While she'd remained quiet most of the drive, she looked downright sullen now. Was being back in Oak Haven really so bad? Or was it something else? We'd never been all that close. Would she even tell me if it was me?

Digging deep for optimism, I said, "It won't be so bad. You've always healed quickly, and we'll all be here to help." Her lips pinched like she'd eaten something rotten. Doubt curdled in my stomach. Maybe it *was* me.

"Oh honey," mom said, catching her expression as she opened the back door to help Carmen out of the truck. "Needing help doesn't make you any less of a strong, independent woman."

"Says you," Carmen grumbled under her breath as she painstakingly got out of the vehicle.

I blamed the endless hours of vigil by her side at the hospital for why I didn't make the connection sooner. Carmen *hated* asking for help for anything. And honestly, I got it. I wasn't any better at asking for help. The last thing I wanted to be was a burden or an imposition.

On cue, my phone dinged with a text message. Carmen glanced at me over her shoulder as best she could. "Someone's popular. That thing's been going off every few hours like clockwork. Care to share?"

"How about we get you inside and off your feet?" I sidestepped, my face heating. Carmen grunted, but didn't push.

There wasn't a doubt in my mind it was Mason reaching out to see if I needed anything or if there was anything he could do to help. As much as I loved that he cared enough to offer, we were still too new. I didn't want to risk putting him off because I was so needy. And fuck did I feel needy. Texts and video calls were a poor substitute for getting to hold him.

It took some doing to get Carmen settled, even after everything we'd done to prepare the house for her extended stay. We'd completely rearranged her old room to make her situation as easy as possible, but there were things we hadn't accounted for. Like Carmen taking one look at the poster-covered walls of her youth and looking like she wanted to gag. I'd thought the nostalgia would be comforting. Clearly, I was wrong.

"I'm as good as I'm going to get," Carmen declared acidicly when Mom fluffed yet another pillow for her. She sighed, and her fierce expression softened when she saw the immediate hurt on Mom's face. "I've been surrounded by doctors and nurses and physical therapists poking and prodding me for days. What I really need right now is some space. You've done an amazing job making sure I have everything I need easily at hand and a bell for anything I don't." She rang the small handbell Dad had found at the antique store, and a perfect chime emerged that would be easy to hear clear across the house.

"Right, of course, honey. I just..." Mom trailed off, and Dad wrapped an arm around her shoulders.

"I know, Mom," Carmen replied gently. "Of all the things to happen." She shook her head. A move she seemed to instantly regret. Rather than say anything, the rest of us left her in peace.

Somehow, I became the person to bring Carmen whatever she needed. Mom helped with the personal things and Dad helped with changing the bandages, but I ended up spending the most time with her. The only problem was I had no idea what to say or even how to act. She was seven years older than me, career-driven, and possibly the fiercest person I'd ever met. When I'd been graduating high school, she'd been conquering boardrooms.

"Oh my God, would you please sit already? Watching you flitter about aimlessly is making me anxious," Carmen declared. She winced as she scooted herself into a more comfortable position propped on the bed as she was, and I bit my tongue to stop from offering to help.

"Sorry, I can go. I didn't mean to—"

"You're not upsetting me, Atticus. Needing so much help is... hard for me. I'm trying not to be a bitch, but I know I'm kind of failing at it." I started to protest, and she held up a hand. "Whether or not anyone will say it to my face, I know it's true. So rather than continue to snap at everyone and have you walk on eggshells around me, I figured I'd try something new."

"Okay..." I said, not entirely sure where this was headed. We were basically strangers, so I didn't even have a good guess.

Abruptly she laughed, then clutched her side. "Ow, ow. Ooh that stings like a motherfucker. But your face." She released a smaller laugh, and I was pretty sure it was the first genuine, non-drug-influenced smile she'd worn since I first went to see her. "Not over there, you goose. Come sit by me. I'm going absolutely bonkers with no one to talk to."

"Mom and Dad would be happy to talk to you if you'd let them," I grumbled, moving the chair to be beside the bed.

"I know," she said with a sigh. "But when they look at me, I know they see Jess. And I can't... I can't bear it." She looked down. "Why did I get to walk away, and she didn't?" I don't know why it never occurred to me that Carmen would miss Jess just as much as the rest of us.

"I don't look at you like that, do I?" I asked tentatively.

She snickered. "No, you look at me like you've gotten caught in a net with a barracuda."

"I do not," I argued adamantly.

"Okay, maybe it's not that extreme, but we don't really know each other very well, do we?"

"I guess not. But I know you're a totally badass project manager," I added with a hopeful grin.

Her smile returned. "As long as you've got the important stuff." I laughed, and her grin widened. "And I know that you're a ridiculously talented glass artist, who for some reason is spending all of his time with me instead of impressing people with his crazy skills."

"That's, um, generous." I cleared my throat and glanced around, at a loss for what to say next.

"Come on, Atty. Surely there's something better you could be doing with your time than hovering around an invalid like me. If not your art... a boyfriend?" My face heated like I was three inches away from the furnace. "Aha! I knew it. Do Mom and Dad know? You know what? Forget I asked that. *I* know, and now I want to know more. Is that who keeps messaging you?" she asked with more enthusiasm than she'd shown anything in days.

"Only some of them are from Mason. The others are Maria checking in from the shop and friends wanting to know how you're doing," I countered.

"So Mason, huh?" She smirked, and despite my embarrassment, I went with it, telling myself it was to keep her spirits up.

"Mason Albright. He manages The Literary Lighthouse on Main."

"Damn, I haven't read a good book in ages. Never had the time." She snorted. "Got plenty of it now."

I hated how the thought seemed to make her sad, though she tried to make light of it. "You'll be back to slaying corporate dragons in no time."

"We'll see," she said with a wry twist of her lips. "But enough about tomorrow. Tell me about this boyfriend. How did you meet? How long have you been dating? Details, bro."

I chuckled. "Let's see, we met a couple of months ago and started dating not too long afterward. The official part is new." I didn't need the heat burning my cheeks to know I was blushing, and I didn't even bother to rein in my smile.

"That is the sweetest," she crooned. "My baby brother's all grown up and catching feels." She wiped away a fake tear, which, now that I was looking, might not actually be fake. "Okay, what else? What's he like? Is he local?"

Her enthusiasm to know about who I was dating wasn't at all what I'd expected and I couldn't help but puff up a little with pride.

"Mason is great. He has an amazing smile and eyes so blue it's like you're looking into a cloudless sky. Moved here a few years back with his best friend, so not a local, but seems like he plans to stick around." She nodded along, a smile on her face, as I continued on dreamily. "He's smart and unbelievably funny, even if his humor is on the sarcastic side at times."

"I like him already," Carmen interjected.

"Would you want to meet him?" I asked tentatively.

"Duh. Anyone who makes my baby brother smile like that, I *have* to meet."

Excited and flustered all at once, I said, "Yeah? Okay. I'll, uh, talk to him and set something up." I didn't realize I'd reflexively taken out my cell to do just that until it vibrated in my hand with an incoming message.

Carmen's eyes lit up and she leaned as close as her precarious position would allow. "Ooh, is that him?"

"Uh, yeah. But it's weird. He's asking if he can come in..." I trailed off, already typing a reply.

Atticus

First, you don't ever have to ask if you can come in. Second, I'm not at the hot shop today.

Mason

That's good to know ;)

> I'm not at the hot shop either

> I'm standing in front of an alarmingly green door.

I stared at my phone, trying to make sense of the messages, but my brain was having none of it. The piece I needed was just out of reach.

"Atty? Is everything okay? Where is he?" Carmen pressed.

The last piece slid into place. "He's here."

"What?"

I lurched to my feet. "He's at the house. He's outside." She said something in reply, but I was already out of the bedroom and making a beeline for the front door. Before my doubts could catch up with me, I flung open the door. And there he was, his golden hair shining in the afternoon sunlight and his blue eyes wide like I'd startled him.

"H-hey." He awkwardly waved a hand and gave me a sheepish smile.

"Mason. You're here. Like, actually here. But how did you know where I was?" I asked, already reaching for him. How long had it been since I'd last touched him? It felt like forever.

His grin grew. "I asked Maria."

Pure joy expanded in my chest. I yanked him toward me and pressed my lips to his. He inhaled sharply and let out the smallest of moans when my tongue traced along the seam of his mouth and slipped inside. I knew how long it had been since I'd touched him now. Too damn long.

I got completely lost in the kiss, in the feel of our mouths moving against each other, in the heat of his body pressed against mine. The desire I worked to keep in check roared to life much like it had when he'd dragged me to his car to make out. Except, my parents' front stoop was not the place for a handjob or any of the other sexy things I desperately wanted to do with this man.

Someone loudly cleared their throat behind me. I reluctantly pulled away from Mason's amazing mouth and glanced over my shoulder. The fog I'd been in cleared in an instant. "What are you doing? You're not supposed to be moving around."

Carmen rolled her eyes and drove her nifty scooter-thing closer. "I *would* have asked for help, but you raced out of there like your ass was on fire. Hi, you must be Mason. You'll have to forgive me. I'm not exactly at my best," she said, smiling and extending a hand.

"And you must be Carmen."

"That I am. Now, the more important question is, what's that?" She pointed to a large basket I hadn't even realized he was holding.

He smiled broadly and held it up so we could see better. "This is a goody basket. Atticus wouldn't tell me how I could help, and I know healing is boring as hell. So I brought some books—a few different genres since I didn't know what you liked—several snacks that I pray you're not allergic to, and some fun spa-at-home stuff."

"Are those cookies?" I chimed in, noting how the container didn't really match with the rest of the arrangement he'd put together.

His cheeks colored, but his smile remained. "Don't get too excited about those. I can't bake worth shit. Shanae learned what I was doing and wanted to contribute her famous 'Better Than Sex' chocolate cookies."

"Oh, hell yeah." Carmen made grabby hands for the basket, which Mason helpfully placed in her lap. Then she promptly turned around and zoomed back the way she'd come. Not sure what to say, I turned my attention back to Mason.

"I hope it's okay that I'm here." His earnest gaze betrayed his nerves.

"Of course it is." I gave him a quick kiss before pulling him into a tight hug. Damn, it felt good to have his arms around me again. I'd never thought of myself as a really touchy guy, but I certainly struggled to keep my hands off of Mason. "I just can't believe you're here," I said when I finally released him.

"And I can't believe you weren't going to let me help," he fired back with a smirk.

I was still floundering for words when Carmen's shout carried down the hall. "Well, don't just stand there, you two! Come help me explore all my new goodies!"

With a laugh, Mason officially stepped inside. "She's a trip. I like her already."

"Funny, she said the same thing about you." I planted a kiss on his cheek and reached for his hand, lacing our fingers together. "I'm sorry I've been so absent. I'm really glad you're here."

Mason leaned in and brushed a soft kiss on my lips. "I'm really glad I'm here too. Now we should probably get back there before your sister eats all the cookies."

Chapter 15

EXCITED BUTTERFLIES FLUTTERED IN my stomach as Atticus and I stood outside his apartment complex. Our first date since Carmen's injury had been absolutely perfect. I still couldn't get over how well I'd hit it off with Atticus's sister. I knew how much it meant to *me* that she liked me, and I could only imagine how Atticus felt. Add to all of that not having to worry about Jasper showing up at the worst time, and there was really only one way the evening could get better.

"I really enjoyed the play tonight," Atticus said as we moseyed closer to the entrance of his apartment building. "I don't know how I've lived here my whole life and never gone to see the Oak Haven Players." He shook his head.

I bumped his shoulder. "Probably has something to do with the old theater not getting renovated until a few years back."

He nodded, glanced up at the facade of his building, then over to where I'd parked at the far end of the temporarily uncrowded lot. Finally, he looked at me with a shy smile. "Would you like to come up?"

"I'd love to." The butterflies migrated to my chest, where they went absolutely bananas.

We walked inside, the air of anticipation tightening around us. The elevator ride was a blur of shared smiles, then we were standing outside Atticus's apartment. I willed myself not to look at Jasper's door, or worse, poke my head inside to verify he was truly gone, and kept my focus on Atticus.

"So this is it." He dropped his keys into a decorative glass bowl that I suspected he'd made himself. "I'd offer you the grand tour, but I'm pretty sure you're familiar with the layout."

"You could say that." I gave him a cheeky grin before returning to my perusal of his space. I gestured to the end table beside his couch, which was facing away from the doorway. "Do you always leave a lamp on when you go out?"

"Can't say I really think about it so much as it's a habit. On late nights when I'm exhausted after a full day at the hot shop, the last thing I want to deal with is flipping on bright lights."

"Makes sense," I mused as I wandered across the open floor plan to admire another glass piece, this one an intricate design that looked like waves crashing against each other. "This vase is stunning. I know I've said it before, but you are incredibly talented. I've always wanted to be good at art, but as Jasper likes to tease me, there's not a creative bone in my body." I turned away from the artwork and was surprised to find a small frown on Atticus's face. "Did I say something wrong? Fuck, it's not a vase, is it?" I covered my face to hide my rising embarrassment.

Moments later, Atticus gently pulled my hand away from my face, his expression surprisingly tender. "Just because you may not have the artistic skills you would like, doesn't mean you're not creative. Everyone shines in their own way. Look at how you're reorganizing the bookstore."

"It's nothing," I scoffed, my face heating.

He placed his knuckle under my chin and gently turned my face to look at him. "It's not 'nothing'." The earnest way he said it had my heart stuttering. The things this man did to me. I'd never felt so *seen*. He searched my gaze another second, then leaned in to press his lips gently against mine.

I happily returned the sweet kiss that turned into another and another, each one getting slightly more intense. He dropped his hand from my face and lightly gripped my sides. Smiling into the next kiss, I looped my arms around his neck, pulling us closer. I wasn't sure who deepened the kiss first, but I certainly wasn't complaining, especially when his grip tightened so that we were flush against each other. Then Atticus palmed my ass, and I groaned into his mouth. I might have been self-conscious about how I was shamelessly rubbing against him if he wasn't doing the same damn thing.

I pulled out of the kiss with a ragged breath and looked at him. "I really want to taste you right now."

He buried his face against the side of my neck. "Fuck, Mason."

"Is that a yes?" I asked playfully.

He snorted as he lifted his head. "That's an enthusiastic yes."

"Good." I pressed another firm kiss to his lips, then dropped to my knees. Thankfully, the area rug was plenty plush. I glanced at him from my new position, pleased to see how he was watching me with rapt attention.

His belt was a minor obstacle and swiftly dealt with, along with the subsequent button and zipper. I resisted the urge to dive right into blowing him and instead pushed up his shirt so I could kiss his abdomen and nuzzle the thick hair trailing down.

He gently carded his fingers through my hair, and I hummed in appreciation. "You're fucking beautiful. You know that?"

Thankfully, my current position made it nearly impossible for him to see the blush burning across my face. I tugged the waist of his jeans down while I nibbled along sensitive skin just above the band of his briefs. His small gasps of pleasure were the perfect backdrop as I stroked his thick length through the fabric. When I mouthed his cockhead, the gasps turned into a full moan, and he briefly tightened his fingers in my hair.

"You're killing me, Sunshine."

"Certainly can't have that," I said as I hooked my fingers on the elastic and freed his impressive cock. My man was *thick*. This time it was my groan that filled the living room. On cue, a drop of precum beaded at the tip. I eagerly licked the pearl away, savoring the salty musk that was pure Atticus. Torn between swallowing him down so I could feel the weight of him on my tongue and wanting this to last, I stroked his base while I mouthed his shaft.

When I couldn't take the delay a moment longer, I slowly took his cockhead into my mouth, my lips fitting perfectly under the crown. I sucked lightly and gradually took more of his length, prompting a burst of precum on my tongue. Moaning, I bobbed my head, stroking him as I alternated between swallowing him down as deep as I could and swirling my tongue around the sensitive head.

"You look way too good with my dick in your mouth," Atticus said, his voice that husky personification of sex I was quickly becoming addicted to. He rolled his hips, making shallow thrusts into the cavern of my mouth that turned me on even more.

I relaxed my jaw so he could move as he liked and tried to adjust myself surreptitiously. Though apparently I wasn't as sly as I thought. He tugged lightly on my hair to keep me from chasing after his erection as he slipped free of my lips.

"Come up here." He held out a hand, and I let him help me to my feet while I tried to hide my pout behind wiping my mouth. He chuckled and ran his thumb under my bottom lip. "Don't be sad. There's plenty of time to do all the things. But tonight... tonight I don't want to stop touching you." He pressed his lips against mine before I could process that epic feelings bomb.

"Don't suppose we could do the touching without clothes?" I asked with a crooked grin.

He kissed me again, then slid his hands beneath my shirt, coaxing it higher. "Did I forget to mention? No clothes is kind of a requirement."

"Is that so?" I replied, giving his shirt the same treatment.

"Oh, definitely." He finished tugging my shirt off and dropped his head to trail kisses along my neck. My breath caught, and I raked my fingernails across his back when he hit a particularly sensitive spot. "I don't think we need these either," he whispered in that *voice*. He deftly freed the button of my pants, sliding the fabric down a little further. Then, he pushed both hands past the material to squeeze my ass, and I let out a loud moan as I practically collapsed into him.

"Fuck, that feels good," I said when he trailed a finger along my crease, once more shamelessly rubbing against him.

He teased a little more, then continued pushing my pants and briefs to the ground, following them to remove my shoes. I swallowed thickly when I saw the way he was looking at me. It was so much more than lust. The way energy ebbed and flowed between us was a unique connection we shared that honestly broke my brain a little. He flashed me a wicked grin before placing a soft kiss on the head of my now throbbing dick.

"Now who's killing whom?"

Laughter played in his eyes as he straightened and finished divesting himself of his clothes. I hungrily devoured the sight of him, from his broad shoulders and hair-dusted pecs to his thick thighs and impressively thick cock, that for some unknown reason was no longer in my mouth. Before I had the chance to pout about it some more, he pulled me close, our bodies slotting perfectly together as he sealed my mouth with another breath-stealing kiss.

I groaned as I tangled my fingers in his hair and his hands coasted over my bare back down to my ass. "I want you to fuck me," I panted when I could finally pull my mouth away. "I really *really* want you to fuck me," I repeated, my voice pitching high in the middle when Atticus dipped a finger in my crack and brushed the edge of my hole.

"Yeah, I think you're still the one killing me." My breath caught as Atticus edged his finger further until he could rub the wrinkled muscle. Then he lightly pressed, dragging another moan out of me and making my cock jump against his abdomen. "You're so damn responsive," he practically growled in my ear before nibbling along my neck.

"Then what's taking you so long?" I quipped, aiming for sassy and landing somewhere closer to desperate.

He snatched another quick kiss, then grabbed my hand and led us to the bedroom, where, surprisingly, another lamp was on. We stumbled back toward the bed, still making out like our lives depended on it, but stopped shy of falling on it. He slowly coasted his hands down my sides and around my waist, causing goosebumps to prickle my skin.

"What's your stance on rimming?" Atticus asked, pulling away enough to meet my gaze.

"Never done it before, but always been curious," I replied honestly.

His grin broadened, and something a little wicked gleamed in his eyes. "Then prepare to have your curiosity satisfied."

"Babe," I began, looping my arms around his neck, "you can do anything you want to me so long as your dick eventually ends up in my ass." We were pressed so close that his deep chuckle vibrated through my chest, and I added, "Preferably sooner rather than later."

"Mason Albright, you are something else." Before I could slide down the rabbit hole of what that might mean, he placed his lips against mine in a tender kiss that ramped me up and settled me all at once. "Do you need a minute?"

I shook my head. "I was sort of hoping this is how the evening would end."

"Guess that makes two of us. Get on the bed. Back, stomach, or knees, however you're most comfortable."

My heart stuttered at the overwhelming consideration of this man. I shuffled to do as he asked and after a moment of indecision, I opted to lie on my back so I could see him. And man, was it a sight. Those broad shoulders and defined biceps were the things of my dreams, not to mention how thick he was below the waist. Even his slight belly was sexy as fuck.

Atticus crawled up the bed and lay over me, supporting most of his weight with his forearms. He ran his nose along my jaw before peppering kisses along my neck, across my shoulders, down my torso. He paused to run his tongue around my navel, then resumed his trail of kisses. I thought I might die when he bypassed my leaking cock to taste my thighs, then he dragged the flat of his tongue up my shaft and swallowed me down to the root.

"Fuck!" My shout filled the room, and my hips reflexively bucked off the bed.

He gagged, but didn't pull off right away. He tortured me with several more swallows until I was clawing and fisting the sheets. When he finally relented, I counted it a miracle I hadn't already blown my load.

I was still trying to catch my breath when Atticus dipped lower to nuzzle my balls. Then he spread my cheeks and licked a firm stripe up the middle. If my previous shout was loud, it didn't hold a candle to the sound I made this time. Not that it deterred Atticus in the least. He licked and licked, teasing my hole, before finally thrusting his tongue past the sensitive quivering muscle.

Every nerve ending lit up, and even though it was physically impossible for my eyes to roll back in my head, I was pretty sure they did it anyway. *Fuuuck* why had I never done this before? The way Atticus's tongue fucked into me as if a preview to how he planned to fuck me with his cock teetered on the border of so much pleasure it was almost pain. Then he added a finger, and I was positive I wouldn't last, but I also didn't want it to end.

Abruptly, I realized my fingers had snaked their way into his hair and I was pushing his face closer, desperate for more of what he was giving. I quickly released him and muttered a mortified, "Sorry." Atticus's only response was to grab my hand and put it right back on his head.

I moaned as he continued to take me apart, writhing beneath his touch. His name came out in chanted fragments along with a host of other unintelligible babble. My release promised to be epic and was so close, hovering just out of reach. I reached for my leaking cock to push it over only to have Atticus once again grab my hand.

"Not just yet, Sunshine." He flashed me a grin and placed a firm kiss first on the inside of one quivering thigh, then the other.

I actually fucking whimpered when he took his amazing mouth and fingers away, too far gone to care if I sounded pathetic and needy. I watched through sex-hazed eyes as he wiped the saliva from his face and rose to his knees. He paused in reaching for the condom and lube he'd set nearby and looked at me with wonder.

"You have to be the sexiest man I've ever had the privilege of having in my bed. I don't just want to make you feel good, I want to make you fly."

I grunted in pain as I quickly wrapped a too-tight hold at the base of my cock to keep from coming. "Atticus," I begged, not entirely sure what I was begging for, but knowing I needed it more than anything. Mercifully, I didn't need to find actual words.

He rocked back on his heels, quickly tore open the foil, and rolled the condom onto his thick cock. I probably looked half-wrecked as I watched him slick up and push a generous amount of lube into my expectant hole. I moaned deeply when he brushed over my prostate, inadvertently loosening the strangling grip on my cock.

He removed his fingers and lined up the fat head of his cock with my entrance. Even after all the work he'd put into opening me up, he was still a tight fit. He slipped past the first ring of muscle with a steady press that continued through the second. Pleasure merged with the familiar sting of being stretched, then there was only pleasure and the incredible sensation of being perfectly filled.

"Full disclosure, it's been a while. I'm not sure how long I'll last. And you feel incredible," Atticus said on the heels of a deep groan.

I nodded in agreement. "Yeah. That. Me too." I reached for him, desperate for more contact, and yanked him down to capture him with a fierce kiss, loving the way his larger body covered me. The movement caused his dick to move inside, prompting both of us to groan as he slipped a little deeper. "Need... Need you to move," I stuttered through faltering breaths.

He continued to kiss me as he slowly pulled almost all the way out, then just as slowly pushed back in. He shifted his position, and I wrapped my arms around him to keep him close, not ready to let him go. That didn't stop him from sitting up enough to grip the back of my thighs and push them closer to my chest.

I was worried he planned to turn me into a pretzel—not something I'd ever quite managed—when he repeated the slow thrust. Stars exploded behind my eyelids as he rubbed perfectly across my prostate. "Fuck. Atticus," I gasped, rocking into the next thrust.

"Mason," he groaned into my neck, maintaining the deliberate, slow thrusts. "That's it. You squeeze me so tight."

Pleasure spiraled through my body. My awareness zeroed down to the roll of his hips. The feel of his breath puffing against my fevered skin. How amazingly full I was. And the perfect angle he'd found to drive me absolutely wild.

Gradually, he increased his pace, each thrust threatening to scoot me that much further up the bed. I locked my ankles behind his back and gave up my death grip on his shoulders. That seemed to signal him to go harder. I threw my head back onto the mattress, moaning with abandon.

"You gonna come for me, Sunshine?" Atticus panted as he continued to plow into me.

"Uh-huh." I snaked my hand down and stroked my throbbing cock in earnest. My release didn't gradually dance closer. It crashed over me without warning. Cum splattered my chest and abdomen as I milked myself through the most intense orgasm of my life.

Atticus dug his fingers into my thighs with bruising strength as his release hit with brutal force. He thrust a few more times before collapsing over me, barely catching himself from settling all of his weight on top of me. Not that it would have mattered if he did. I was no wilting flower, and the idea of his weight settling on me was heaven.

"You. Are. *Amazing,*" I whispered. I couldn't remember the last time I'd been so thoroughly satisfied.

He placed a tender kiss on my shoulder as I lightly brushed my fingers along his arms. "You say that like you aren't," Atticus replied with a hum, lifting enough to look at me. My heart squeezed at his sweet words. Seriously. This man.

I cupped the side of his face and brought his lips down for a languid kiss. I released a small gasp when he pulled out of my now gloriously tender ass. Logically, I recognized it was far too soon in our relationship for how big my feelings for him were becoming. But at this point I wasn't sure there was anything I could do about it. Or if I even wanted to.

Atticus groaned as he pulled away and got up. "I'll be right back." He leaned down to brush a chaste kiss on my lips and moved to the bathroom.

I heard the water running briefly, then he was back. Before I could even think of taking the damp cloth from him, he was gently wiping down my chest, and decorating each cleaned area with more featherlight kisses. Once he finished, he settled beside me, and I turned to face him.

"I wish you could stay," he said softly while he traced my bottom lip with his thumb.

"Me too," I replied with a sigh. But there was another poorly timed delivery due at the bookstore, and I didn't want to risk possibly bumping into Jasper when I tried to leave in the morning.

Aaaaand there was my mood killer. What the hell was wrong with me? How did I think this would end? Jasper was going to lose his shit when he found out. And he *would* find out. I had to be the worst friend in the history of friends. How could I do this to him?

"Hey." Atticus's urgent whisper pulled me out of my spiralling thoughts and I looked at him. "I didn't mean to upset you. It was selfish to say anything. I, of all people, understand that time isn't always our own." He slid back off the bed, taking his warmth and comforting presence with him.

My heart squeezed again at his overwhelming compassion. I scrambled off the bed and attacked him with a fierce hug. "I'm not upset, not really. Just also wishing I didn't have to go." That I could be confident that what we were building wouldn't come crashing down around me like so many things in my life had. Jasper had been my only constant, and here I was betraying him.

He squeezed me back, then we parted and began gathering our clothes, regularly passing items to the other as we found them. While I put on the clothes I'd worn earlier, Atticus tugged on a pair of loose joggers. Then we were at the door doing a terrible job of saying goodnight. Eventually, I steeled myself to stop kissing him and reached for the handle.

"I'll text when I get home." It wasn't that he'd ever asked me to, but his sweet smile told me how much he appreciated the gesture.

"I'll wait up. Goodnight, Mason. Sweet dreams."

I gave him a cheeky grin. "Like I could have any other kind after such an incredible evening." I stole one more "last" kiss, then made a break for it, trying to keep my giggles to myself as I raced to the elevator.

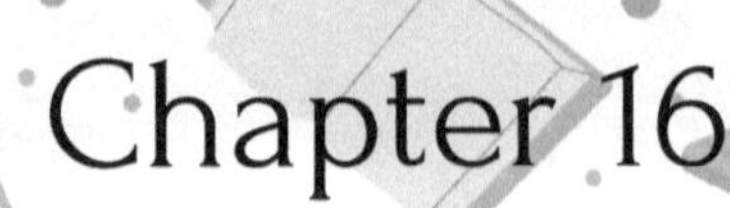

Chapter 16

I STEPPED BACK FROM the slightly less overstuffed bookshelf and cracked my back. "How the hell did I ever let Mr. Forester convince me to let things get this bad?"

"Because you're a total people pleaser and don't know how to say no," Mickey responded without missing a beat.

I gave him an incredulous look. "I am not. I can say no when I want to."

Mickey snorted and finished boxing the current stack of overstock before turning to face me. "Don't get me wrong. You're a great boss, Mason, but when's the last time you *didn't* pick up a shift for me or the others? It wouldn't hurt you to say no once in a while."

"I don't always say yes," I grumbled.

He crossed his arms. "Yeah? Name one time."

I floundered as I struggled to come up with a single instance. "There was that day the week before Christmas two years ago," I said triumphantly. Except now that I heard it out loud, it didn't feel like such a victory. A feeling emphasized when Mickey shook his shaggy hair.

"Doesn't count. *No one* could work that day thanks to the freak snowstorm. The store never even opened."

I finished labelling the box I'd been filling with a touch more force than necessary. Mickey made me sound like a pushover. I wasn't. Was I? "Yeah, well, maybe I don't want my employees feeling beholden to their jobs and missing out on living their lives," I said with a huff.

"Like you?" he challenged softly.

I purposefully kept my head down and my back to him so he couldn't see the traitorous heat pinking my cheeks. "I don't know what you mean. I live my life just fine, thank you very much. Ask anyone."

Mickey laughed quietly, then called out, "Hey Denise?"

"Yeah?" she shouted back from a few aisles over. I cringed inwardly as I heard her approach. "What's up? Oh, wow, you guys have made a lot of progress."

"Thanks," Mickey said, but clearly wouldn't be put off. "I was wondering if you knew the last time our dear Mason here didn't pick up a shift for one of us."

"Well, um, I haven't been working here that long, so I couldn't really say." I nearly turned at her pause, then she added, "But I'm pretty sure Casey was supposed to be working today."

I finally turned to look at them in time for Denise to give me a sheepish expression of apology before scuttling back to the front desk. At least her reaction was better than Mickey's smirk.

"Exactly my point. You cannot honestly tell me that there wasn't anything you would have rather been doing today instead of getting up at the ass-crack of dawn to play with dusty books. Or maybe *someone*." His smugness only grew when I failed to respond. "What about that guy? You know the one."

He had me there. I absolutely would have preferred to be doing Atticus this morning. Or, at the very least, waking up with him holding me close.

"Damn it, why am I blanking on his name?" Mickey rapped his knuckles on his temple as if he could shake loose the information. "Argh! This is going to drive me nuts. He's in here like all the time. I *know*, I know his name."

"Who comes around all the time?" Jasper asked immediately behind me, and my soul damn near left my body.

I quickly spun to face my best friend and mentally crossed my fingers that Mickey wouldn't magically remember Atticus's name. "You, obviously," I said with a forced laugh.

Jasper narrowed his eyes at me. "You're acting weird. Why are you acting weird?"

"I'm not acting weird. What makes you think I'm acting weird?" Good grief, what was it with everyone digging into me today?

"You mean besides every word you just said?" Jasper arched a dark eyebrow and leaned slightly to look behind me at Mickey. "Has he been like this all day?"

"Pretty much." Mickey grunted as he picked up the heavy box of overstock and trotted off to the storeroom.

Jasper shook his head and returned his attention to me. "I knew cancelling movie night was a mistake."

"What? No! You were so excited about the exhibit, and it's good for you to get out and rub elbows with other creatives," I argued. Besides, if he hadn't gone, I never would have gotten to finally have sex with Atticus. Or at least not without constantly worrying about getting caught.

"So you keep telling me." He placed his hands on his hips as he surveyed what he could see of the store. "Wow, I can't believe you're really rearranging this place."

I bristled at his tone. "What's that supposed to mean?"

"Whoa! No need to get your knickers in a twist. I know the chaos bothers you. I just never thought you'd actually do anything."

Well, that was a fucking punch to the gut. "Damn, tell me how you really feel."

"Don't be like that. Especially when all I wanted to do was treat my bestie to lunch." He gave me the sad puppy face that never failed to work on his parents, and I wasn't willing to challenge.

"Fine." I released a heavy sigh, trying to force out my burst of irritation with it. "Where did you have in mind?"

A broad smile instantly replaced his over-the-top sad face. "Let's pop over to the diner and grab an early lunch. It's been ages since we ate there."

I chuckled. "And by 'ages' you mean last week."

"That's literally like a lifetime ago." He nudged me with his elbow, prompting another laugh from me. "I'll even throw in a slice of cherry pie." Which he undoubtedly planned for us to share.

"Make it pecan and you have a deal," I countered. See? I could say no. Sort of.

He rolled his eyes. "Ugh. Fine. But if I can't finish my slice, you have to help me." Rather than point out that he'd never once in his life had an issue finishing a slice of his favorite pie, I nodded.

After checking with Mickey and Denise that they had everything covered and making them promise to call if they needed anything, I let Jasper drag me the couple of blocks to the diner. To my surprise, the diner wasn't crowded. On a Saturday, that was unheard of.

Jasper eyed the plethora of available seating dubiously. "Do I want to know why no one is here, or should we turn around and find somewhere else to eat?"

"Hush you." Mabel Whethers flicked the hand towel she kept tucked in her light blue apron at him. She had her gray and white streaked hair pulled back in a bun that had probably been tight earlier in the morning, but now looked ready to succumb to gravity at any second. "Don't be implying there's anything wrong with the food. You've just missed the brunch crowd, and the lunch crowd isn't due for another twenty minutes. I suggest you boys take advantage of all the seats and sit."

"Yes, ma'am," we replied in unison.

A warm smile crinkled the many lines on her face. "I'll be over in a jiff with some water and to take your orders."

"Thanks, Mabel," I said before following Jasper to a booth by the window. The red vinyl seat creaked as I slid in. Despite years of wear and the not at all subtle patches decorating it, the booth somehow remained comfy.

Silence fell as we took a minute to decide what we wanted. Then, as promised, Mabel arrived with two glasses of ice water, took our orders, and was off again.

"So... How was the exhibit?" I asked tentatively.

Jasper shrugged and gazed out the window. "Wouldn't know. I didn't go."

I spat the sip of water I'd been taking back into the cup. "What?"

"I didn't go," he repeated with another shrug as he began tearing his napkin into tiny pieces.

"Yeah, I heard you. But why?" And when the fuck did he get back to the apartment? Had he seen anything? Was this really what this lunch was about? My confidence in going back to Atticus's apartment last night now felt horribly misplaced.

He tossed the remnants of the napkin down and flopped back against the backrest of the bench. "Don't say it like that. I had... reasons," he sidestepped when Mabel dropped off our food.

"And those reasons would be?" I pushed once she was out of earshot. Neither of us was keen on being the center of small-town gossip. A tense conversation at the local diner—even a mostly empty one—was like taking a bullet train while everyone else was still using horses and buggies.

"You. Okay?" he snapped defensively. Before I could press for details, he surged on. "Look, I felt guilty as heck for cancelling movie night basically at the last minute and abandoning you."

"I'm perfectly capable of entertaining myself," I countered half-heartedly. My brain was too caught up in panicking to do much more.

He rolled his eyes and stabbed at his grilled chicken. "I know that. Doesn't change the fact that I felt like a Grade-A jerk. We were about to leave when I couldn't take the guilt anymore. So I bailed and tried to call you to see about meeting up. Only *someone* never picked up." He narrowed his gaze at me as if it were somehow my fault that he'd forgone going to the exhibit. Then I realized this wasn't about me at all. It was about him and his guilt.

"I put my phone on silent and turned in early." It was the easiest lie to stick with and, honestly, not that far from the truth.

Jasper groaned and smacked his head against the backrest. "See. I knew it. I can just see you curled up with your over-salted popcorn on your couch watching a sad movie by yourself. I should have just gone over to your place when you didn't answer."

I wasn't a fan of his plan to come to my house, especially since I wouldn't have been there. Nor was I too fond of his image of me. But I wasn't in a place to address either of those. I needed other answers first. "Where did you go instead?"

"Where else?" he scoffed. "Back to the apartment."

I pushed back the psychotic need to know exactly *when* he'd gotten back to his place. "I'm sorry your Friday night turned into such a bust."

"You can make it up to me later," he said, waving away my half-assed apology. "Get this though. It's a good thing I *did* come back early. Otherwise, I might never have known."

"Known what?" I asked, swallowing thickly as my panic surged again. Sometimes I really, *really* hated his tendency to build up to a big reveal.

"Atticus-the new neighbor," he clarified as if I could somehow forget the name of his latest obsession, even if I wasn't dating him, "he's totally seeing someone." His drawn eyebrows and pursed lips told me exactly how much he didn't like that.

Feeling my way carefully, I asked, "What makes you so sure?"

"Because I *heard* them. No way was he was in there by himself. And don't even suggest that he might have just been watching really loud porn. Porn doesn't shout your name like that."

Fuck. fuck. fuck.

For once, my ridiculous tendency to blush didn't betray me. Namely, because all the blood was currently draining out of my body through my feet into the floor. Or that's what it felt like. "Could it have been a casual hookup?"

The frown he gave me said my voice sounded just as weird to him as it did to me. "I suppose it could have been. Ugh, what if he's one of those app-obsessed guys? He didn't *look* like the kind of guy who wants to have sex with a different guy every night," he complained.

Of course, that's when Mabel dropped off our pieces of pie. She gave us a curious look, but mercifully didn't prod. I was waiting to resume our conversation until she got farther away, but Jasper wouldn't be stalled.

"That would be just my luck. He's secretly a jerk face that likes to use 'em and lose 'em. Mace, why does this always happen to me?" he griped as he shoved a spoonful of cherry pie into his pouting mouth.

I don't know what came over me. Maybe it was watching the cherry filling ooze out of the fresh pie Jasper had tried to coerce me into sharing. Maybe it was the way the sunlight was glinting off the metal napkin holder and shining in my eye. Or *maybe* it was because I was sick to death of having this conversation.

I threw down my fork without taking a bite of my pecan pie. "For fuck's sake, Jasper. This has got to stop." And not just because he was badmouthing *my* boyfriend.

"What's your deal?" he demanded.

"My *deal* is that you keep complaining about the guys you like not living up to your expectations and magically falling into your lap. You bitch and moan when you do absolutely fucking nothing to make something happen." I exhaled hard through my mouth and tried to claw my temper back into submission.

"Dang. Tell me how you really feel." Jasper rolled his eyes and scooped up another bite. "For the record, I *have* talked to him. All I'm saying is the least he could do is give me some kind of clue if he's interested or let me know he's not on the market," he said around his bite.

"No, it's not the least he could do. He doesn't *owe* you anything. You don't own him. Or anyone else you've had one of your ridiculous crushes on." I pushed away my plate of untouched pie and scooted out of the booth. "I'm going back to Lighthouse. I have a lot of work to do."

Jasper stared at me with wide, disbelieving eyes, his spoon hanging listlessly from his fingers. "What's gotten into you? Why are you acting like this?"

He was right that this was out of character for me. I rarely pushed back against whatever inane thing had captured his focus, but maybe that was on me. Indulging him all these years because I didn't want to risk offending him and ending up back out on my ass clearly hadn't done him any favors.

I'd worked hard when the Rivers took me in not to see Jasper as a spoiled only child. I mean, what right did I have to judge anyone's family when mine had proved so shitty? But much as I loved him and what had become a cherished friendship, he'd never grown past being a spoiled brat.

I blinked, breaking our staring contest, and pulled enough cash from my wallet to cover both of our meals and leave a generous tip. "Consider this me making up for not answering the phone last night." I threw the cash down and stalked out of the diner without looking back. I didn't need to see him to know his gaze tracked me through the double-glass doors, past the long window of the diner, and across the street. I could feel the heat of his stare burning into my head with every step I took.

Chapter 17

I WAS NEVER GOING to grow tired of kissing Mason. The way he wrapped his arms around me and pressed close so that we slotted together perfectly. The way he met each curl of my tongue with a swipe of his own. Or how his kisses seemed to tell me everything I needed to know.

Mason released a despondent groan and pulled out of the kiss. "Much as I would like to keep doing that, if we don't leave now we'll be late to meet your sister."

I rested my forehead against his. "I know." It was amazing how well he and Carmen got along, and I didn't want to do anything that might jeopardize that growing friendship.

He brushed a kiss over my lips and placed his hands on my chest. Then he gave a small push so he could step away from the wall that separated the hot shop from the other creative spaces. "Is there anything else you need to do before we leave?" he asked as he looked around the shop.

"Besides you?"

His cheeks darkened from the blush that never seemed to truly leave him, but his smile said he liked it. "Besides me."

I took a mental inventory of everything I'd used and visually checked to make sure it was back in its place. "Don't think so. Everything looks in order to me."

"All right then, let's get to gettin'." He slipped his hand in mine, then slid back the barn door separating the hot shop from the rest of the Artists' Co-Op and pulled us through.

It didn't take long before we were rolling into the neighboring town of Mist Wood Springs. Finding somewhere to park, however, wasn't as easy. Then we dove into the winding crowd, trading car traffic for foot traffic.

"I thought you said this was like Oak Haven's Makers' Market?" Mason glanced at me in confusion while being careful not to bump into anyone in front of him.

"It is. It's just *a lot* bigger," I said with a smile, lacing our fingers together so we wouldn't lose each other in the throng of people. "Don't worry. It'll get better once we're inside."

"I thought you said the festival was an outdoor event?"

"It is. It's sort of cordoned off and there's a main gate to control the..." I trailed off when I noticed Mason was struggling to contain a smile. "You're teasing."

He nodded his head, his bottom lip firmly caught between his teeth, undoubtedly to suppress a laugh.

"It's a good thing you're cute." I pressed a quick kiss to the side of his head, then guided us to the main gate. As I expected, once inside, the crush of people dispersed in every direction, leaving plenty of room to breathe, though the grounds were far from empty.

The Mist Wood Springs Art Festival boasted over a hundred artist booths, several food trucks, and even a band. It had been a long time since I'd come here. Not since I'd discovered my now ex-boyfriend, Tom, had been living a double life. It was one thing to find out you were being cheated on. It was a whole other thing to learn there was a wife and kids in the picture, two seconds *after* I walked up and kissed the man that was supposed to be my boyfriend.

Things had gotten rough after that. Seemed the wife was just as clueless about where her husband spent his time. At first, I had empathy for her. How many times had Tom done this over the years? How many idiots had he fooled into believing that he cared? Then the angry calls started. I'd expected them from Tom—hoped for them even—but they'd come from her. Part of me understood why I needed to be the villain in her story. The other part wanted to tell her explicitly all the things Tom and I had done together. Maybe then she'd see who the *real* home-wrecker was. Either way, I was past letting that man take anymore joy away from me.

Mason shook our clasped hands, pulling me away from the dark shadows of memory lane.

I glanced at him and took a wild guess why he was getting my attention. "Right, I should message Carmen and let her know we're here," I said, my phone already out of my pocket.

"I already did that," he said casually, because of course they already had each other's numbers. His brow wrinkled with a worried frown. "Are you okay? You seemed... far away and not all that happy."

I gave him a guilty smile. "Sorry, the last time I was here wasn't so great."

"How long has it been?" he asked, his frown deepening.

"Three years."

He stepped close enough that our chests brushed each other and dropped his voice to a whisper. "Shit, Atticus. I never would have agreed to Carmen's suggestion to check out the festival if I'd realized it would bring up bad memories." He was so earnest, so considerate. I couldn't help but tilt his chin and seal our lips in a kiss.

"That's *why* I wanted to come." I stole a smaller kiss. "I'm looking forward to making new memories. Better memories," I added. So close, I could actually see the dark of his pupils expand across the brilliant blue of his irises. And now I was trying to decide if I was brave enough to follow through on my innuendo. Then again, I was pretty sure not even Oak Haven would be okay with me doing all the things I wanted to do to Mason on the open grounds of a festival. At any rate, another—*mostly tame*—kiss was still perfectly acceptable. I smiled and leaned in, ready to take his lips again.

So, of course, that's when Carmen showed up. She zipped her scooter so close that Mason and I practically leapt apart so she wouldn't crash into us. "Hey, break it up, you two." She lowered her sunglasses like some movie beat cop. "You can fuck each other's brains out later."

Mason snorted and held his fist to his mouth to hold back laughter. I'm glad he found it funny. My face felt like I was standing in front of the furnace with both doors open, and I absently wondered if Misty Wood was prone to sinkholes and if I'd be lucky enough for one to swallow me now. Carmen's response to my complete embarrassment? She laughed so hard she nearly fell off her scooter.

"Aw, Atticus, I'm sorry," Mason said, wrapping me in a tight hug before stepping back. "I shouldn't have laughed. I guess I've forgotten how awful it is when your siblings embarrass you."

It took me a second to realize why that sounded off. It sounded like *Mason* had siblings, plural. But he'd never mentioned having any brothers or sisters. Much as I wanted to ask about it—and I definitely did—I didn't want to do it now. That was a conversation for just us. And I wasn't going to let it dim our beautiful day.

"It's okay." I squeezed Mason's hand, then I looked over at Carmen. "What gives?"

"Atty, you may be bigger than me, but I'll always be your big sister. And there are certain... responsibilities that come with that." Her grin made the hair on the back of my neck stick up. "Getting to mercilessly tease and cockblock you are just a few of them." She hiked her shoulder. "I'd also kill for you. I'd add that I'd die for you too, but that's hella morbid. Now come on, slowpokes, I've been here over an hour and I've only seen a quarter of the artists."

I watched as she angled her scooter toward a display a few booths down, then glanced at Mason. "*That* was the morbid part?"

"Eh. Technically the rest was more disturbing than morbid," he clarified with a smirk.

"Come on, I'm curious if some of my favorite artists are still here." I slipped my hand into Mason's and we set off in the same direction as Carmen. We'd almost made it to where my sister was inspecting what appeared to be a birdhouse constructed of license plates when Mason tugged on my arm.

"Look at these," he whispered in awe, reaching up to delicately brush the bronze tube of a wind chime. Even that light touch elicited soft musical tones. "It's so beautiful."

I wrapped my arms around him from behind and placed a kiss on the side of his neck. "Not as beautiful as you, Sunshine." Okay, that was a hell of a cheesy line, but I was hard-pressed to feel bad about it when I saw the blush darkening his face. Damn, he was adorable. *Especially* when he didn't know how to respond to compliments.

I caught sight of Carmen waving impatiently for us to join her. Not wanting to rush Mason as he continued to admire the various designs, I gave his middle a light squeeze. "Did you want to go inside?"

"Huh?" He glanced at me. I waited as his brain slowly came back online. I loved that I could do that to him. I loved... a lot of things about Mason.

"The tent. Did you want to go in and see some of the other designs?"

"Oh! Uh, maybe later we can come back. I'm looking forward to exploring the festival with your sister." He stepped out of my arms, and I reluctantly let him go. Then he looked at me over his shoulder and added with a wink, "And you too, of course." He laughed and took off toward Carmen, who was now clear across the festival, before I could grab him.

By the time I caught up, he and Carmen had their heads together as they admired some impressive wood carvings. With Carmen conveniently between me and Mason. He gave me a cheeky grin behind her back, and I arched an eyebrow at him. Grinning to myself, I took a closer look at a carved set of goblets with the most incredible twisting pattern. I couldn't help but wonder if I could replicate its like in glass.

"As I live and breathe, Atticus Garner."

I looked toward the owner of the booth and the source of the enthusiastic greeting. "Will Stevenson. Holy shit, man." How had I forgotten he'd taken over his father's carpentry business? Hell, I had at least two of his pieces in my apartment.

Will stepped from beneath the shade of his tent and met me in a massive bear hug complete with stinging back slaps. "Never thought I'd see you here again. Not after that ass—" I cleared my throat, and he let it drop. Determined to move past the whole Tom disaster didn't mean I wanted to talk about it. "You on a mission for somethin' or just exploring?"

"Just exploring. Had to get this one out of the house." I gestured over my shoulder, then stepped aside so he could see who I meant. "I believe you already know my sister, Carmen," I said, knowing damn well that they had a history.

Will's gaze raked over Carmen, barely pausing at the yellowed bruising and evidence of stitches. "You've grown up, baby doll. Still chasing the dream?" he asked with a knowing smile.

Her cheeks colored slightly, and she sniffed. "I will be. And I see you haven't changed. Still playing ball?"

"I might be, but nothing official. Just some of the guys getting together on weekends to throw the ol' pigskin," he said, leaning to rest his forearms on the table displaying his wares. The move accentuated his shoulders and thick arms, which Carmen diligently pretended not to notice. Yep, he hadn't changed one bit. Neither of them had. "You should come sometime. Could always use someone to cheer me on."

She gave a derisive snort. "Like your ego needs any help."

"Or you could just come by to say hi," he suggested, his gaze softening. Will had always had it bad for Carmen, even before she transitioned. Then it got worse. It wasn't that he couldn't respect "I'm not interested" so much as she'd never said it. And so the dance went on.

Deciding that was enough payback for embarrassing me earlier, I gestured for Mason to step closer. "You might know this ray of sunshine. This is Mason Albright, my boyfriend." My stomach fluttered both at the label I still couldn't believe and at the smile that split Mason's face as he extended a hand.

"Can't say I've had the pleasure." Will shook Mason's hand and glanced at me. "Finally decided to dive back into the dating pool?"

I probably looked sappy as fuck staring at Mason. "How could I not?"

Mason's adorable blush rose from beneath his collar to suffuse his cheeks. "*Atticus,*" he hissed.

"They're fucking cute as hell," Will said, crossing his dark arms across his chest.

"Tell me about it," Carmen added with an over the top eye roll, but there was a hint of wistfulness in her voice. Abruptly, she cleared her throat. "Right. We have a festival to see, and we can't do that standing here." She snuck a glance at Will, then angled her scooter to continue down the line of artists' displays.

Will's sigh threatened to send some of his finer carvings tumbling to the grass. "She's still just as stubborn as ever. But I think she might actually be hotter now."

"Ew, that's my sister."

Mason laughed and tugged on my arm. "It was nice meeting you Will! Maybe we can all get together sometime." I beamed at him. It had to mean something if he was already making future plans with my friends, right?

We walked at a more sedate pace on our way to catch up with Carmen, pausing periodically to check out the impressive pieces on display and for sale. While Mason was checking out some prints, I snapped a few pictures of a sculpture that was reminiscent of the original piece I was working on. Then I stole a few minutes to talk with the artist about how they'd worked out the connections before joining Mason at the next booth.

"So... You going to tell me what all that was about?" Mason asked as we continued on.

I missed a step and played it off as stumbling over an exposed root. "What 'what' was about?" Did he see the sculpture? Could he have connected it to the piece he'd helped start with me? How the hell was I supposed to surprise him if he'd already figured it out?

"Uh, Carmen and Will. But seeing that panicked look on your face makes me *really* curious what you thought I was asking about." He slipped an arm around my waist, tucking his hand into my left back pocket. "Except now you look extra freaked. So let's stick with Carmen and Will. If that's okay?" he asked with an uncertain smile.

"More than." I wrapped an arm around his shoulders and pulled him closer to plant a kiss on the side of his head. "Will was Varsity Right Guard in high school and Carmen... was a cheer-leader."

"No fucking way."

I smirked. "Way. And..." We rejoined Carmen at a booth selling every kind of crystal you could imagine, some of which were arrayed in truly impressive designs. And now Mason was officially filled in on the drama of Carmen and Will's school days, "Will they/Won't they?" drama.

Carmen eyed us suspiciously before returning to her perusal of the stones. Once she completed her purchase, she angled her scooter to the opposite corner of the festival where several trucks and closed trailers were arranged. "I don't know about you, but all of this scootin' has me famished."

I glanced toward Mason to get his thoughts on food, only to find him gone. Something way too close to panic tightened my chest, then I saw him at an adjacent booth. I walked over to him, relieved and trying not to show it.

"Hey. Sorry, I should have given you a heads-up before wandering off. These beauties caught my attention, and I couldn't resist." He held his hands out in a helpless gesture and gave me an abashed smile.

I looked down at the display table to learn what had caught his attention. A laugh burst out of me. "You manage a bookstore. I imagine you have dozens of bookmarks."

"Who says I don't?" He raised an eyebrow in challenge, and I surrendered. "You looked like you wanted to say something when you were coming over here. What's up?"

"Carmen is voting for food. And for the record, I think your continued joy in all things bookish *despite* being surrounded by it all the time is pretty great." Mason's smile made my stomach flutter and my heart beat faster.

He stepped closer and dropped his voice to a whisper. "I could eat."

A surge of lust went straight to my dick so fast I got lightheaded for a moment. I held out my hand, savoring how warmth spread through my palm when he took it. "Come on. I think I saw a trailer selling funnel cake."

"Why didn't you start with that?" His eyes danced with merriment as he tugged me toward Carmen, who was already halfway to the food truck circle.

Chapter 18

I COULDN'T BELIEVE HOW perfectly the day was going. I'd bumped into several old friends and familiar artists. Carmen was having a blast, though I suspected I'd be carrying those bags to the car. I hadn't spotted anyone who looked even remotely like Tom or his angry wife. It wasn't overly hot thanks to a pleasant breeze. And Mason. Fuck. He was just... perfect. The way the sunlight caught his golden hair and made his blue eyes shine. The smiles he kept sending my way. Even the enthusiasm with which he greeted the artists and complimented their designs had warmth spreading through my chest. If I didn't already know that I was falling for him, this would have sealed it.

Mason finished tossing our trash from our lunch at the food trucks and walked back to me. He paused mid-dusting his hands when he caught me smiling at him. "What?" he asked, glancing around as if there was anyone else I wanted to be looking at.

"Come here." He stepped closer, his blue eyes wary. "You have powdered sugar on your cheek." I brushed it away with my thumb, letting my hand linger on his jaw.

I was debating whether to kiss him when his gaze flicked to look just past me. His eyes widened in what looked to be panic, then before I could process the expression, he was gone. I caught a glimpse of his back right as he rounded a food truck. Worried, I took off after him. It took a little more searching than I expected, but I eventually found him peeking out from behind a different food truck.

"Is everything all right, Mason?" I asked as I walked up behind him.

He let out a muted cry and spun around to face me, clutching his shirt over his heart. "Holy mother of God. You scared the shit out of me."

"I'm not surprised given how intently you were staring in the opposite direction. What are you looking at anyway?" I stepped up beside him and peered around. There were a few familiar faces—a couple that had commissioned a custom piece last year, my dark-haired neighbor from across the hall, the boyfriend of the owner of Kaleidoscope Coffee—but mostly it was a bunch of random people.

"No one. I mean nothing," he corrected hastily. I frowned at him, and he released a sigh. "Sorry, it was just... someone I didn't expect to see here." Anxiety rolled off of him in waves, and he continued to dart glances toward the seating area in front of the food trucks. Considering I'd avoided coming here for three years to avoid seeing someone, I got it. The last thing I wanted was to make things any worse for Mason.

I held out my hand. "Come on. What do you say we swing by that booth with the pressed flowers again before we meet back up with Carmen? You can finish checking out their bookmarks." And it was in the complete opposite direction of whatever was stressing him out.

The smile that bloomed on his face was equal parts relieved and appreciative. "Have I told you lately that you're the best?"

I leaned forward and dropped my voice. "How about you tell me later? *In detail.*" I wasn't surprised to find his eyes burning with lust or the goosebumps prickling his arms when I pulled back.

"What are we standing around here for? I've got book-marks-I-don't-need to buy." He grabbed my hand, and I couldn't help but laugh as he practically dragged me toward the booth. We'd barely gone a few steps when he glanced over his shoulder at me. "How long did Carmen want to stay? And is she sure she doesn't want to catch a ride with one of her friends?"

I shook my head, still laughing. "You'll have to ask her. She didn't say. And *that*, I suspect, was on purpose."

"Why don't I like the sound of that?" he asked as we stopped in front of the pressed flowers booth.

"Because you've only known her for a month and you already know she does nothing without a reason." We shared an intense look, then we both cracked.

"It's more disturbing because it's true." His grin was finally more relaxed.

I stole a quick kiss, then tugged him toward the interior of the booth. "Come on, you've got some bookmarks-you-don't-need to buy."

For a while, Mason was as relaxed as he had been when we arrived... almost. Carmen rejoined us not long after he'd bought no fewer than four bookmarks *and* secured a card to see about carrying them at Literary Lighthouse. It was pretty cool that the bookstore had such a focus on supporting local artisans. I just wished that he didn't look like some carnival monster was going to jump out at him any second.

Carmen slowed her pace and tugged on my sleeve so that I fell back with her.

"What's up?" I glanced down and noted that her scooter still held a decent enough charge. But she was healing, and the docs had been pretty adamant about her not overdoing any physical activity no matter how good she *felt*. "Are you okay? Do you need anything? Water? A snack?"

"No, no. I'm fine. Good grief, you're such a caregiver. If I need something, I'll ask," she harrumphed. I frowned at her, and her grumpy expression melted into a self-deprecating smile. "Okay, so maybe I'm shit at asking for help, but that's not why I wanted to talk to you."

I glanced ahead, where Mason was now perusing wares several booths ahead while also periodically looking around. "Should I have Mason join?"

"Not yet." She worried her bottom lip and glanced up at me. "Please don't take this the wrong way, but is something wrong with Mason? Did you have a lover's tiff or something?"

"Of course not. Why would you think that?" I asked, slowing to a stop, which she mirrored.

"He seems... off. Different from when we got here. I absolutely adore Mason and enjoy spending time with both of you. If I'm cramping your style though, I need you to tell me and not worry about hurting my feelings. I'm a tough girl."

I laughed and lightly squeezed her uninjured shoulder. "No doubt about that. As for Mason, he saw someone he hadn't expected to see here. I'm guessing an ex considering how jumpy he's gotten."

"*Ohhh.* Okay, I can see that. Wow, that sucks." She paused and glanced around at the busy festival. "Should we go so he doesn't have to feel anxious? I'm worried the man is going to give himself whiplash."

"Maybe? Neither of us wants to cut your outing short, though. Because Mason *does* like spending time with you." I chuckled and shook my head. "Sometimes I feel like *I'm* the third wheel."

She smirked, looking smug as hell. "That's good to know. Then, as his self-declared new most amazing friend ever, I'm calling it. Let's get out of here." She sped ahead without waiting for a response. One thing was for sure: when Carmen decided something, she let nothing get in her way.

By the time I caught up, it seemed Carmen had already put her plan into motion. Mason looked at me askance when I joined them. Sadly, I also caught the almost imperceptible slide of his gaze to look behind me.

"Are you sure you want to leave? You were so excited about it before." The worry on Mason's face was so sweet it actually made my heart ache.

"Pft. You forget I was here *waaaay* before you two arrived. Besides, the doc said to take it easy, and I feel like I'm already flirting with that line." She leaned forward to pat him on the arm. "I promise I'm perfectly okay with heading out now."

Mason's frown deepened. "Is this because I suggested we circle back to Will's booth?"

She stiffened, and I started to laugh. I quickly covered it with a cough, but I clearly didn't fool Carmen since she shot me a nasty look. Suddenly, I realized Mason's lips were twitching like he was fighting back a grin.

Carmen alternated her scowl between us. "You two think you're so funny. Teasing a poor, helpless injured woman. I'll have you know that I've already responded to Will's text about catching up sometime." For a second it seemed she'd stick her tongue out, then she registered what she'd said and her face turned beet red.

"Okay, okay, I'm sorry. We can head back to the car. Who knows, maybe the foot traffic won't be so bad," Mason offered optimistically.

Spoiler: the foot traffic was just as bad, and the car traffic was somehow worse. Eventually, we made it to Mason's car and dropped off Carmen without incident. Then we sat in my parents' driveway trying to decide what to do next. We'd anticipated the art festival taking more of the day and having dinner in Mist Wood Springs before coming back. Now we had an entire afternoon to fill. Good thing I had a great idea.

"What would you say to coming back to the apartment?" I asked.

"No!" he exclaimed, contradicting the ease I thought he'd regained and startling me. "Sorry, that was way more forceful than I intended." He cleared his throat and wore an uncertain smile when he looked back at me. "I was kind of hoping we could go back to my place?"

I instantly forgot the alarming outburst and reached across the console to thread our fingers together. "I'd really like that."

It wasn't until we pulled up to an adorable Craftsman home I remembered he rented a house, not an apartment.

"Welp, uh, come inside," Mason said once he'd put the car in park. Then he promptly cringed and looked at me with pleading eyes. "That's not... I mean, it is... but not... Oh, for fuck's sake. What is wrong with me, Atticus?"

I resisted the desire to laugh and leaned toward him. "Absolutely nothing." I cupped his jaw and pulled him in for a kiss. I could feel the moment all of his tension drained out of him. Our lips continued to move together until we were practically on top of the console.

"Really want to keep doing that," Mason said when we pulled up for air. "But…"

I arched an eyebrow. "But?"

"When did we get so dusty?" He made a face as he patted his sleeve, and, sure enough, a small pouf of dust rose.

"I wouldn't want you to be uncomfortable," I said, running my thumb along his admittedly very dusty cheek. "Suppose we could always rinse off."

His cheek warmed slightly beneath my touch, and lust darkened his brilliant blue gaze. "I'd really like that," he replied, answering the implication that I'd be joining him.

Our gazes kept coming back together as we exited the car and made our way to the front porch. I did my best not to crowd him so he could unlock the door, but all I wanted to do was press his body close to mine. Mason opened the door, pushing it wide. Then he looked back at me and extended his hand.

I gladly took it and let him lead me into the house. I had enough wherewithal to close the door behind us, but other than that my focus was solely on Mason. We walked in a warm, expectant silence, bypassing any semblance of a tour. He didn't hesitate to lead us through the bedroom directly into the ensuite. It wasn't large by any stretch, but not crowded. Or it wouldn't have been with only one person in it.

He released my hand in front of the sink, turned on the water to warm up, then turned back to me. With hardly any words and only a few chuckles, we slowly stripped each other of our clothes. Mason checked the water temperature and stepped into the shower, giving me enough room to join him.

Desire became as thick as the steam as we crowded close to fit and took turns soaping each other. It wasn't some frenzied lust though; it was softer, more subdued. We were existing. I couldn't think of a single partner I'd ever felt this at ease with.

Mason slid his hands over my chest, clearing away the soap he'd put there, then he lifted his gaze. His eyes were the stunning blue of an ocean with no land in sight. Deep and alluring, drawing me closer, a siren's call I'd gladly follow.

I leaned in, brushing my lips over his in a sweet kiss, which I followed with another. He coasted his hands over my shoulders, trailing his fingers across my back before he slid them into my damp hair and used his hold to deepen the kiss. I pulled him closer so that more of us was touching. We both gasped as our erections slid against each other, but didn't stop kissing. Then, with his tongue still dancing with mine, he rolled his hips.

I moaned into him at the feel of the slight, yet nowhere near enough, friction, and felt him smile against my mouth. Each shallow thrust made me wild. I reflexively tightened my hands on his waist, and he stopped moving. Well, that wasn't what I wanted at all. Eager to get things back on track, I broke the kiss long enough to reach down and grab his conditioner.

A smile danced in his eyes when I curled my finger for him to step closer. Our cocks lined back up and I dribbled some of the conditioner on them. Getting the hint, Mason grinned wide, then sealed his mouth back on mine at the same time he wrapped a hand around our lengths. The sudden onslaught of sensation had me instantly wrapping my arms around him, both to steady myself and because I was desperate to touch as much of him as possible.

Mason kept his grip just tight enough to keep us on the cusp without falling over. I slowly thrust into his grip while I trailed my hands down his back and over the curve of his ass. He hummed appreciatively when I massaged the firm muscle, his movements slowing as another sensation fought for his attention.

Lost in the intimacy, I slid my finger along the seam, then slipped past his plump cheeks to brush against his rim. I swallowed his deep groan and applied more pressure. There was still just enough conditioner on my finger for it to slide inside to the first knuckle.

A soft "Oh" escaped him quickly followed by a grumble of displeasure when I removed the digit. Clearly taking a page out of my book, he resumed stroking our dicks together. The extra squeeze as he reached the tips felt amazing, but I wasn't about to be diverted. I grabbed the conditioner once more, a feat in itself since I didn't want to do anything that might lead Mason to stop touching me.

This time when I ran my finger around his quivering rim and pressed, it slid in easily. I abandoned his mouth to kiss along his jaw and neck while I thrust the digit in and out of him at an unhurried pace. Mason's fist continued to slow and stopped altogether when I added another finger. Soon he was writhing with pleasure, trying simultaneously to get friction on his dick and drive my fingers deeper.

"Fuck, baby," he moaned. "I need you inside me."

With how quickly I removed my fingers and turned off the water, it was a miracle neither of us slipped and landed on our asses. Mason chuckled, but that didn't stop him from ripping back the curtain and immediately grabbing towels. Then it became a whirlwind of hands and terrycloth as we tried to resume kissing, dry off, and stumble out of the bathroom all at once. We separated long enough for him to pull some things from the nightstand and toss them on the bed.

I stepped up behind him and wrapped my arm around his middle. He moaned and pressed back against me. Unable to resist, I kissed and nibbled along his neck while I stroked his dick with my free hand.

"Atticus," he panted, and I could feel how close he was.

"I know, Sunshine." I tightened my grip at the base of his dick, and he bucked against me. Much as I wanted to drag this out, turn Mason's world upside down, I was already so close. "Get comfy," I said with a light nip at his neck before releasing him and turning to grab a condom and the lube. When I turned back to him, I damn near came.

Mason had bent over the bed, legs spread, putting his perfect ass on display. I watched completely mesmerized as he sunk two of his fingers into his eager hole. I wasn't sure who moaned louder, but the sound filled the room.

"You're so fucking sexy," I said, my voice rough. His skin was warm and smooth, golden hair shining in the lamplight, as I ran my palm over his ass. Needing to be inside him, I gently tapped his wrist. He removed his fingers and looked at me over his shoulder. *Fuuuck.* The desire in his eyes nearly undid me.

I stepped closer, lining my cock up with his twitching entrance. In one smooth stroke, I buried my length in his ass. His intense heat swallowed me, and it was all I could do to hang on to him from the overwhelming pleasure of it. He rocked back impatiently, fucking himself on my dick. It might have been the sexiest thing I'd ever seen. He really was perfect. And I was so far gone for him.

I pulled out slowly until only the head of my cock was stretching him open. Then I thrust just as deep as the first time. Again and again. With each pass, I picked up my pace. My orgasm drifted closer, pleasure pooling at the base of my spine.

"I'm close, baby," Mason panted beneath me.

"Me too. You feel so damn good."

"Uh-huh," he replied, slipping his hand between him and the bed to stroke his cock as fast as I was pounding into him. A second later his channel turned into a vice and we were both coming.

I groaned through my release, flexing my hips to milk out every second of bliss. When I had nothing left, I flopped over Mason, blanketing him with my body. Half a second later, I realized I was probably crushing him.

"Shit, sorry," I said, trying to move my weight off of him. Trying being the operative word. I'd scarcely moved when he reached back to hold me in place.

"Not glass," he mumbled into the sheets.

I kissed his shoulder. "I know, Sunshine. Was just thinking about cleaning up a bit before snuggles."

"Oh. Kay."

He released me, and I didn't waste any time darting back into the bathroom to wet a hand towel. When I returned, he was already standing. I forgot what I'd been doing as my gaze travelled over his beautiful body.

"See something you like?" he teased, holding out his hand for the damp cloth.

I waited for him to finish wiping himself and the side of the bed down before stepping in close. "You know I do." I teased him with a kiss that I withheld, making him grin. "So... snuggles?" I wrapped my arms around his middle, loving how he seemed to fit perfectly against me.

He searched my face for a moment, and I was on the verge of asking what he saw, when he said, "Stay."

"Thought you had to open the bookstore in the morning."

He promptly pulled my arms from around him and held up a finger. "Hold that thought." He darted into the bathroom only to return a second later, typing away on his phone. Once he finished, he flashed me a smile that stole my breath and tossed the device on the nightstand. "There. Now I'm not. Do you have any early-morning plans?" he asked with an undercurrent of challenge.

"Nope. Maria's practicing some solo work. If I go in, I'll just hover."

"Good. Now come here and cuddle me." He flipped back the covers and climbed onto the bed. Following his lead, I slid beneath the sheets, and he flicked them back over us. Then he scooted in close, draping a leg over mine and curling against my side with his head on my chest. "Fuck, this is perfect," he practically moaned, placing a kiss on my chest before settling again.

I rubbed my hand along his back while I buried my face in his hair. Yeah, it was pretty damn perfect.

Chapter 19

There was something truly special about waking up wrapped in your boyfriend's muscular arms with his warm chest at your back. I hummed with contentment. It seemed Mickey was right. I did need to be better about putting myself first. And right now, that meant sleeping in and snuggling against Atticus's broad chest.

"Morning, Sunshine," Atticus said in a sleep-rough voice that had goosebumps racing across my skin. He placed a kiss on the back of my neck, then loosened his hold so I could roll over.

"Good morning, yourself," I said once I was facing him. He wrapped his arm around my middle and tugged me closer to press a sweet kiss on my lips.

I hummed again and wiggled an arm free so I could rub my hand along his back. His eyes drifted closed as I continued. Smiling, I lightly tugged on his hair. "Hey, no going back to sleep."

"Mm, not asleep. Just…" he trailed off with a sigh.

"Just what?"

He slowly opened his eyes, and their gray depths pulled me in like a gravity well. I almost didn't catch the tiny smile on his lips. "Just really fucking happy." He brushed his lips over mine again. This time, though, I didn't let him go without stealing a few more.

"Is it wrong that I want to play hooky today?" I asked when I could finally bring myself to pull away. The kissing was not helping with plans to get *out* of bed.

"If it is, then I'm just as in the wrong." He gave me a playful smile that I couldn't help but mirror. Then it fell. "Unfortunately, there's a client coming in for a custom piece. I'd see about rescheduling, but the poor guy has already had to reschedule three times."

"Oh, baby, I didn't mean we should, just that I wanted to. Besides, I would never ask you to move your schedule on a whim." I ran my fingers through his hair, worried that I'd upset him.

Atticus shifted, and suddenly I was on my back with him hovering over me. "And that's just one of the many things that make you perfect." I snorted. I was *far* from perfect. Before I could say as much, he adjusted his position, and our cocks rubbed against each other.

"Fuck, that feels good," I moaned. "And I really *really* want to see where this goes, but—"

"We're adults with jobs and people relying on us."

I pouted. "Adulting sucks."

"It has its perks," he replied with a devious grin and rolled his hips.

Sparks of pleasure lit up inside me. Maybe we'd have enough time. I was sure we'd have enough time. I leaned up for a kiss, except he pulled back.

Clearly seeing my disappointment, he added in that sexy as sin voice, "We could make out here. *Or* we could relocate to the shower."

He laughed as I shoved him further away and practically leapt out of the bed. I was probably a sight, with my hair mussed from sex and sleep, not to mention my erection proudly showing exactly where my thoughts were at. It was reassuring to see that when Atticus got out of the bed that I wasn't the only one insanely turned on this morning.

"I'll start the water, and I think I have a spare toothbrush," I declared, making my way to the bathroom. "Grab some more towels from the hall closet?" The ones we'd used last night were in a wet pile we'd left on the floor.

One extra steamy shower and two mutual handjobs later, we were dressed and out the door. All too soon I was dropping Atticus off at the Artist Co-Op, then I went in search of somewhere to park. Finally, I gave it up as a lost cause and settled for a cramped parking spot and a long walk. I blamed my distant space for why I didn't see Jasper until he basically leapt out at me from the antique shop.

"Fucking hell, Jasper!" I clutched at my chest and fought to get my heart rate under control. When I finally met his gaze, he at least had the decency to look abashed.

"Sorry! Sorry. I was just worried you weren't coming in today at all. When you didn't open like you usually do on Fridays, I wasn't sure if I should call or..." If I hadn't been looking right at him, I'd have missed the blip of genuine worry tinged with fear that swept across his face.

"I'm fine. Decided to take Mickey up on his offer to cover my shift and sleep in." It was a bit of a stretch. Mickey hadn't offered so much as demanded that I stop covering everyone else's shifts and ask someone to cover mine for a change.

Jasper ran his hand through his hair, which was already pointing in every direction, then rubbed the back of his neck. "Yeah. Of course. Makes sense. That's what Mickey said."

I narrowed my eyes at him. Jasper could be awkward at the best of times. It was one of his most endearing qualities. But this wasn't awkward, or not just awkward, behavior. I could feel the anxiety rolling off of him.

Before I could ask if something was wrong, he blurted, "Are you still mad at me?"

"Mad at you. Why would I be mad at you?"

"You don't have to be nice, Mason. I know I messed up. It was wrong to talk like that about someone I barely know." He took a deep breath and added, "You had every right to be angry."

It was probably shitty, but I'd forgotten all about the argument at the diner. "Okay," I said, not really sure what I was supposed to say. To my surprise, he cringed.

"And I really should have been more supportive about the changes you're making at the bookstore. It's not that I don't believe you can do it or that I don't think it's great. You're just always so worried about upsetting Mr. Forrester. But what I said came out cruel. I'm really sorry, Mason. Please don't be mad anymore."

I was officially taken aback. While Jasper was capable of self-awareness, he didn't exercise it all that often. And now he'd apologized for two different offenses. What's more, he looked genuinely contrite and, frankly, sad. "I'm not still mad." I wrapped him in a tight, albeit brief, hug to underscore my sincerity.

"You're not?" he asked when we stepped apart. It wasn't until he wiped the heel of his hand across his cheek that I realized he'd started to cry. "I figured you were, and that's why you avoided me at the art festival. When I saw you, I was hoping to apologize then, but you ran off so fast it was clear you didn't want to be around me." He sniffled and I was pretty sure a knife to the gut would have hurt less.

"I, uh…" I should come clean. Tell him the truth about why I was there and with whom. Only the words that came out of my mouth weren't anywhere close to that. "Yeah, not my finest moment." At least, that was true. "Apology accepted, though I didn't mean to leave things like that for so long. So I'm sorry too."

Jasper was already shaking his head. "Nope. You don't get to take any of the blame for this. It was my wrong, and I'm owning it."

The being-a-shitty-friend feeling intensified, but I was also oddly proud of him. Maybe he was finally taking being an adult seriously. "Did you, uh, want to check out some changes we've made?"

"Only if you promise to tell me about what else you plan to do. And tell me if there's anything I can do to help. Oh! And show me the bookmarks you bought at the festival."

Cold fear slid down my back. Had he seen me with Atticus? We hadn't exactly been shy about being publicly affectionate. Which, now that I thought about it, was a little weird, at least for me. "H-how did you—"

He smirked. "I saw those super cool pressed flower bookmarks, and I *know* you. No way you'd pass those up if you saw them." His smirk became a full-on grin as he reached into the bag at his side. "And if you *didn't* see them, I got you these. I hope they're designs you like. Or didn't already buy," he added as an afterthought. He held out a pair of bookmarks from the booth where I'd gotten mine.

"Wow, Jasper. Thank you. These are beautiful." I accepted the gift with a measure of disbelief. One of them was one I'd debated getting, but couldn't justify buying *five* bookmarks when I already had like a hundred. The other was a design I hadn't seen at all. It must have been the one the artist was saying always sold out first. It was stunning. He'd even gotten the special protective sleeves she had for them.

"You really like them?" His uncertainty was surprising, but then again, I was doing my best impersonation of a statue.

"I love them. And before you ask," I said, cutting him off when I saw him open his mouth, "I saw the booth, but I didn't get these designs."

"Yay!" He wrapped me in an enthusiastic hug right there on the sidewalk. I laughed and hugged him back. "I don't like it when we fight," he whispered, still clinging tightly. "You're my best friend, Mason. I don't know what I would do if I ever lost you."

I squeezed him a little tighter. "Me neither." Okay, now I was getting teary-eyed, and I still had to go into the bookstore and face people. I released him and met his gaze, giving him a little smile. "Movie night?"

His eyes practically glowed with excitement. "Totally. Since you didn't open, I know you'll be working late. I'll grab the takeout so you can come straight over. How about that pho place you love? And no sad rom-coms." A laugh burst out of me at his mock-serious expression.

"Sounds great," I said with a grin, and I meant it.

Jasper waved at someone in the antique shop, then fell in step with me for the short distance to Literary Lighthouse. "Okay, regale me." He held out his arms to encompass the full interior of the bookstore.

"You are the most." I chuckled and up-nodded to Casey at the register, then led Jasper deeper into the store. "You already saw me working on some of it. Mickey and I moved the impulse buys and tchotchkes to the front and replaced them with that disaster of cramped shelves."

"They don't look too cramped to me. Actually, they don't look cramped at all." He leaned forward and plucked a paperback from the middle shelf. "Huh, what's this?" he mused to himself.

I threw my hands out in a dramatic gesture. "This! This is why!" Apparently it was a touch too dramatic, because it spooked Jasper enough that he jumped and fumbled the book he'd grabbed.

"Dang it, Mason. Are you trying to scare me to death? What are you shouting about, anyway?" He huffed and resumed trying to read the back of the book.

My face heated slightly, and I gave him an abashed smile. I really hadn't meant to be so loud. "Sorry, it's just you did exactly what I knew cleaning up the shelves would do, and I got a little excited."

He lightly smacked my middle with the book. "A little, huh? So what did I do that was so awesome?" He tilted his head as if considering something and added, "Besides the everything I already do."

"Cheeky shit. You picked up a book."

Jasper blinked at me. "Uh, yeah. It's a bookstore. Isn't that kinda the point?"

"The difference is you didn't come in here to get a book, but because you could see them without being overwhelmed, one of them caught your attention." Okay, I could admit I was maybe too excited. It was just so fucking vindicating to see it work in real time.

"That is," he paused and glanced around, taking in books still competing for space and the now strategically organized books in front of us. "That's freaking genius. Who'd have thought such a minor change could have such a big impact? It's going to look amazing in here when you're finished."

I swelled with pride. "Trust me, it didn't feel minor when we lugged that heavy-ass bookcase clear across the store. I thought for sure the dolly we use for book deliveries would have worked or at least helped. Instead, we almost broke the damn thing." We'd also dropped the stupid thing on our feet several times. On the bright side though, because we caught it with our feet, neither the case nor the flooring was damaged.

"I'm really excited for you. And I saw the other day that you moved the kids' section to be in the lighthouse display. It makes a great impression when you first walk into the store."

"Yeah? It was—" I cut myself off, nearly biting my tongue. *Fuck.* I'd almost told him it had been Atticus's suggestion. I pounded a fist against my chest and coughed in a weird attempt to explain my weirdness. "Sorry. I was going to say it was an endeavor." That was technically true, though it hadn't been a hardship spending time with Atticus, playing with books and eating pastries.

"This will probably take a while," he gestured to the remaining overcrowded shelves. "Do you know what your next project will be yet?"

I squinted. "Sort of? I want to put something on the wall by the lighthouse display now that it's more of a feature. Like art or something. Problem is that none of us can figure out what should go there that wouldn't overwhelm it. That would defeat the point."

He crossed his arms, tucking the book he was still holding to his side, and made his way back to the lighthouse display. I watched him consider the blank spaces on the wall, and I could have smacked myself. Jasper was *literally* an artist. Why hadn't I thought to ask him in the first place? Oh, right. Because I was too busy hiding my relationship with Atticus from him. No time like the present to remedy that.

"Would you maybe be interested in helping me come up with something or even possibly... design something?" I asked because I was a coward and couldn't bring myself to admit that I'd been sneaking around behind his back.

Jasper turned wide, surprised eyes on me. "Really? You'd trust me with that?"

I frowned. "Of course I would. You're the art expert."

"Yeah, but you know," he gestured vaguely at the wall, "this store is kind of like your baby. And you're finally making the changes you always wanted."

I wrapped an arm around his shoulders and tugged him against my side. "All the more reason to get my bestie involved."

"Okay," he replied excitedly when I let him go. "I'll put together a few concepts, and you can see what you think." He gave the wall another long look, then made his way toward the front of the store.

It wasn't until he angled toward the register that I realized he intended to buy the book he'd picked up. We got up to the counter Casey was currently manning. I smiled at him and reached for Jasper's book. "Here. I'll get that."

"I can get it," he said, twisting to keep the book out of my reach.

"Yeah, but you're getting dinner," I argued.

He stopped pushing me away and straightened. "I may not be its biggest fan, but I feel you don't understand how commerce works," Jasper said with a flat expression.

Casey snorted where he was waiting for us to buy the damn thing. My mouth hung open, and I couldn't think words, let alone push any out of my mouth. He smirked at me in triumph, and I found my voice.

I laid my hand on the where he'd set it on the counter, preventing Casey from ringing it up. "Fine. But you're using my employee discount." I gave Casey a meaningful look. It was clear he thought we were ridiculous by the smile twitching at the corners of his lips, but he didn't argue as he took the book.

"Ugh," Jasper grumbled. "Now who's being extra?"

"Pretty sure it's still you," I teased.

Chapter 20

THE HEAT FROM THE furnace washed over my face and forearms as I gathered molten glass onto the metal pipe. I wiped what I could of the sweat from my forehead onto my shoulder. My arms ached as I spun the pipe to keep the gather from dripping onto the floor. I carefully pressed the molten goo into the shattered pieces of color bar Maria had set out for me, then swung round to the glory hole right as she opened the door.

Exhaustion made my muscles burn as I kept the pipe moving, but determination kept it at a steady pace. This would be my fourth attempt at a rondel. Not that anything had really been wrong with any of the other flat discs; they hadn't even cracked. That wasn't the point, though. I wanted it to be perfect. And so I kept spinning.

"Thought I might find you here."

I looked up at the sound of Carmen's voice. It took me a moment to register why she looked odd. The scooter was gone. In its place was a cane with an adorable trio of tennis balls covering the feet. Abruptly, I realized I'd stopped spinning the pipe and resumed the steady motion. Hopefully, I hadn't stalled long enough to cause lasting harm.

"Hey, sis. When did you lose the ride?" I asked, even as I returned my focus to the glob of glass I was trying to coax into being a sun.

"Today. Figured I'd stop by and show off my new walking stick." Bemusement edged her undeniable excitement at being more mobile.

I glanced at her, sure to spare the bland walking aid a disparaging look. "You know, I bet Will would be more than happy to carve you something more your style." I caught the tinge of red darkening her face and ducked my head before she could call me out for laughing at her.

"Yes, well." She cleared her throat without finishing. I suspected Will had already made such an offer, given her interesting reaction. "What's all of this for?" she asked, walking over to the worktable littered with glass shards, discarded sketches, and who knew what else.

"Maybe he'll tell you, because he certainly hasn't clued me in," Maria said with a huff. She opened the door so I could remove the heated glass and closed it once I was clear and the pipe safely nestled in the cradle. "First original piece he's worked on in months. And what's he told his devoted apprentice? Nada." She pulled on heavy mitts and squatted in front of the slowly flattening disc.

I sighed, risking a glance over at Carmen. "The sketches are there if you want to see them. It will be a standalone piece with water and light elements coming together to make a rainbow curtain." Out of the corner of my eye, I saw her pick up a few of the sketches and scrutinize them.

"Looks complex," Carmen said just as the disc was cooling enough to see the streaks of color we'd added. "Beautiful, but complex. What made you decide on this design?"

Maria gave me an intense look I interpreted as "I told you so" when she opened the glory hole once more.

I carefully maneuvered the growing disc back into the heat. Only after it was safely nestled in the cradle and the doors were closed, did I respond. "It's for Mason." Even though there was no way Carmen could see it, I was positive she heard the grin in my voice.

"Well, that explains why none of the other rondels have been good enough. They were showpiece perfect, by the way." Maria gave me a knowing look. But was the smirk really called for? Okay, maybe it was.

"You've made your point." I sighed and nodded for Maria to reopen the doors. "I have been a little more obsessive with this piece than I've been with any others in a long while."

"Just a little?" she teased, grabbing the cork paddles to help smooth the disc while I spun.

Carmen's laughter filled the hot shop. Her cane made a muffled thump-slide noise as she moved closer. "I get it. Mason is pretty special."

There wasn't a doubt in my mind that I was sporting the goofiest, sappiest grin. "He really is."

"I like seeing you so happy. I also really like that we've gotten to spend time together and get to know each other."

"I love that you two get along so well," I replied absently. The rondel was coming along nicely, the streaks finally laying the way I wanted. I indicated for Maria to take another pass with the cork paddles. Recognizing that I'd reached the point of possible over-shaping, I grabbed a jack to score the glass, waited for Maria to get into position with thickly padded gloves, then tapped the rondel free of the pipe into her waiting hands.

Carmen followed us to the annealer, her lips twisted in a wry smile. "Oh, my dear, sweet baby brother. I was talking about you and me getting to know one another better. Though I'm obviously a fan of the beau," she added with a wink.

"I'll be sure to tell him when I see him tonight." I hung my heavy apron on its designated hook while Maria confirmed the annealer was sealed and began gathering tools.

"Oooh. And what do you two lovebirds have planned?" Carmen wiggled her eyebrows suggestively, and I barked a laugh.

"Movies. We're going to curl up on the couch, binge on movie snacks, eat salty popcorn, and have ourselves a Meg Ryan marathon." I smirked at her exaggerated expression of disbelief. "It was *his* idea."

She shared a look with Maria, who said, "I know, right? They're so cute it's gross."

I gave my sister a meaningful look as I finished cleaning off the worktable. "You could be cute-gross with someone if you wanted. Not pushing. Just saying." I held up my hands defensively.

She smiled and patted my cheek. "I know. Go enjoy your evening with Mason."

"I'll tell him you said hi. You good here?" I asked, turning to Maria.

"Totally. Is it cool if I work on a personal project before closing up for the day?" She nodded toward the sketch she'd pinned on the workboard. "I'm determined to master that pull technique if it's the last thing I do."

"Of course I don't mind. This is your workspace too. Promise you'll message or call if you have questions?" I held up a hand before she could argue. "I'm still your mentor, and Mason is just as supportive of your journey. You won't be intruding."

She gave me a somewhat defeated smile. "Okay, yeah. Prome-to."

Satisfied, I turned back to Carmen. "Don't suppose you could give me a lift? I'm assuming you're using Dad's truck."

Her enthusiastic "Yes" caught me off guard. "Oh, don't look at me like that. I never got to drop my little bro off at his sweetheart's for a date. This is older sister *gold*."

I shot Maria a concerned look, and she gave me an unsettling smile. Officially concerned, I followed Carmen to the old pickup. We chatted casually as we made our way to Mason's place, with me providing directions as we went. I took for granted how much Oak Haven had grown around me over the years and forgot that most of the "newer" additions would be foreign to her.

We pulled into his drive, where Carmen gave me another lasciv-ious waggle of eyebrows. Chuckling to myself and doing my best to block out her "helpful" advice, I got out of the truck and made my way to the door. I waved to Carmen as she pulled out and drove back the way we'd come. Then I rang the doorbell.

"Wow, when you say thirty minutes or less, you take that shit seriously," Mason said, his voice getting louder as he got closer to the door. Surprise dominated his features for the smallest fraction of a second then undeniable joy brightened his entire face.

"Hey, Sunshine. Is it okay that I'm early?" I asked, unexpectedly anxious.

He snorted and tugged me inside. Though he glanced around outside before shutting the door. "You being here will always be okay." He stepped close, sliding his hand around the back of my neck, and pulled me in for a kiss sweet as honeysuckle. "So..."

"So?" I lightly squeezed his hips and brushed my lips over his again.

"I was thinking about which movies to watch first," he began, stepping back and lacing our fingers before tugging me toward the livingroom, "and I found one I've never seen."

"Just one?" I teased, giving his hand a shake. He laughed as I hoped he would.

"Okay, there were a couple," he admitted. "But one of them really caught my eye, and I was wondering if we could start with that one."

"Color me intrigued. Which caught your fancy?"

"French Kiss?" he said uncertainly.

I swept him up in a hug, firmly pressing our lips together. "Have I told you lately how perfect you are?"

It took him a moment to blink away his dazed expression. "I'm far from perfect, Atticus. In fact, I'm actually a terrible human." The undertone of conviction in his voice at the dire statement made my heart hurt. I was more convinced than ever that there was a darkness in his past.

"Mason."

"Kidding. I'm kidding." Much as I wanted to believe that, his smile was off and his eyes were too bright. I continued looking at him, and his smile slipped when I didn't say anything. "What?"

I rested my forehead against his for a moment and then met his gaze once more. "You've said some things here and there that have given me pause. I'm not demanding you share anything you're uncomfortable with, but if there's something I could be there for you, I'd like the opportunity."

He let out a sigh, nodding to himself. "Yeah. You're right. And for a first, I *want* someone to know." He grabbed my hand once more and led us over to the couch. He took a deep breath when we sat as if psyching himself up.

"Hey, I meant what I said. If this is too painful–"

"No, it's okay." He cupped the side of my face, his thumb making a slow arc over my cheek as he stared into me. "You have to be hands down the sweetest man I have ever met. It's no wonder I'm..." Instead of finishing his sentence, he brushed a light kiss over my lips then sat back, holding my hand in his lap. "I grew up just outside of Boulder, Colorado. When I was fifteen years old, I was kicked out for being gay. The worst part was that it completely blindsided me.

"We were in Colorado, for fuck's sake. My parents had always given the impression that they fully supported the LGBTQ+ community. When I came out, I learned it *was* okay... for everyone else." Sadness swam in his eyes along with a flicker of anger, but the most heartbreaking was the resignation.

I squeezed his hand. "What did you do?"

"They'd let me pack some stuff so I at least had more than the clothes on my back. What I didn't have were nearby relatives, and I didn't really have any friends. I'd been on my own for about a week when Jasper stumbled across me going through my luggage in some bushes behind the school." Mason huffed a laugh, presumably at the memory. "I remember trying to figure out if we had any classes together and how I was going to explain what was happening. He didn't even give me a chance. He looked from the open luggage to me and said, 'My mom is trying a new spaghetti recipe. It'll probably be awful, and she always makes way too much. You should totally have dinner at my place, then we can play games and have a sleepover.' He goes on without ever pausing, talking about how he'd been looking for a new best friend and his mom said that the best things always happen when you least expect them."

I held up a hand. "Wait. So, *did* you know him from one of your classes?"

"Nope." He laughed, his gaze far away like he was reliving the memory. "It wasn't until we were nearly at his house that he realized he'd forgotten to introduce himself. The look on his parents' faces when he casually walked in the backdoor, rolling my suitcase behind him, promptly announced that I was his best friend and that I'd be staying over."

I gave him a skeptical look. "And they were just okay with that? Didn't they want to talk to your parents?"

"Maybe." He shrugged. "I vaguely remember them asking me about myself, but I was living in a daze by that point. I'm sure they did some kind of responsible adult thing. Honestly, I was so fucking relieved to have a roof over my head again and actual adults in charge, I never questioned that they never asked me to go home."

"They sound like... interesting people." Insane was more like, but then how many people nowadays would step up to help a kid in need without wanting some sort of compensation?

Mason's laugh sounded more relaxed and like himself this time. "That they are. Calling them quirky comes close, but doesn't really do them justice. Still, they're wonderful people. And Jasper and I have been besties ever since. Sometimes the universe really does give you exactly what you need. You know?"

"Yeah, I do." After all, it had sent me Mason. "What about the rest of your family? Siblings?"

Sadness swept over his face, and he dropped his head to stare at our joined hands. "I'm also a middle child. My oldest brother,

Abel, was four years older than me, and I idolized everything about him. Then my brother Noah, who was only a year older. Then me. And finally, my little sister Abigail, who's two years younger.

"I haven't..." He paused to take a shuddering breath. "I haven't seen or heard from them since the day I left. Hard to imagine them all as adults when my last memory of them is as teenagers. Sometimes I wonder who they've become. Did Noah ever get to go on a safari like he always dreamed? Did Abbie set a new record climbing Mount Everest? Nothing could slow her down. Carmen reminds me a lot of her. Abel... Abel and I were more alike. He was going to be a scholar or a librarian at a prestigious library."

At his sniffle, I dragged him into a hug. "I'm sorry. I shouldn't have asked. You would have told me when you were ready." He wrapped his arms around me and squeezed back, though I could feel him shaking his head.

"No, no. It's fine. It was my choice whether to share, and I made it."

"I appreciate you trusting me with such a painful time in your life. If you're not interested in watching a bunch of movies now, I would understand," I said once I released him.

He scoffed and playfully pushed at my chest. "The movies are happening. Snacks, takeout, and everything. But, uh, you think we could maybe keep it to just cuddling tonight?"

Hearing how uncertain he sounded made me want to go out and find every asshole that had ever made him feel like it wasn't okay to just cuddle. "You listen to me, Mason Albright. Sex is always optional. Enjoyable? Definitely. But never expected."

His lips twitched with a smile. "Has anyone ever told you that you're like the champion poster child for mental health advocacy?"

"Oh, hell. I'm doing it again," I grumbled. Because, yeah, when you had mental health issues, you were painfully aware of all the things that contributed to them.

Laughter burst out of Mason. He looked at me and did a double-take. "Holy shit! You're serious. People have actually said that to you before? More than once?"

I cringed and nodded. "It happens from time to time. Now what movie were we starting with?" I asked as I stood, then promptly answered myself. "Right, French Kiss. Then of course we have to watch You've Got Mail. Did you want to get the movie set up or get started on snacks? You know what? I'll just go ahead with the snacks." My teeth clicked as I finally got my mouth to stop moving and beat a hasty retreat to his kitchen. Not that it provided much coverage since his house was just as open-concept as my apartment. But the way his laughter filled the room made every babbled word worth it.

"You really are a wonder, Atticus."

I glanced up from tearing the plastic from the popcorn to see Mason smiling softly at me. Worried I'd done something wrong or even more embarrassing, I glanced around, then finally asked, "What?"

"I don't know how you do it, but it never fails. No matter how upset I might be about something, you somehow always make me smile again."

Well, damn, if that didn't have all the feel-goods sparkling in my chest. I cleared my throat and went back to organizing snacks before I could do something reckless like blurt out how I'd fallen for him. "Now I'm really looking forward to meeting Jasper," I said as I pressed start on the microwave and filled a small bowl with sour gummy worms.

He snorted. "I'm positive you've already met him a few times and seen him at least a couple dozen. You know, since he's your neighbor and all."

"True. I may have already met him." Though for the life of me I couldn't ever seem to remember his name and connection to Mason when I did. "But I wouldn't be meeting my neighbor."

"Oh yeah? And who would you be meeting?" There was an odd edge to his playful question, but it wasn't worrisome enough to chase down.

I finished emptying the bag of candy-coated chocolates into a small bowl before responding, "I'd be meeting my boyfriend's best friend, a man who was there for him when no one else was."

Chapter 21

It was past-time I came clean to Jasper about dating Atticus. How else was I going to be able to introduce them properly? Besides, keeping the best relationship I'd ever had a secret was killing me inside. I just hoped that telling my bestie who I was dating wouldn't irrevocably damage our friendship. Jasper was my family. He might not be related by blood, but, like Atticus had said, he'd been there for me when it mattered most. I couldn't lose him. Which really made the fact I'd hidden this from him for so long that much more despicable. First though, I needed to find him.

"Hey, Mickey?" I asked as I stepped out of my little office behind the counter.

He finished supervising Denise ringing up a customer. Once he'd given her his feedback and encouragement of how well she was doing, he turned to me. "Sup, boss?"

"Have you seen Jasper recently? I thought he said he'd be coming by today, except his phone went straight to voicemail when I tried to call, and it doesn't look like he's seen any of my texts today." I tried not to overthink why my best friend wasn't responding. It wasn't uncommon for him to get so involved in a photography project that he forgot to charge his phone. It didn't mean he'd already found out about Atticus and me dating.

Mickey and Denise shared a conspiratorial look, and I narrowed my eyes at the two. Mickey whispered something to Denise that had her grinning and nodding enthusiastically, then she stepped from behind the counter to wind her way toward the back of the store. Sadly, I hadn't gotten the chance to finish moving the shelves currently blocking my view.

"Why am I afraid to ask what's going on?" I leaned over the counter as if it would magically enable me to see past the shelving that was mid-relocation and dividing the front of the store from the back.

Mickey clapped me on the shoulder. "Because you are a very smart man." Suddenly, Denise scurried back into sight and gave him a thumbs up. He gave her a nod and turned to me. "To answer your first question, Jasper arrived while you were out at lunch and has been here since."

"No way." I snorted and walked around the counter to stand in the entryway. "I wasn't gone that long, and besides, I'd have seen or at least heard him since I got back."

Mickey joined me in the front, wearing an annoyingly knowing smirk. "You sure about that? You went to lunch at 11:30."

"Yeah, and that was," I checked the time and altered what I'd planned to say. "Holy shit, that was three hours ago." I huffed. "In that case, I *definitely* would have noticed he was here by now."

He chuckled as he walked in the same direction Denise had gone, while I followed half a step behind. "Hard to notice anyone when you're locked in your office, eyeballs deep in reports."

Okay, he had a point. I tended to get a little cross-eyed whenever I dug into the books. Even then, why hadn't Jasper let me know when he got here? I didn't like this one bit. And it was sketchy as hell that two of my employees were apparently in on it. I warily followed Mickey around the obtrusive shelving, increasingly concerned about stepping into an ambush surprise party. Not that there was any reason I should have one or why Jasper would throw one.

"Um, a little to the left. Little more. Perfect!" I heard Denise say.

My curiosity got the better of me. I surged past Mickey, who seemed to be intentionally taking his sweet ass time, and rounded the last section of shelving hindering my line of sight. Then promptly came to a shocked standstill. "What the..."

Denise let out a startled squeak and quickly climbed down the store's "tall" ladder. "You were supposed to stall him," she hissed at Mickey as he joined me.

"I did! You gave me the thumbs-up. It's not my fault you decided to make last-minute adjustments," he argued.

"Could someone please tell me what I'm looking at?" No sooner did I ask than Jasper emerged from behind another set of shelving. I dared a glance at him. "I was expecting a few mockups to review, but this is..." I trailed off, still taking in the intricate clusters of photos in different sized frames. There seemed to be some sort of pattern or design to their placement, but I couldn't quite make it out.

"Okay, so please don't be mad," Jasper began.

"Mad? Why would I be mad? This is incredible. How the hell did you do all of this? *When* did you do this?" I stepped closer to the veritable collage of images and realized they were a mix of book covers and people shopping. "Wait. Are those *Literary Lighthouse* patrons?"

Jasper moved to stand beside me, crossing his arms as he surveyed the wall with a smile. "Do you really like it? I thought about trying to sketch out the idea or use some software to mock it up, but I couldn't see the vision until I really *saw* it."

"That... makes no sense. But yes, I do really like it. You've put an unbelievable amount of work into this. My real question is how you managed to keep it from me." I mentally cringed. Considering how good a job I was doing *not* being around him, hiding anything from me wouldn't have been difficult.

He shrugged, his gaze still coasting over the images he'd put together. "I wanted to surprise you. It wouldn't have been possible without the help of these two crafty devils. Seriously, Mickey, how on Earth did you convince him to move those shelves into the perfect spot to hide what I've been doing?"

"That was me, actually." Denise beamed. "And it wasn't all that hard. I simply suggested we use the more austere shelves for the horror section. You know, for *thematic* reasons. Just so happens that section is at the complete opposite end of the store. Easy peasy."

Jasper dropped his crossed arms. "Ooh, that reminds me. Mickey, think you and Denise and scoot those further across for the big-big reveal?"

Denise appeared reticent, but Mickey chuckled. "Don't worry, they're not nearly as heavy as they look. Not with only a third of the books on them. Plus, I might have conveniently forgotten to remove the flat cabinet dollies. Don't worry, boss, I locked the wheels so they couldn't accidentally go anywhere," he added to me with a wink.

"Awesome." Jasper rubbed his hands together and stepped closer, gesturing for me to do the same. "While they do that, tell me what you think of the images I chose. If you don't like any of them, I have plenty more we can use to switch out. Of course, I figured you could do that anyway whenever you wanted to focus on something. Holidays, events, whatever."

"These are amazing. I love getting to see real moments happening in the store." There were little Ender and his mom looking through a picture book together. In a smaller frame was Denise ringing someone up while wearing what was becoming her trademark smile. And even some of me helping customers. All in different-sized frames and interspersed with book covers. "But when? How? Why—"

"Who and what," Jasper interjected playfully. "Ugh, no reason to make that face. You basically walked right into that. Staring at the top. When—it's pretty easy to take pictures when no one is expecting you to take pictures. How—with my fancy schmancy camera, obviously. And why—I'm assuming you mean the overall color scheme. You'll better understand that when we go to the front of the store."

"Okay... Much as I love the Kodak moments, we'll need to get everyone who's displayed to sign agreements." I hated raining on his parade, especially since he'd clearly put an unbelievable amount of work into this.

He slung an arm around my shoulders. "Way ahead of you. That's another piece where your minions were pivotal. Mickey can get you the agreements we collected so you can have them in the store's records." He glanced behind us, and his grin somehow got even wider. "Now for the best part."

I glanced back, surprised to find the bookshelves already moved and a clear line of sight to the front door. Before I could do anything else, Jasper grabbed my hand and dragged me toward the entrance where Denise was practically bouncing on her toes,

Mickey looked smug as fuck, and a small crowd of customers had gathered.

As abruptly as he'd begun dragging me, Jasper released my hand and spun me to face the back once more. My breath immediately caught as I took in the display in its entirety. As amazing as the pictures were individually, they came together in a larger image that incorporated their coloring, size, and frames.

"This is… How did you… Fu–dge me," I quickly amended at catching sight of a little girl out of the corner of my eye.

"So, what do you think now?" Jasper asked, the confidence in his tone suggesting he knew exactly how impressive the display he'd created was.

I took a minute to appreciate the nuances that he'd taken into account to create the masterpiece before me. In the center, of course, were the impressive lighthouse shelves, now the home of the children's section. Around it, Jasper had meticulously arranged each frame and image to create the impression of waves crashing around the lighthouse. He'd even collected the lighter images to form clouds.

Finally, I huffed a laugh. "I think this is way outside the store's budget and worth every single cent." I glanced at my best friend, overwhelmed with what he'd put together. "In case I don't tell you enough, you are outrageously talented."

His cheeks darkened, and he replaced his arm around my shoulders. "I'm just relieved you like it."

Chapter 22

"Seriously, you've got to check this out," Carmen said as she passed my phone with the pictures Mason had sent across our parents' kitchen table to our mom. Dad moved to look over her shoulder and let out an appreciative whistle as she swiped through the images.

I couldn't help but laugh to myself as they oohed and ahhed at the new art installation at Literary Lighthouse. Mason had been talking through different ideas for a while now, but had yet to hit on anything he liked. So when he'd sent me several pictures of a piece already installed, I'd been more than a little surprised. Turned out his photographer-bestie was rocking a shit ton of natural talent. I'd have to ask him what sort of "light" in the lighthouse I could make to complete Mason's original vision that also melded with what he'd created.

"And that's enough of that," Carmen declared as she plucked my cellphone from my mother's hand.

"But I wanted to see the pictures from the festival," Dad argued in perfect sync with Mom's pout.

Carmen shot me a devious look. "It's generally best not to keep scrolling through pictures on someone else's phone." Mom frowned, but before she could ask anything, Carmen passed me my phone. "Though I have to say, your boyfriend's got a spectac-ular ass."

I spluttered, spitting most of my coffee back into the cup. "Seriously, Carmen?"

"What? It's not my fault you didn't think to make a hidden folder for your naughty pictures." She shrugged and finished rinsing her cup. "In my defense, I was left unsupervised."

"You could always try *not* scrolling past pictures I'm showing you." I rinsed my cup as well and set it beside hers on the drying rack.

She snorted and rolled her eyes. "Why do you think I got the phone back from Mom? Call it a benefit of being the oldest. I already know the things that need to be looked out for and that Mom has a tendency to want to look at *all* the pictures she can." She hiked a thumb at where our parents were still sitting at the breakfast table doing a poor imitation of innocence. "It's even worse when they're looking together."

"Guilty," Mom replied, sounding almost proud.

"We're curious about your lives. We know you don't share everything with your poor, old, forgotten parents." Dad made an exaggerated sad face, and I had to bite my lip to keep from laughing. Carmen had no such compunctions.

Once she stopped laughing, Carmen looked at our parents with a fond smile. "Don't ever change." It was so great to see that they'd been able to reconnect during her time back. "All set, little bro?" she asked, turning her attention back to me.

"If you are."

We said our farewells to Mom and Dad, then made our way outside where we hopped into our dad's old pickup that Carmen had been using. Before long, we were cruising down one of the country roads on the outskirts of Oak Haven, and I realized I had no clue where we were going.

"Is there an actual place we're going or are you kidnapping me?" I asked as we turned down a gravelled road. If it could even be called that, given how much of the gravel was now straight dirt.

"Have a little faith, Atty. I used to love coming out here, and when I saw the place was still open, I thought it could be a great spot to hang together." She flashed me a smile, her brown ponytail swinging behind her.

"And somehow, that still doesn't tell me where we're going."

She shoved me, but held up a hand when I went to shove her back. "Ah-ah, driving. So impatient. Didn't you used to like surprises?"

It was a small, yet stark reminder of how little time we'd spent together in the last decade-plus. While she knew I had anxiety, she'd never seen it in full force. "Surprises can be nice. I just like having something to narrow down the possibilities so my brain doesn't go berserk coming up with things."

"Oh shit! Atty, I'm so sorry. I wasn't even thinking."

"Hey, hey. It's okay. Not a big thing, and I trust you." I patted her shoulder lightly. "Unless you *are* kidnapping me..."

A laugh burst out of her. "No kidnapping today, pinky swear. There's a quaint little B&B out here that has a kick-ass lunch. Brunch too, which is what we're here for. Not that their dinner isn't just as amazing. Okay, so all of it is good." I snickered, and she rolled her eyes. "*Anyway,* while my friends and I never actually stayed here, it was a great place to eat and chill for however long we felt like it."

"Sounds like fun. Also, considering how far out this place is, it's no wonder Mom jokes that you never had a curfew you couldn't break."

Carmen made an indignant gasp. "She does not! Does she? Ugh, she probably does. But we were teenagers, breaking curfew kinda comes with the territory."

"Does it though?" I asked as she pulled into a grassy spot in front of the cutest little bed-and-breakfast. It was maybe three stories tall, which felt like a lot until you realized the entire first floor was communal space. The gray-blue exterior somehow made it look vintage and modern. But the wrap-around porch littered with benches, rocking chairs, and swings was the real showstopper. Unsurprisingly, my first thought was whether Mason would enjoy coming out here. We could spend a weekend in the beautiful countryside, making memories and getting lost in each other.

Carmen rapped her knuckles on the passenger window, and I jumped. "You planning on sitting in the truck all day, Mr. I-Never-Broke-Curfew?"

"Why do you assume I was a goody-two-shoes?" I finished getting out of the truck and shut the door behind me. We were still in Oak Haven, so neither of us worried about locking it. Instead of responding, she gave me a knowing look. "Fine. You win. I never stayed out later than I was told."

Looking smug as hell, she waltzed into the B&B and immediately turned toward the restaurant portion. "Two for Garner."

The hostess's head shot up. "Carmen? Is that really you? OMG, I can't believe you're here!" She let out a squeal of delight as she moved from behind the podium to embrace Carmen. "I'm so sorry. I heard about the accident. The healing must be going well, because, gurl, you look fabulous. Though I'm surprised you're still in town."

"Seemed like sticking around for a while was the thing to do." Carmen glanced my way, where I was undoubtedly looking awkward as fuck. "Bella, this is—"

"Pft. No introductions necessary. This has to be little Atty. Though not so little anymore." Bella's gaze started at my feet and travelled up. "Damn, when did you get so freaking *tall*?"

I would have argued that six feet really wasn't all that tall, but compared to her petite frame, I was basically a giant. "Nice to meet you."

She beamed and turned her focus back to Carmen and the task at hand. She plucked some menus from the basket, then guided us to our table. "It's so rad you're here. Almost like old times."

"Almost," Carmen agreed as she took her seat. "So, you work here now?"

Bella snorted a laugh. "Sorry. I'm just helping today since our scheduled host is out sick. I actually own the joint now."

"Holy shit, Bells. That's amazing! Way to go, you."

Bella finished putting the menus down, then flipped her hair. "It is pretty amazing. Right. I'll let you two enjoy your time together, and we can catch up later, doll."

"Sounds like a plan. I'll touch base before we head out." Carmen waited until her former schoolmate had returned to her post before shaking her head in disbelief. "She used to always talk about owning this place. We all assumed they were the usual big dreams of teenagers. But she went and made her dream a reality. Go figure."

"Okay, don't get upset, but I gotta ask. She seemed pretty surprised to find you were still in town, and I confess I am too. Not that I don't absolutely love having you here," I hastily added. "It's been wonderful getting to spend real time with you. I think this might be the longest you've ever been in town outside of growing up here."

She looked thoughtful, but the server arrived before she could reply. Luckily, it took only a quick glance to know exactly what I wanted. I got the chicken and waffles, while she ordered eggs Benedict and some orange juice. Once that was taken care of, she turned to me.

"I hadn't intended to stay so long. The plan was to head back once I was mobile enough to get around my apartment. But every time I went to pack my things or schedule a car, I couldn't."

I took my time unrolling the silverware. "Have you considered staying?" I peered up at her when she remained silent and was surprised to see how thoughtful she looked.

"Honestly? It's crossed my mind. A few times. Even... even before the accident."

My fork slipped through my fingers to clatter on the table. "Is something wrong at work?"

She shook her head. "Yes. No. The work itself is the same. There's always some big client to win, another pitch to create. And even though each project is unique, it's also... Well, it's all the same. I could make a million pitch campaigns, and there would always be another. I want to feel like I make a difference."

"Here you are," the server said as they set down our plates. "Anything I can get you?" We confirmed we were both good.

"Sounds like you've been thinking about it a while," I said cautiously once the server had left. "Would it be too soon to ask if I can look forward to spending more days like this with you?"

She gave me a cheeky grin and finished chewing her latest bite. "It would not. But speaking of timing…"

"Uh oh, why don't I like the sound of that?"

She rolled her eyes. "Don't be so dramatic. It's nothing bad. I was just curious about how things were going between you and Mason." She took a delicate sip of her orange juice, the gleam in her eyes far from innocent.

"Stop."

"What? I didn't do anything." And yet, she struggled to contain a grin.

"Uh huh. You know what you're doing. As for me and Mason, I think things are going well."

She raised an eyebrow and stopped suppressing her grin. "Just 'well'?"

"Okay, really well. He's so funny, and smart, and charming. He's wonderful, though he doesn't believe it. Whenever he's around, he lights up the space." I shook my head and let out a soft chuckle of wonder. "It's been so long since I trusted anyone with my heart, but I can't help it. I'm falling for him."

"Sounds to me like you already have. The better question is, have you told him how you feel?"

I used the excuse of taking a bite to find the right words. Sadly, by the time I washed it down, none had appeared.

Chapter 23

I STOOD ON MY tip-toes and craned my neck in an effort to peer around Maria. The woman might be a full head shorter than me, but she was doing a damn good impersonation of a solid wall. I wasn't about to let that stop me from trying, though.

"How you doin' back there, boss? Your boyfriend's getting persistent," Maria said over her shoulder.

Atticus's laughter drifted from the back of the hot shop. "Nearly there."

I dropped back to my heels and crossed my arms with a huff. "I still don't understand why I can't see how the piece is progressing. Not like I helped in getting it started." I grumbled to myself, much to Maria's amusement.

"Maybe I want it to be a surprise." Atticus placed a hand on Maria's shoulder, and she flashed him a grin. "Thanks for keeping this handsome, *nosy* troublemaker at bay."

"No problem." She gave me a cheeky wink as she stepped aside, and I couldn't help but chuckle.

Atticus finished hanging up his thick leather apron. "Oh, I looked at that piece you're worried about. Try not flashing it for so long and reduce the time between flashes. That should clear up the issue you're experiencing."

Her shoulders slumped. "Damn it. Should have gone with my first instinct. Guess I'll be starting over... again."

"I wouldn't say that. Except for trusting your first instinct. That you should always do."

I nudged Atticus with my shoulder. "Eh, not always."

He wrapped an arm around my waist and tugged me close to smack a kiss on my temple. "*That*, my incredible Sunshine, was a first impression, not an instinct."

"Oh," I replied with an extra helping of drama. "So what you're saying is that your initial instinct was to berate me in the hallway, while mine was to fuck with you." I smiled extra wide at his baffled expression.

Finally, he shook his head. "Fine, not all initial instincts are the best. You happy now?" He looked from Maria to me.

"Exceedingly. Though I'll be even happier once we're back at my place. After we enjoy a movie in the park, of course," I added belatedly.

Atticus grabbed my face with both hands and smacked a big kiss on my mouth. "What am I going to do with you?"

I wiggled my eyebrows. "I can come up with a few ideas."

"No," Maria interjected, holding her hands out. "No more cuteness. You can go be sappy somewhere else. See you on Monday, boss. Maybe by then I'll have a piece worth showing."

"I think that means she's kicking us out," I whispered loudly to Atticus. Dropping the faux whisper, I turned to Maria. "Have more faith in yourself. Atticus has shown me the pieces you've worked on. You're incredibly talented."

"Thanks, Mason. That's really nice of you to say."

I shrugged. "Just telling the truth. You ready to go, babe?" I asked Atticus. To my surprise, he was gazing at me with a soft expression I couldn't place. I cleared my throat to hide my sudden nerves. "That a yes?"

"Yes." He reached for my hand, lacing our fingers together. "Come on, let's get out of here. Call if anything blows up!" he shouted back to Maria as we made our way through the sliding barn door to the rest of the Artist Co-Op.

The dividing door had already shut behind us when I came to a stop and looked at Atticus askance. "Wait. Things don't actually blow up, do they?" Instead of giving me an actual answer, he laughed and continued walking, leaving me to catch up. "Seriously. Do they?" I repeated with more urgency. His response was, of course, to laugh more.

I unlocked the door to my house, glad I'd remembered to turn on the porch light for a change. "What do you think it would take to get on the committee that decides what movies to show?" I asked as we stepped inside.

Atticus pulled up short, his hand still on the handle in the process of shutting the door. "You know, I have no idea. But I bet I know who would."

"Oh yeah? Who?"

"Carmen." He finished locking the door and flicked off the porch light. My heart fluttered at how natural it was, and I was more than thrilled at the wordless confirmation that he'd be staying the night. Then what he'd said registered.

I snorted. "She's only been here a couple of months. There's no way she would know that. I've been here almost five years and I don't know that. Hell, you've been here your whole life and *you* don't know."

"Don't ask me how. She just *knows* things. It's always been like that. Even our parents don't know how she does it." He held his hands out from his sides in a show of defeat.

I stepped into Atticus's personal space, close enough to dance my fingers up his chest. "Then I guess we'll have to ask her." I slipped a finger beneath his shirt collar to stroke the skin beneath. "As much as I enjoy talking about your sister, she's not who's been on my mind all night."

"And who has?" he asked, teasing me with the possibility of a kiss. He wrapped his arms around my waist, drifting his hands lower to get a double handful of my ass, and pulled me against him. My breath caught, and a groan slipped free when he rubbed his growing erection against mine. Not even the layers separating us could diminish how good it felt. That didn't change how much better it would feel without them, though.

"Fuck, Atticus," I panted, dropping my head back so he could continue a trail of kisses. I ground my hips against him, craving more friction. "Bedroom. We should go there. With the bed. Clotheless."

He chuckled, the sound vibrating through my neck briefly before he pulled back. "You are so freaking cute when you're scattered." He pressed our mouths together before I could get indignant. His soft lips massaged mine, and when he teased at the seam, I gladly opened for him, revelling in the glide of our tongues against each other.

My brain was one hundred percent on holiday by the time we came up for air. Now we were both fully hard, basically frotting in the living room, and we were still wearing too many clothes. "Bedroom," I moaned, getting dangerously close to painting the inside of my jeans when he used his hold on my ass to grind our clothed dicks together.

He nipped at the side of my neck, then led us toward the bedroom, where he caught me with another intense kiss that liquefied my insides. "You taste like chocolate malt. I can't get enough."

"That good thing?"

"It's a great thing," he rumbled before going back to devouring my mouth.

We stopped kissing long enough to ditch our clothes and toppled onto the mattress. Then we were back to being all hands and mouths. I slid a hand over the curve of his ass while he kissed my shoulder and tweaked my nipple. He groaned when I raked my nails along the backs of his thighs, and I gasped as his kisses turned into love bites.

I writhed beneath him as he blazed a trail down my torso, along my hip, and down my leg. Then he slipped off the bed entirely. "What are you doing?" I sat up to see him better, but that proved no more enlightening. With a crooked grin, he hooked his hand around my ankles and pulled me toward him. I let out an "Oof" as I fell back.

"Getting comfortable," he said, dropping out of my line of sight.

I levered up on my elbows to see him kneeling on the floor, looking at my dick like he planned to devour it. He shifted his focus to me, and the hungry expression nearly undid me. As if he could read my mind, he wrapped a firm hand around the base of my cock. Then he licked me from root to tip without breaking eye contact. He swirled his tongue around the head, dipping into the slit, and suckled on the tip.

"Let me hear how you feel," he said in that voice that was pure sin.

My arms nearly gave out at the sexy command. "Good. So so good," I moaned while he circled the head again. Tingles of pleasure radiated from where his incredible mouth held me captive. I shifted my weight to one arm so I could thread my fingers through his hair. "You're so hot. You look so damn sexy bobbing on my cock."

He made a pleased sound that sent delicious vibrations through my cock. He continued to jack me as he licked and sucked, steadily driving me insane. Then he swallowed me down without warning.

"Fuck! Atticus." I didn't know what I was trying to say, only that his mouth felt fucking amazing. The intense wet heat combined with the suction had me clawing at the sheets, my balls already tightening. But I wasn't ready for it to end. I tugged on his hair a tad harder than I intended when he swallowed around me and I reflexively thrust my hips up.

He popped off with a smug grin. "How you doin', Sunshine?" It might have been easier to corral words into a sentence if he weren't slowly stroking me while he waited for my response.

"I'm n-not gonna last if y-you keep that up."

He placed a sweet kiss on my tip, getting his lips glossy from the precum pearled there, and I about swallowed my tongue when he licked his lips. "We certainly can't have that, now can we? Scoot back up." He gave my thigh a playful swat, leaving me to awkwardly reposition myself while he grabbed lube and condoms from the nightstand.

There was nothing remotely graceful about my frantic shimmy to get higher on the bed. My cocked bounced obscenely against my stomach, glistening with spit and throbbing for more attention. There wasn't any doubt in my mind that I looked absolutely ridiculous, splayed out and waiting for him. But when I met his gaze, it wasn't laughter I saw in his eyes.

"You have no idea how incredibly sexy you are. How did I get so lucky?"

My face burned at the sincerity both in his voice and clearly written on his face. Had anyone ever looked at me that way before? There was lust there, but also something that scared and excited me. Whatever it was, I knew I didn't want to lose it. If anyone was lucky in this scenario, it was one hundred percent me.

The mattress sank as he knelt on the bed and positioned himself between my legs. He nudged my legs further apart and tapped at my entrance with a slick finger. Where he would normally look down to watch, he kept his gaze firmly on my face.

Shocks of pleasure rippled through my body as he opened me up. As much as I yearned to close my eyes and bask in the sensations, I couldn't bring myself to look away from his intense gaze. I swallowed thickly and shuddered as he brushed along my prostate. We'd had sex plenty of times now, but this was different. I'd never felt more exposed. I'd also never felt safer.

He replaced his fingers with his cockhead, and we'd yet to break eye contact. My eyes threatened to flutter shut as he slowly pushed inside. The burn of being stretched barely registered before fading to the ecstasy of being full. Once he was buried to the hilt, he leaned over me, bracing his arms to either side of my head.

"Atticus," I whispered, completely overwhelmed.

"I'm right here, Sunshine." He closed the distance to claim me with a sweet kiss, and I finally let my eyes drift shut as I gave into it whole-heartedly.

Our kisses remained tender and unhurried. I clung to his shoulders and rocked into him to meet each slow thrust. My cock received the slightest friction from rubbing along Atticus's abdomen. Too much and nowhere near enough. Sensation sparked when the next drag of his cock rubbed my prostate just right, and I moaned.

"Fuck, you feel so good. I want to stay buried inside of you all night," he said between kisses peppered along my jaw and shoulders.

"Yes, please." I wanted that. Wanted more than anything for what we had to never end. Even if it did terrify me a little.

His pace slowly increased until we were panting into each other. My release slid closer and closer until it was a wonder I hadn't already come. His rhythm faltered, and he gave a hard thrust, pushing as deep as he could. "Mason."

Atticus groaning my name was the last push I needed to fall over the edge. My balls drew up, and I clung to him for dear life as my climax crashed over me. His final stuttering thrusts coaxed out every last sensation until I existed in a puddle of bliss.

Aside from the sting of when he slipped out, his getting up and cleaning us off was a blur. It could have been a few minutes or a few hours before he pulled the covers over us and tugged me close.

I snuggled into his chest. "Goodnight, Atticus," I hummed contentedly.

He tightened his arms around me and placed a soft kiss on the top of my head. "Sweet dreams, Sunshine," he whispered. My heart fluttered at the endearment, and I sighed happily as I drifted off.

Chapter 24

I SET DOWN THE book on glassblowing I'd bought from Literary Lighthouse what felt like ages ago and reached for my coffee on the nightstand. The book was proving to be as entertaining as it was informative, thanks to the author's humor. It was always refreshing when professionals didn't take themselves so seriously. None of that changed that I'd spent the last ten minutes attempting to read the same paragraph. It was definitely not the reading material that was making it a struggle to focus, though. That honor belonged solely to the man sitting beside me.

The sheets pooled around his waist, leaving his tanned chest bare, and he was clearly engrossed in the novel he'd been devouring for the last hour. Every now and again, I caught him making faces at the book, almost as if trying to mimic what he was reading. It would have been funny if it weren't so fucking adorable.

Spending a Sunday morning reading in bed wasn't ever something I saw myself doing. Not that I didn't enjoy reading—far from it—more that I rarely had the time to indulge. For the last few years, my life had been nonstop work, though that was more by design than happenstance. It was easier than being alone with my thoughts or dwelling on how unlucky I was in love. I didn't even realize how much I was isolating myself after the disaster with Tom. It rankled a bit to admit that Maria and Barry had been right, but then again, if I had followed their advice to put myself out there when they'd given it, would I have met Mason?

I set my empty cup down and looked at the man in question, still absorbed in his reading. This may not have been the kind of morning I'd ever considered myself having, but it was certainly one I could get used to. There was peace in the quiet companionship. Mason flipped to the next page, his face screwing up into a weird frown that morphed into an expression of confusion before returning to neutral. A smile twitched at my lips, but I didn't resume reading, preferring to gaze at him instead.

Finally, he realized I was staring and did a double take. "What?" I smiled, unable to help myself, especially after his latest face-making.

"Just love you." Right. So that was *not* anything remotely similar to telling him how cute he looked as he read. Mason's eyes widened, and his book threatened to tumble free of his lax grip. Maybe it was too soon, but I couldn't take the words back, and wouldn't if I could. They were my truth.

The room remained unnervingly quiet as we looked at each other. Then, the corner of his mouth twitched before blossoming into a shy smile accompanied by a light stain of pink suffusing his cheeks. "I love you, too."

"Yeah?" I asked, a little dumbfounded.

The blush faded from his cheeks, and his smile settled into his naturally sweet one. "Yeah. Pretty sure I have for a while." Apparently, I'd been really worried about that, considering how relieved I felt.

"Thank fuck," I blurted without thinking. Mason threw his head back and laughed. I joined him, letting the last of my latent tension go as I scooted closer to him and laced our fingers together. Once we sobered, he looked at me, his blue eyes sparkling.

"You know, I don't think I've ever said that to a serious boyfriend before."

I raised my eyebrows. "Oh, so we're *serious* boyfriends. What if I don't want to be serious? What if I'd rather we were silly instead?" To emphasize my point, I tackled him, dragging him down onto the pillows so I could pepper his face with kisses. He wiggled and squirmed, laughter spilling out of him to fill the room and my chest with a golden glow. I only relented when we were both out of breath. I rolled to my side next to him, and we gazed at each other, the smiles on our mouths dancing in our eyes.

"In case I haven't told you lately, you're amazing. Oh! And I'm completely in love with you," he added like it was an afterthought.

"You're pretty damn amazing yourself." I cupped his jaw, letting my thumb glide along his cheek. The heat of his minor blush warmed my hand. I leaned forward to press our lips together in a tender kiss that made me feel like I was floating. A sigh slipped free when I pulled away. "Yep, definitely in love with you."

He laughed, then scooted toward the edge of the bed. Except he didn't pick up his book like I expected. Instead, he pulled back the sheets and got up. Not that I was arguing with the view of his beautiful body or the way his lounge pants hugged his ass.

"Where do you think you're going?" I grumbled playfully.

"*I'm* not going anywhere, but you might want to get a move on if you still plan on having lunch with your family." He nodded toward the cute little clock he kept that was an open book with digital numbers hovering above it.

"Shit. You're right." I threw back the covers and scrambled to get dressed. While I scurried about, he walked out of the room.

By the time I was finished, he'd returned with a glass of water, which he handed me right as I fished out my travel pack of meds from my pocket. "Thanks," I said with an appreciative smile. I couldn't remember a time I'd been with someone who didn't treat my anxiety like it was a separate part of me—preferably a part they could ignore. It wasn't like that with Mason, and it never had been.

His lips twitched into a smile. "You planning on actually eating with your family or staring at me all day? Not that I mind, but I'd hate for you to end up late on my account."

"I always lose time around you, Sunshine. And for the record," I said, lowering my voice and noting the reaction it had on Mason as I stepped close enough for our breath to mingle, "there are worse reasons to be late than getting distracted by my sexy as fuck boyfriend." I wrapped my arms around his middle and sealed our lips in a kiss. Finally, I pulled myself away and reluctantly relinquished my hold of his warm waist. "So what are you getting up to today?"

"Going to knock out a few house chores I've been putting off, maybe go to the store, and I think..." He paused then gave a firm nod of his head. "Yes. I'm going to see about a time we can meet up with my bestie. That way, the two of you can get to know each other better, and..."

"And what?" I prompted him when he left the sentence hanging. It was already weird that we'd been seeing each other for almost five months and I still hadn't gotten to sit down and talk with his best friend. But I also recognized that Mason's best friend was virtually all the family he had now and trusted he'd make it happen when he was ready. Seemed like we'd finally gotten to that point.

He gave a self-conscious laugh. "And I can stop feeling like I'm being pulled in two directions," he replied with a grin and a light shove to my arm. His playful demeanor didn't fool me. I could see the truth of his words in his eyes, and it broke my heart a little that he felt that way.

"You know I don't mind you spending time with your best friend, right? He's your family. I would never come between that."

"What? No, of course not." His smile was more authentic when he looped his arms around my neck. "How the hell are you so kind and supportive all the time? It's like your superpower."

"Ah-ha! I knew you had the newest superhero romance."

He snorted and let me go. "Whatever would make you think that?" It was almost believable, but then his gaze darted to the book he'd been reading.

We both made a dash for it. Luckily, I was closer. I held up the hardback triumphantly. Sure enough, the book jacket on it was not the one that went with the book. "Sneaky sneaky."

"How'd you guess?" he asked with a huff that didn't sound nearly as put out as I'm sure he intended.

"Not once have I ever heard you refer to someone as having a superpower. The inspiration had to come from somewhere, and it seemed the likeliest source. Why not tell me?" I asked as I carefully replaced the wrong book jacket.

"Because it's technically an advance copy. I knew how excited you were for the next installment, and Casey won the coin toss to read the other ARC we received. To be fair, empathy *is* kind of your superpower."

I twisted my face into an exaggerated frown, making him laugh. "Is there an exchange option? I'd much rather have something to do with fire. Now *that* would be cool."

"I think you mean hot." Mason gave me a cheeky grin and winked. "Now go on before you really are late."

"Yeah, yeah," I grumbled as we made our way to the front door. He held it open for me, and I turned back to steal one more kiss. "Love you."

"Love you, too," he replied with zero hesitation and the brightest smile. "Tell the fam I said hi."

"Will do. Now I just need—" Right on cue, Carmen pulled up in our dad's truck, which I was increasingly sure he was never getting back. A quick double honk ensured I didn't come up with more reasons to dally. "I'd better go. *Someone's* superpower is not patience. I'll talk to you later." We shared a chuckle, and Mason waved to Carmen.

Catching Carmen's "get your ass in gear" expression, I opted not to angle for another kiss. Mason waited in the open doorway until I slid into the cab of the truck and closed the passenger door. Only then did he go back inside.

"You two are too much," Carmen said as she pulled away from the curb, her tone fond. "You going to tell him how smitten you are?" She tossed me a smile before returning her attention to the road.

"Already did. We, uh, maybe told each other this morning." I wasn't sure why it embarrassed me to admit. Maybe it had something to do with how precious it felt. Like Venetian glass, it was extraordinarily beautiful but equally as fragile.

Carmen smacked my arm with enough gusto that we swerved. I shot her a look. "Eyes on the road, I got it. But come on, can you blame me for being excited? My little brother's in love. That's so stinkin' cute I could cry." The warmth that had spread throughout my chest when Mason told me he loved me too glowed brighter.

"Oh shit," she said out of nowhere, shooting me a worried glance, and just like that tension wound tightly around my chest. "Did he say it back?"

"Damn it, Carmen," I said once the tightness relented enough that I could let out a relieved breath.

"What'd I do?"

"For starters, you nearly gave me a heart attack." I glowered at her, and she cringed, giving me an apologetic smile. "Yes, he said it back. I didn't realize I was worried that he wouldn't or hoping that he would or—whatever. Either way, I was relieved when he said it."

Carmen rolled to a stop at a red light. "And happy?"

"So fucking happy. Like, holy shit, I didn't know it was possible to *be* this happy. I really love him, Carmen." I smiled softly to myself, thinking of how much I would love more mornings like we'd spent this one.

"Ugh," Carmen grumbled, mostly to herself. I glanced at her, and she gestured toward the street ahead. "Looks like we're taking a detour. Mulberry Street?"

I weighed the alternatives. "You could. But if you take Fig Moore, we could swing by my apartment."

She gave me a dubious look. "And why would we need to do that?"

"There's something I've been meaning to give Mom and Dad, but I keep forgetting it. Also, I just realized we match and just, no." I waited while she mentally debated whose plan to go with.

"Okay, we'll swing by your place. But you better be quick about it," she said with that eerily ominous big sister voice. When she pulled up in front of my building, she reiterated I needed to hurry or she'd leave my ass here.

I was still shaking my head at her insistence that I had "Five, no, *three* minutes or else" when I stepped off the elevator onto my floor. Thankfully, I wasn't at the far end of the building. I'd just unlocked my door when I heard another door close behind me.

"Oh! Atticus, hey."

"Hey," I replied without fully turning around. I wasn't trying to be rude, but I only had "maybe three minutes".

"I was wondering if you maybe had a minute? There was something I wanted to run by you," the guy said, who I finally recognized as my neighbor.

I finished opening the door and pushed it wide. "Uh, yeah. I can talk for a minute, but would you mind coming inside? I'm kind of in a hurry."

"Of course. No problem." He followed me inside, but remained hovering by the bar-top counter in the kitchen.

I took a moment to mentally high-five past me for cleaning up before heading to the Co-Op yesterday, then surged around the couch to look for the other books I'd grabbed on a previous visit to the bookstore. "So, what did you want to talk about?" I asked as I flipped through the stack of books on the coffee table for the one I was looking for. Of course, it would be at the bottom.

"Right. I was wondering—if you're free sometime—if you'd maybe like to…"

"Like to what?" I asked as I replaced the books. I had an uncomfortable feeling I knew where this was going. Letting people down easy had never been a skill I'd mastered. But maybe I was wrong? I cleared my throat when he still didn't respond.

"Where did you get that?" he asked.

I followed his line of sight to the travel mug sitting on the counter. "Oh, that? My boyfriend lent it to me. Actually, thanks for reminding me, I've been meaning to get this back to him for ages."

The man turned to face me, his face unnervingly blank. "Who is your boyfriend?"

"Mason Albright." Just saying his name brought happy flutters to my heart. "Do you know him?" His face twitched, and I could have smacked myself. "Shit. Of course, you know him. Jasper, right? Is that what you wanted to run by me? A time for the three of us to get together? Damn, he didn't waste any time. Well, I suppose it did take a while for him to want us all to get together."

Jasper stepped closer to the counter. "I got him this. Years ago. It was the last one like it." He wrapped his fingers around the mug almost possessively. "How long?"

"How long, what?" I asked, increasingly confused by his odd behavior.

"Have you two been dating."

"Um... four/five months?" Okay, his low monotone was officially starting to creep me out. I inched closer to the door, hoping he'd get the hint. "But yeah, in a bit of a hurry. Do you think maybe you could figure out when to meet with Mason? He can just tell me what you two decide."

His grip tightened on the mug so much that his knuckles turned white, and I was a little afraid for Mason's favorite to-go mug. "Yeah. I'll talk to Mason." Without so much as a goodbye or talk to you later, Jasper turned on his heel and walked out of my apartment, taking Mason's mug with him.

I debated retrieving it since I'd technically been the one to borrow it, but I got the impression Jasper was on his way to talk to Mason now, so he'd get back either way. Besides, they were best friends. Mentally berating myself for trying to overcomplicate everything, I shook off the weird interaction and stepped back into the hall to lock up. I was confident I'd made good time until a sharp HONK split the air. Well, damn.

HOLY SHIT, I TOLD Atticus I loved him. And I meant it. Fuck, did I ever mean it. And he loved me back. A couple of hours of housework later and I still couldn't believe it. Giddiness kept flooding my chest like one of those massive bubble wands that makes hundreds of bubbles in a single go. I didn't ever want it to stop.

Despite all of my excitement though, there was still one major hurdle I needed to overcome. I never should have waited to tell Jasper about Atticus and me. It was juvenile to hide our relationship from my best friend, and for the life of me, I couldn't figure out *why* I had waited so long. I'd justified it in the beginning of not wanting to hurt him over something that might not even go anywhere, but those reasons had grown thinner with each day that passed.

I paused mid-loading a plate into the dishwasher as it finally hit me. I didn't want to share. Things had a way of inevitably being about Jasper, and I hadn't wanted what Atticus and I had to be as well. Just once, I wanted it to be all about me. Something I hadn't had since before my parents kicked me out.

I finished the dishes and set the dishwasher to start as that realization sank in. Did that make me selfish? Probably. But why couldn't I have something that was purely mine without having to compromise? Subconscious reasons aside, I was overdue to clue in my best friend with what I'd been up to. But first, a shower.

Refreshed and ready to conquer the day, I grabbed my cell off the charger and walked to the living room. A quick glance at the screen showed I'd received a message from Atticus while I'd been cleaning. Before I could look at it though, a familiar head of hair poking over the top of the sofa caught my attention. For a hot second I wondered how he'd gotten in, then I remembered he had a key to my place just as I had one for his apartment. It was easy enough to forget since he so rarely needed to use it.

I tucked my phone into my back pocket and walked around the sofa. "Hey, Jasper! You must be sharpening your psychic abilities. I was literally about to call you," I said with a grin. A grin that slowly slipped off my face when he met the greeting with a blank stare. "Um, what brings you here? I didn't forget we had plans, did I?"

Jasper picked up a travel mug from the end table as he slowly stood. "I brought you your mug."

Why was he saying it like that? And why was he acting so strangely? He hadn't even said hello or given me a hug or any-thing. I frowned as I tried to remember the last time I'd used the mug. "Thanks. Where did you find it?"

"It was on the bar-top." He held it out to me. Upon closer inspection, I realized it was actually the one-of-a-kind travel mug he'd gotten me when we graduated college and decided to move to Oak Haven.

That was weird. It wasn't like me to leave things lying about, especially not something I treasured. No matter how I racked my brain, though, I couldn't remember having it at his place in the recent past. Not to mention the last time I'd put coffee in it had been for... Oh shit. *Shit. shit. shit.*

"Atticus's bar-top," Jasper said flatly with a disturbing undercurrent of danger.

While I'd been dragging my heels, he'd gone and found out anyway. "I can explain," I rushed to say.

"Yeah? Can you explain the last five months?" He narrowed his eyes, and a spike of fear tore through my chest. This was worse than the worst case. Not only did he know I was dating Atticus, he knew for how long. And he hadn't heard any of it from me.

"It started as an accident, I swear." I cringed. Saying it out loud was even worse than hearing it in my head.

Jasper crossed his arms and continued to glower at me. "Please enlighten me how you 'accidentally' date someone for five months. Did you just happen to be at all the same places at the exact same time?"

"I mean, well, sort of."

"And you just happened to forget to mention you were seeing someone? Oh, but not just any someone, my neighbor. The guy you *knew* I was interested in."

"You don't have a monopoly on men! You can't call dibs on a person," I snapped. "This is real, adult fucking life, not an afternoon at the playground."

He threw his arms wide. "You don't think I know that? The only reason I was even in Atticus's apartment was because I was following *your* advice."

I snorted. "Yeah, five months after the fact. And in the meantime, I have to put up with your precious 'crushes' and your ridiculous expectation that no one else is allowed to touch them even though you're too much of a chicken-shit to do anything about it."

"That's a lie, and you know it."

"Is it, though?" I challenged him. "This isn't a new pattern for you, Jasper. You've been doing it for our whole lives. You go through crushes like you're binge-reading a series, but I can't so much as look at the cover without you getting bent out of shape. Even after you moved on, it was never worth pursuing any of the guys you'd crushed on. Not without risking that I would succeed where you had failed."

"Why is that my fault? If you really felt that way, why didn't you *say* something?"

"And what was I supposed to say? You took me in when I was homeless. Gave me a life. How could I risk jeopardizing that after already losing so much?"

"Wow." He shook his head and gave a humorless laugh. "*Wow.* I don't know, Mason, maybe you could have trusted me to be your fucking friend."

Hearing him curse was like a slap in the face. It took me a moment to rally, and I should have taken another to consider my words before I let them spill out of my mouth. "And how the hell was I supposed to do that when you consistently act like an immature teenager when it comes to anything remotely serious? For fuck's sake, you're thirty and still can't seem to get your life together—personal or professional. Take some fucking responsibility instead of waiting for someone else to do it for you."

Red splotches bloomed on his cheeks, and he balled his hands into fists at his sides. "Maybe the reason you think I'm so childish is because you keep treating me like one."

"It's not like you've ever given me a reason not to," I fired back.

"You've got some nerve to say that to me. I'm not the one who went behind their supposedly best friend's back. I'm not the one who *lied* for months. And I'm not the one currently acting like an immature teenager sneaking around. All I've done is be there for you since the day you came to live with us. I cancelled plans because I didn't want you to feel lonely. I helped with your art installation at the bookstore. *I have done everything for *you*.*"

I rolled my eyes. "Please, let's not pretend you bailed on that art show for any other reason than being scared of having to be responsible for your own damn career. You're getting *paid* for that art piece. And as for 'doing everything for me', I don't know who you think you're fooling. You brought me home like some wayward *dog* you found wandering the streets. You barely even knew me. That wasn't for me. You did that for *you*."

"Are you fucking kidding me! No one made you stay. No one *made* you be my friend. Those were your decisions," he snarled.

"Like I could have made any other. I was fifteen, alone and scared. My entire family turned on me, treated me like I was completely worthless. In the span of one afternoon, everything I'd ever known was *gone*. My parents, my siblings, any sense of security or belonging." I paused in my tirade to suck in deep lungfuls of air. "You never could understand that. Eventually, I realized you didn't *want* to. It would ruin the perfect fantasy you'd built in your head."

His eyes widened with indignant outrage. "What fantasy?"

"The one where you have a loyal lapdog you call a friend. Someone so beholden to you they'd never consider leaving."

His mouth opened and closed a few times before settling into a grim line and a death stare. After an unbearably tense standoff, he threw up his hands. "Forget this. I have better things to do than fight for a friendship you clearly don't want. At least now I know how you really feel after all these years. But hey, at least you don't have to worry about not having a roof over your head."

I recoiled at his vehemence and dropped my head as the acid of shame ate away at me. He was right. I'd been so consumed with fear of losing everything again that I'd gone out of my way never to upset him. We *hadn't* been friends when he brought me to his home. But then we *were* friends, and I didn't let go of that fear. I'd been clinging to it, letting it define me, define our friendship. Sure, he played a part, but at the end of the day, the disaster I found myself in was entirely of my own making.

"Jasper, I..." I let out a heavy breath. How did I even begin to fix any of this? The distinct sound of footsteps filled the silence. "Jasper?" I looked up, but he was already halfway to the front door. "Jasper, wait." I rushed to catch up with him.

He paused with his hand on the doorknob and turned his head to the side without looking at me. "I'm done. I hope you have the life you deserve." With that final vindictive comment, he opened the door and left. The door slammed shut, and all my fears crashed down on me. Unable to bear the weight of losing the last person I considered family, I crumpled to the ground, right there in the entry hallway.

I wasn't sure how much time passed before I could drag my sorry ass into the living room, where it took a Herculean effort to get onto the couch. Once I was situated on the cushions, I wrapped a blanket around myself and burrowed deep into the depression and self-loathing that had dogged my heels for months. Not even the persistent ringing of my phone could pull me out of my fugue state. It wasn't Jasper. It wouldn't be Jasper. Once again, my decisions had stripped me of my family.

"Mason?"

I huddled deeper into myself. It was likely my imagination that it was Atticus calling to me. Guilt surged like a tidal wave at the *hope* that it was him. But that wouldn't make sense. He'd been here this morning, then had left for a standing family lunch. We hadn't made plans for him to come back.

"Sunshine?"

Yes, definitely a manifestation of my misery. A fully deserved misery. I'd destroyed a fifteen-year friendship, and for what? The *chance* of a relationship? Thrown away my entire second family, because I wanted to feel special? There was nothing special about what I'd done unless you counted how spectacularly I'd betrayed my best friend.

I looked up at a sudden sharp intake of air. It took a few blinks to focus the blurry image in front of me. "Oh. You are here."

In the blink of an eye, Atticus went from standing on the opposite side of the room to hovering in front of me, concern etched deeply into his face. "Mason, are you okay?"

I shook my head and turned my head to the side. He was so beautiful, and kind, and sweet. He loved me. And I didn't deserve any of it. Didn't deserve him.

He moved to sit beside me, putting him back in my line of sight. Immediately my eyes stung. "What happened?" he asked, brushing the hair back from my face.

My lip trembled as I looked into his worried gaze. In a whisper that was closer to a croak, I said, "I've ruined everything." Then I broke. Great heaving sobs tore through me, and I collapsed into his arms. Fresh waves of guilt crashed over me at so desperately wanting that comfort when it was that want which had led me to this point.

"Sh, I'm right here," he crooned over and over while he rubbed my back and I completely fell apart. He continued to hold me even after the tears stopped and silence overtook the room. When he finally pulled away, it was only to wipe my face with the hem of his shirt.

"You shouldn't be so nice to me." I ducked my head, ashamed of myself.

He gently tilted my chin up. "How about I be the judge of that, hmm?"

"You don't understand. I'm a terrible person. Maybe that's the real reason my dad kicked me out. It wasn't just that I was gay, but he could see what a horrible person I was inside."

Atticus's brow furrowed, and anger flashed in his eyes. "I don't believe that for a second. Why would you possibly believe that?"

"Because good people don't go after the guy their best friend fancies. And they certainly don't lie about it for months on end," I admitted bitterly.

"What are you talking about? I barely know your best friend. Half the time I barely remember his name. Hell, this morning is the most we've ever spoken."

"Haven't you ever wondered why that is? Why I've never set up a time for all of us to get together? He lives across the hall, for fuck's sake. It's not like it would take even minimal effort for the three of us to be in the same space." Self-directed anger made my tone sharp, bordering on cruel. "I knew he wanted you, and I selfishly pursued you anyway."

Atticus frowned, amplifying his confused expression. "Okay, but he's never said or done anything to give me the impression that he was interested."

"That doesn't matter!" I shouted, my hurt and anger getting the better of me. "*I* knew. Jasper is supposed to be my best friend. He's practically my brother. He gave me a life, a *family*, when I thought

I'd lost mine and never asked for anything in return. And I still stabbed him in the back."

"That seems a bit harsh."

I looked at him in disbelief. "I went out of my way to hide our relationship. From the moment we interacted in the hallway outside his apartment until this morning, I have done everything in my power to make sure he didn't find out. I've kept you like a dirty secret. The person I was afraid of running into at the Mist Wood Springs Art Festival? It wasn't the random ex I let you believe it was. I didn't want Jasper to see us together. So I hid, and I made you hide. If all of that doesn't make me a terrible friend and human, I don't know what does."

"But, Mason—"

"No, Atticus. Just... no." I abandoned the comfort of his embrace to sink in on myself once again. "I think... I think you should go."

He placed a hand on my shoulder, and I fought the urge to lean into him. "I'm sure we can work through this."

"There's nothing to work through," I mumbled, refusing to meet his beseeching gaze.

His gasp might as well have been a razor blade across my heart. "Please don't do this." The couch shifted as he vacated his seat. "Mason, please." I buried my face in my arms so I couldn't see my heartbreak reflected in his eyes. "You don't have to do this. I love you," he added in a broken whisper.

"Please. Just... go."

Chapter 26

My entire body was shaking as I made my way out of Mason's house, softly shutting the door behind me. I didn't understand. Everything had been perfect this morning. *Better* than perfect. He told me he loved me. Had he not meant it? Only saying it because I had?

I stumbled down the paved path toward the street. Once I got my balance, I pulled out my cell phone, nearly throwing it across the front lawn in my haste to free it from my pocket. Anxiety continued to tighten around my chest as I pulled up my favorited contacts. But who to call? I couldn't call Carmen. Not after gushing about being so fucking happy and in love this morning when she'd picked me up. Or after making her drop everything and bring me back when Mason didn't answer his phone for several hours.

Of course, who would pick me up wasn't my only problem. I couldn't bring myself to return to my apartment either. Jasper lived across the hall. Jasper, the man I'd been so excited to get to know as Mason's best friend, and who had effectively torpedoed our relationship. Logically, I knew it wasn't actually his fault that Mason kicked me to the curb. I *knew* that. But that didn't stop me from wanting to blame him.

Mason broke up with me.

The crystal-clear thought was a veritable gut-punch of heartache. It was enough to make my breathing falter, and suddenly I was struggling to drag in more than sip-fulls of air. I squinted at the screen, my vision increasingly blurry with tears I fought to keep in check. I just needed to hold it together a little longer. Desperation had me pressing a name at the top of the list. To my surprise and relief, it wasn't Carmen who answered.

"Sup, boss?" Maria answered in her usual chipper tone.

"I n-need you to p- pi-... come get me," I stuttered out through increasingly violent shaking.

"Where are you?"

I could have wept at her lack of twenty questions. Bless Maria and her ability to be serious at the drop of a hat. "I'll text the address." No way in hell would I be able to say "Mason's house" or his name at all, not in my current state.

"I've got it. Be there in five." She ended the call before I could say more, which, honestly, I wasn't remotely mad about. Now I just had to make sure I didn't pass out from hyperventilating before she got here.

Had five minutes always been so long? I checked my phone—again. Sure enough, we'd just hit the four-minute mark. My efforts at measured breaths were failing. Each time I thought about what he'd said, how he turned away from me, they shortened a little more. Then someone was hugging me and encouraging me to shuffle forward. They even buckled my seatbelt. It wasn't until I heard a car door slam that I realized it wasn't all in my head. For a fleeting second, I thought it was Mason, that I'd imagined the whole breakup, and we were still stupidly fucking in love. Reality came in the form of a light bronze face with worried brown eyes and a halo of bright pink hair.

"I'm right here, Atticus. Everything is going to be okay." It wouldn't be, but it was nice of her to say. Maria put her car in gear and pulled away from the curb. "To your apartment?"

The thought of catching even a glimpse of Jasper made my pulse quicken and fucked up my losing battle with hyperventilating. I vehemently shook my head in the negative.

"Okay, um, your parents'?" she asked uncertainly, and I shook my head again. "Wait. Duh. I can take you to Mason's."

It was the final crack in the thin wall I'd erected between myself and the overwhelming hurt. The last syllable of his name left her lips, and the wall shattered. I drug in a ragged breath and shattered right along with it. I gripped the seatbelt angled across my chest like a lifeline as great, heaving sobs tore at my body.

"Oh shit. That was his house, wasn't it? No, don't answer that. Holy fuck, Atticus." She flicked the blinker on, and we made a right turn. I fought the urge to look back, though I knew it'd be impossible to see his house now. "Okay, here's what I'm going to do. You clearly don't want to be at your place for some reason, and I totally get why you wouldn't want to go to your parents', especially with your sister staying there. I'm taking you back to mine. And not a damn word about how messy it is. I've got a pullout bed you can use until we figure everything out. And by 'we' I mean, you tell me what the fuck is going on and who I have to kill."

The days of the week became meaningless. I eventually went back to my apartment, first for a few clothes, then for good. Not that I was spending more time there than absolutely essential. I'd heard

Jasper's voice a handful of times and knew without a doubt I couldn't handle seeing him, or whoever might be with him. Now I practically lived at the hot shop. I worked until the small hours of the morning, dragged my ass home for a shower and a few Z's, then went straight back to work.

On the bright side, my bank account was looking better than ever, both from the increased project output and from foregoing my guilty pleasures. I was careful not to look too closely at any of Kaleidoscope Coffee's patrons whenever I had to walk by the shop. I also wasn't bringing food to the Sunday family lunch, because I wasn't going. The downside of working as close to twenty-four-seven as my body would allow was that the commissions ran out, leaving me with nothing left to focus on. Like now.

Unwilling to risk an idle mind, I dug into the original creations. I should have remembered. The only original in progress was the glass sculpture I'd been making for Mason. Technically, it was finished and only needed to be assembled.

I didn't feel in charge of my body as I carefully relocated each part to the worktable. Then I spent an inordinate amount of time painstakingly putting it together. I had to string the light fragments together, attach them to the sun, and lastly hang it all from arced water. All without breaking any of the delicate pieces.

It was every bit as beautiful as I knew it'd be. The way the light caught the colored glass to form a rainbow between the sun and the water was breathtaking. I'd been planning to give it to Mason once I'd told him how I felt. A physical representation of my love for him. It was absolutely perfect.

I hated everything about it.

A burst of anger flooded me with heat. I grabbed the base of the custom piece that I'd devoted hours upon hours to and hefted it off the table. It was a testament to how much of a workout I'd been getting that I could lift it high over my head. Fragments of light twinkled around the shop as I hurled it at the nearest blank wall. The violent crash sent shards of glass flying and sound smashing into the walls. It was almost enough to obscure a gasp of surprise.

I didn't look toward the door. I had a feeling I knew who it would be. Instead, I stood there with my fists clenched at my sides while I glared at the shattered remains of my beautiful piece, which felt like the perfect metaphor for the disaster I called my love life. An ache blossomed in my chest, intensifying until it became acute. I stumbled back a step and dropped my head into my hands as yet another wave of grief pulled me down. Fuck, I was so tired of crying. I was so tired of hurting.

"Atticus," Carmen said softly by my shoulder. "Come on, let's get you seated and some water."

"Go away," I grumbled, though I allowed her to guide me to the workshop table and the few chairs there.

"Yeah, no can do, big guy." She pressed on my shoulder hard enough to make me sit, then retrieved my neglected water bottle. "You've avoided me long enough. Maria filled me in on what she knows, but I'd like to hear it from you."

Of course, she did. I wiped my nose with the back of my hand and briefly contemplated wiping it on her. That was about as "obnoxious kid brother" as it could get. Maybe if I did, she'd leave me to my heartbreak in peace. Rather than be gross, I settled for frowning at her.

"You know, Atty," she began as she pulled one of the other chairs closer, "I have to admit I'm really hurt that you called Maria and not me."

I gave up my glower, which obviously wasn't working, to stare at my clasped hands on the table. "Why would I want to compound my humiliation?"

She sighed, resting her hand on my forearm. "Okay, I get that. But I would hope that after spending these last few months getting closer that you'd know I would never tease you over something you have no control over. Or—"

"Was it out of my control?" I interrupted bitterly. "Why didn't I push to be introduced to his circle? Looking back, it doesn't make any sense. He talked about Jasper all the time."

"Um, who's Jasper? Is that someone I should already know?"

"Yes," I deadpanned. Then I let out a defeated sigh and added, "Jasper is his best friend." Carmen remained unusually quiet. I turned my head to look at her and was surprised to find her scrutinizing me with unmistakable concern. "What?"

She licked her lips, her gaze darting away from mine before returning with a glint of stubborn conviction. "Is that all he is?" She raised her eyebrows for emphasis that was lost on me.

"What are you talking about?"

Her gaze softened. "Please don't make me say it."

My realization of what she was asking hit me like the glass hit the wall. I'd have laughed if I still could. This was one worry I'd never entertained. "They were more than friends, but not in the way you're suggesting. More like brothers than lovers."

"And you're sure about that?"

"Positive," I replied without hesitation.

She smacked her thighs and popped out of her chair. "Okay then, I'm going to need context. And that context needs a drink. Up and at 'em, Atty."

Carmen all but dragged me out of the hot shop and into the truck. From there, she navigated to the Twisted Pine Brewery, where she promptly ordered beers and bar food without asking if I wanted any of it. Once they arrived, she gave me an expectant look, and I gave her the context she'd requested. We stayed until it was dark out as I told her everything over several beers and two more orders of food.

Chapter 27

I'D HAVE BEEN SURPRISED at how quickly Jasper seemed to forgive me if I hadn't also been so desperately relieved. I couldn't lose my family again. I just... couldn't. Thankfully, we'd said most of what we should have said *years* ago during our shouting match. All that remained was to apologize, promise each other to do better, and go back to the way things had always been. Before Atticus.

The days bled together in a haze of routine. Wake up. *Don't text Atticus.* Respond to Jasper's midnight messages. *Remember to show an interest in his latest art project.* Get dressed. *Avoid wearing clothes that remind me of Atticus.* Stop by Kaleidoscope for a coffee fix. *Pretend I'm not secretly hoping I'll run into Atticus.* Continue rearranging shelves at the bookstore. *Try not to think about how instrumental Atticus had been in making that happen.* Check in or hang out with Jasper. *Pray I'm not expected to be social or smile.* Go home and stay busy until I'm too exhausted to stay awake. *Lie in bed, failing not to think about Atticus, wondering how he's doing, and hating myself for hurting him.* Then, in the silence before sleep claims me, listen to my heartbreak again and again. Rinse and repeat.

Today was no different from any of the other dozen or so days before with the small exception that it was Thursday. At least, I was pretty sure it was Thursday. That in itself wasn't what was remarkable. That it coincided with the Literary Lighthouse owner's biannual visit was.

I couldn't decide if it was a blessing in disguise that the store was unusually slow today or if the lack of patrons would ultimately hurt my cause. Not that worrying would do any good. Mr. Forester would be here any minute, and it wasn't like we could magically put the store back to the way it was. Still.

"Relax," Mickey said beside me.

I snorted. *Relax?* I hadn't been relaxed in weeks. At the rate I was fucking up my life, Mr. Forester was likely to walk in, take one look, and fire me for going behind his back.

"Seriously, this place looks incredible. Not to mention we have the proof to back up the changes," Mickey insisted.

"I know. I just…"

The door to the bookstore opened, letting the crisp autumn air inside to ruffle the pages of the books on display. An elderly gentleman with a head of tight silver curls, dark deep brown skin textured with countless fine wrinkles, and a warm smile stood in the entry as the door swung shut behind him.

"Mr. Forester. Welcome in. Always a pleasure to see you," I said, stepping out of the line of employees that had gathered to greet him. Out of the corner of my eye, I saw Denise give a shy wave while Mickey smiled enthusiastically. Fuck, I really hoped he was right and Mr. Forester liked what we'd done. "How are you doing today?"

He grinned as he shook my hand. "Woke up still breathing. Can't complain." His gaze swept the breadth of the store, and he raised an eyebrow. "I see you've made a few changes."

I shoved down the demented desire to laugh hysterically and cleared my throat. "About that—"

"It's about damn time, my boy." Mr. Forrester clapped me on the back, and I stumbled a step. No one in their late eighties had any business being that strong.

"So... you like it?" I asked cautiously.

"That remains to be seen. But I'm glad you've finally put your own touch on things. Was starting to think you never would, no matter how much backstock I insisted you to have on the floor."

I nearly swallowed my tongue. "You were doing that *on purpose?*" I spluttered.

He shrugged and tapped the side of my leg with his cane, which seemed to be more for appearances than out of any need. "Now show me what you've done to the place." He glanced at Mickey and Denise. "Did either of you assist in this remodel?"

To my surprise, Denise stepped forward. She struck quite the image with her blond hair pulled back in a tight ponytail, her shoulders squared, and her apron as impeccable as ever. "We both did, sir. And if I may add, Mr. Mason is an amazing manager, and the changes he's implemented have increased both foot traffic and overall sales. Now, even with the overflow, we can't keep some sections fully stocked."

"That's quite an interesting problem to have. Thank you, Denise, for being forthright and an invaluable member of this team." It was clear from the startled expression on her face that she clearly hadn't expected Mr. Forester to know who she was, let alone praise her. He gestured toward the store with his free hand. "Mr. Albright, if you would kindly lead the way. I'm eager to see what you've done."

I slowly released a shaky breath and nodded before turning to my right to begin the tour through the rearranged shelves. We spent the rest of the day going through the changes we'd made as well as plans I had for a spotlight section featuring local authors. He not only fully supported the idea, but finally caved to my request for an updated point of sale system with the caveat that the antique register remain as a store feature.

Traffic in the store had picked up by the time Mr. Forester was leaving, giving him the opportunity to see the new arrangement in action. He was obviously pleased with everything we did, and I knew I should be ecstatic, but all I felt was numb. Even half an hour after he'd gone, the most I could bring myself to do was stare blankly at an inventory report on my desk. There were likely a million and one things I *should* be doing, but... yeah.

"Holy crap, that's amazing!" an all too familiar excited voice exclaimed from the front of the store. Deeply ingrained reflex had me securing the reports and venturing to the front before I realized what I was doing.

"Hello Jasper." Could he hear how hollow I sounded? Did he care? I clenched my jaw at the ugly thought. It was cruel and unfair.

He glanced at Mickey and Denise, who were hovering by the counter. His jovial grin faltered before he pinned it firmly back in place. "So, um, he liked everything? Even the art? Because if he doesn't, I can totally change it. I'd hate for anything I did to come back on you."

"Oh," Denise piped up, "Mr. Forester was very impressed."

"That's, um, good," Jasper replied, darting an anxious look at me. I almost sighed in exasperation. I didn't know how else to reassure him that our friendship was solid.

Mickey walked around Denise, bringing him closer to me. "We've got things handled. Why don't you duck out early? I'd say you've earned it," he suggested. Jasper's face noticeably lit up at the prospect, which basically guaranteed the outcome.

"As long as you're sure…" I looked askance at Mickey and Denise.

"We're very sure." Denise gave me an encouraging grin. "Go on. Enjoy the rest of your day."

"Um, okay. I just need to—" Mickey dropped a small stack that included my phone, lunchbox, and water bottle, on the counter, though I didn't know when he'd moved to retrieve them. "Get my things," I finished awkwardly. If I didn't know any better, I'd think they were trying to get rid of me. Not that I could blame them given the funk I'd been in since the breakup.

Jasper helpfully gathered my things and walked toward the exit, forcing me to trail after him. "Come on, I'm rescheduling movie night to right now."

"Why?" I asked as we walked to my car.

He gave me a long look. "Because I think you need it. Now, A or B?"

I wanted to argue that I didn't *need* anything, but like so many other things these days, I couldn't muster an appropriate level of give-a-damn. "B, I guess."

"Excellent. Pizza it is."

I started the car and turned in the direction that would take us to Brickyard Oven. "Out of curiosity, what was A?"

He glanced up from his phone with a cheeky grin. "Also pizza."

I snorted. "You could have just said you wanted pizza."

"Where's the fun in that?" he countered. He glanced up as I pulled into a parking space. "Wait." He placed a hand on my arm to stop me from continuing to get out. "I placed the order online. We can sit here until they message that it's done."

"Okay. And do what while we wait? You know it can take up to thirty minutes to get a fresh pie. Sometimes longer," I added belatedly.

He fiddled with a loose thread on his sweater. "I was kind of hoping we could talk."

The frustrated sigh I'd repressed earlier escaped. "What do you want from me, Jasper? I've told you we're fine."

"Except we're not. *You're* not."

"What the hell is that supposed to mean? I'm here, we're hanging out, and about to have movie night like always." I gripped the steering wheel, leaning forward to rest my forehead on the worn fabric. "I don't know what else I can do to convince you."

"Did you break up with Atticus?"

I fought back a surge of anger. As if he had any right to ask me that. "Of course I did. You won. What else could you possibly want?"

He looked as if I'd slapped him with a wet fish. "What I..." he spluttered. "I *never* asked you to do that. Would never."

It was impossible to keep the sneer from my voice. "Didn't stop you from making it really fucking clear that it was the right thing to do." He opened his mouth to say fuck only knew what, and his phone beeped. A quick look revealed the notification that our order was ready. "Look, can we please drop this already? We're fine. I'm fine. Or I will be. I just need time. Okay?"

"Okay."

"Good. Now I'm going inside to grab the pizza, and you can put together a list of movies for tonight. Just please no rom-coms." I waited for him to nod before getting out of the car.

If I expected our movie night to be like normal, I was not only depressed but daft as well. I also hadn't expected Jasper's solution to "no rom-coms" to be a collection of horror movies that had us turning on all the lights in the apartment and clinging to each other in fear. Then again, at least a movie about a possessed autopsy where everyone died didn't shove someone else's happy ending in my face.

I opted not to stay the night for a multitude of reasons, the most obvious of which was that I wasn't sure I could handle running into Atticus in the hall like when we'd met. Though we had forgone any alcohol. Possibly our only wise decision of the entire marathon. But as I pulled up to my dark, painfully empty house, I second-guessed my decision to leave.

"Whatever," I grumbled to myself. "If a chainsaw-wielding serial killer shows up at my door, I'll deal with it." I hadn't even made it to the kitchen when there was a loud pounding at my door. Mercifully, no one was around to see me jump, though whoever was on the other side of the door undoubtedly heard me squeal like a terrified toddler.

I mustered what little remained of my dignity and crept back toward the front door. Inches from peering through the peephole, another round of knocks shook the door. I gripped my chest where my heart was doing an admiral job of trying to break through my ribs.

"I know you're in there, Mason. Open the damn door."

With my serial killer fears abated, I yanked open the door. "Carmen? Were you *trying* to scare me to death?"

"Maybe not to death," she said as she pushed past me.

Well, there was absolutely nothing disconcerting about that. I shut the door and followed her deeper into the house. "What, uh... what are you doing here?"

She paused mid-rummaging through my fridge to give me a scathing look. "Why the fuck do you think I'm here?" She turned back to the fridge, emphasizing the rhetorical nature of the question. "This is just fucking sad," she declared, shutting the door none too gently. I winced, feeling the words encompassed a lot more than my pathetic lack of food.

"There's some chips in the cabinet," I offered half-heartedly.

"They'll have to do." She helped herself to the bag of potato chips and a glass of water, then made her way to the living room, where I was still standing and feeling lost.

"Carmen, I... I'm not sure what you want me to say."

She settled herself in my sole armchair. "I don't want you to say anything. I want you to sit down and listen."

"Okay..." It should probably say something that I was more scared of hearing what she had to say than I was of the horrors I'd watched that evening.

"And to make sure you stay quiet, these are for you." She pushed the chips and water across the coffee table toward me.

"But I'm not—" I immediately shut my mouth at her sharp look and promptly sat down. Beneath her watchful eye, I opened the bag and stuffed a few chips in my mouth.

She gave an approving nod and settled back in her chair. "I don't want to know why you broke things off with Atticus. He already filled me in. And, honestly? I kind of get it. I'm not in any way, shape, or form condoning it, but I can see your logic. A logic that I might add is incredibly fucked up."

"I know."

She leaned forward so abruptly, I almost dropped the bag of chips. "See, it's that shit right there. I know you know. Just like I know you broke my little brother's goddamn heart. And like how I know I shouldn't have skipped the 'if you hurt him, I hurt you and no one will find the body' big-sister-chat."

I swallowed thickly and reached for the water.

"What I don't know is what the fuck you're waiting for."

"I don't know what you mean. Waiting for what?" I asked with no small amount of trepidation.

Carmen rested her forearms on her thighs. Her hair swung around her face as she shook her head. "If you're expecting him to fight for you or make some grand gesture to prove his love, one—that's total bullshit, and two—he won't. I love Atty dearly, but that's not in his character. You're the one who ended things, so you're the one who has to fix them."

I set the bag of chips beside the now half-empty glass of water. "And how the fuck am I supposed to do that? Whatever I do, I have to choose. I can either forfeit having a family—again, I might add—or I can be with the man I love."

"Mason, I'm going to tell you something, and I need you to really hear me." She paused, likely to see if I'd interrupt. When I didn't, she continued. "That's not a choice. No one who truly cared about you would ever ask you to make that decision."

I looked down at the faded carpet rug. "He didn't." I took a deep breath and met her confused gaze. "Jasper never asked me to choose."

"But I'll bet he didn't encourage you to go back to him, did he?" Carmen stared at me without blinking until I had to look away. "That's what I thought." She sighed heavily and slumped back in the chair. "I'm not just here as Atticus's sister."

"You're not?" I asked, more than a little surprised at her soft tone.

"No, Mason, I'm not. I'm also here as your friend. Which, God help me, I hope we still are." My nose stung with the sudden emotion flooding through me, but she wasn't finished. "Atty is a complete wreck, and from the look of you, you're not doing any better. So, I'm going to ask you again, Mason. What are you waiting for?"

Chapter 28

I STARED AT THE design I'd sketched out. It bore a disturbing resemblance to the piece I'd smashed. Maybe that was why I was unsatisfied with it. Or maybe it was because no matter what I tried to create, it always came back to Mason. I sighed heavily, sending loose scraps of paper fluttering across the worktable. Clearly, I was going about this all wrong.

"You sure you'll be alright?" Maria asked for the fifth time that day. "I can always stay."

"I'll manage fine," I replied without looking up. Maybe if I stared at it long enough, the answer would magically appear on the page.

Maria's footsteps as she made her way to the exit echoed in the otherwise quiet room. So I knew exactly when she stopped and turned to face me. "Okay, but—"

"Maria," I said firmly, finally straightening to look at her. "I get it. You're worried. But I'll. Be. Fine. You've been looking forward to this concert for weeks. Go. In case you forgot, I used to do all of this on my own before you came along." I gave her a reassuring smile. She didn't appear completely sold, and I honestly couldn't blame her. Neither was I. But I refused to let my heartache infect the lives of everyone else I cared about. "Go," I repeated with more emphasis. "Have fun. Come back and tell me all about it so I can gripe about how music these days just isn't the same."

"Díos. You're thirty-five, not eighty." I shrugged and smiled. It seemed we both believed it this time, because she shook her head and held up a hand. "Alright, alright. I get it. I'm being one of those helicopter friends. Don't hate me for it?"

"Never."

I watched her spin on her heel and make her way out of the hot shop. Once she was gone, I got up and cleared the table of my failed designs. From there, I spent a few minutes puttering around, cleaning, organizing, and generally giving my mind a reprieve. When I ran out of delaying tactics, I resumed my seat at the worktable with a new sketchpad, freshly sharpened pencils, and some cool water. Then I did something I almost never do—I let the pencil roam without a defined purpose.

If I felt like making a curve, I did. The same with straight lines and switching colors. A peaceful quiet settled over me while I sketched. Only the scritch and smooth drag of colored wax across paper broke the silence. I wasn't sure I knew what I was drawing, and I had no intention of stepping back to find out. Getting lost in the motions was what I was really after. It probably shouldn't have surprised me when I finally paused for longer than it took to use the restroom and refill my water that it had gotten late.

Feeling every inch the old man I'd implied I was to Maria, I stood and stretched my arms high overhead. I'd just dropped them back to my sides when the soft scuff of a shoe on the concrete floor reached my ears. I immediately turned to face the front of the hot shop, fully expecting it to be Maria or Carmen come to remind me that food and sleep were not optional.

"Hello Atticus." Even with no sound to compete with, Mason's voice sounded small.

My gaze unwittingly travelled over his familiar body, making my heart ache and my hands itch with the desire to touch him. He was still beautiful. Funny enough, he looked like he was also treating food and sleep as optional. He needed to take better care of himself. A role I'd happily fill if he'd let me. Fuck, I missed him.

"I'm sure you don't want me here, but—"

"No!" The objection rang through the room, and I winced. "Sorry. I didn't mean to shout. Stay. Please." Carmen no doubt would have a myriad of colorful things to say about how this was a terrible idea, but I couldn't find it in me to send him away. Even if it was the smart thing to do.

He cleared his throat and stepped closer. "I've thought a lot about what I would say to you, what I *should* say. None of it came close to being enough to make up for the way I behaved or the way I've treated you. Not just these last few weeks, but months." He stopped to drag in a lungful of air, then abruptly covered his face with his hands. "Ugh. I'm already fucking this up," he muttered.

"Maybe you should sit down. I could get you some water." I didn't register that I was walking closer to him until I stopped and realized we were close enough to touch.

"You're always so kind," he said with a sad smile, "even when I don't deserve it. There's something wrong with me." I immediately opened my mouth to argue, and he amended, "Not *wrong*-wrong. More like not fully healed. I thought I was past the trauma of losing my family, but I'm starting to think I never worked through it at all. That I've avoided it like I've avoided anything else that might generate conflict. Don't suppose you know a good therapist you could recommend?" His uncertain smile had my heart fluttering with hope.

"First, you didn't *lose* your family. Your family left *you*. Second, of course. I know several local therapists. Some of whom specialize in childhood trauma." Not that I'd seen all of them. Just most of them.

A tear streaked down his cheek, and he gave a watery laugh as he quickly wiped it away. "See what I mean? You're so fucking kind, and I miss you so damn much. I don't know how I ever thought leaving you was the right thing to do." Tears streamed freely down his face now, and his laughter took on a hysterical edge.

Unable to take it anymore, I closed the distance between us, wrapping him in my arms. The sheer rightness of holding him threatened to break my heart all over again, only the growing hope filling it kept the abused organ together. "Mason, what are you saying?" I asked after a few seconds to give him a chance to settle. Fear battled with stubborn hope while I waited for his response.

"I don't want to be broken up. I don't want to be the type of person who does what I did to the man he loves," he said, twisting his hands in my shirt and burying his face against my shoulder. Mason sniffled, his hold relaxing as if he intended to step away. No way was I about to let him go now. I tightened my arms around him. "And I know I don't have any right to ask you to forgive me or take me back, but I *needed* you to know how sorry I am. That I—"

I pulled away enough to put a hand over his mouth and look into his shimmering blue eyes. "Do you really mean that? You really want to get back together?" He nodded and sniffled again. I removed my hand so I could wipe away his tears. I hated to see him cry. "Would you believe me if I said I didn't want to be broken up either?"

"But why?" His eyes reflected the broken agony in his voice.

"Because I love you, Mason. You make me happier than I've ever been. I like to think I do the same for you," I admitted with a half smile.

"You do, Atticus. I'm so, so sorry for everything. I wish I could go back and fix the mess I made. Clearly, I need professional help, and who knows how many people I've taken my issues ou—"

A smile broke across my face. This time I put a finger on his lips to stop his rambling. "I love you, Mason Albright, and if it's alright with you, I'd like to keep loving you. I tried doing the other, but turns out I'm pretty shit at not being in love with you." I cradled his face. "What do you say, Sunshine? Wanna give us another go? Without secrets this time."

"Yes," he blurted with a watery hiccup. "Please, yes. Whatever it takes to make things right, I'll do it. I just want you back in my life."

I rested my forehead against his. "You have me. And you've already done the only thing I ever needed." He tilted his head back to look at me askance, and I couldn't resist rubbing my thumb along his mouth. "You're here."

"I never should have left. My head is seriously messed up."

Before he could really dig into the self-recrimination, I grabbed his hand and led him to the worktable where I encouraged him to sit. Once I'd grabbed some tissues—thank you, Maria—and got water for both of us, I resumed my previous seat. "You've already said you need help." I rested my hands, palm up, on the table and hoped my relief didn't show when he took them. "It's hard admitting you need help, and it can be even harder asking for it. This is a really big step. Don't discount that."

"The whole 'the first step is admitting you have a problem' thing, really?" he asked with a laugh that, while wet, was also genuine. My Sunshine was still in there.

"It may be a cliché, but that doesn't make it less true." I squeezed his hands. "We'll find someone you jibe with who can help you get to a place where your trauma stops making decisions for you."

His eyebrows pinched together. "What do you mean?"

"Much in the same way I have an anxiety attack whenever something happens that reminds me of Jessica's death. I believe it was your trauma that made the decision for us to separate. Not you." I studied him to see what he thought about that.

His mouth opened and closed a few times. He tried to tug his hands back, but short of him point blank asking, I wasn't letting him go. "But... but if you really believe that, why did you listen?"

I lifted one of his hands to place a kiss on his knuckles. "Because decisions deserve to be honored, even if I don't agree with why you're making them."

"What did I ever do to deserve you?" He rubbed his thumbs along the back of my hand, his gaze fixed on the small movement.

"Hey. Look at me," I said gently. When he did, I couldn't help but smile softly. He was here, and we were going to work through this together. As for therapy, I'd be there to back him up every step of the way. "You didn't have to *do* anything. Love isn't something you have to constantly earn, Mason." His eyes brimmed with tears once more, but he didn't look away. "You're you. That's enough. *You're* enough."

I wasn't surprised when he broke down again. He had a long road ahead of him to heal not only his past hurts but also every-thing that had developed because of them. I vacated my seat once more and moved to stand in front of him. We clung to each other until he'd cried himself out. Unlike before, these sobs sounded more cathartic than painful. My eyes didn't exactly stay dry either.

"Okay. We're doing this. Again. With honesty." He pulled back and wiped his face with the remaining tissues. "In the interest of honesty, I'm still friends with Jasper."

"I wouldn't expect you not to be."

His shoulders relaxed as if he *had* expected me to have an issue with their continued friendship. "He, um... He doesn't know that I'm here. I didn't tell him. But I will. As soon as possible."

I laughed and brushed his golden hair back from his forehead. "Tomorrow's Friday. You could always tell him at movie night if you don't get a chance before then." His eyes widened almost comically, and he surged forward to wrap his arms around my neck and slammed his mouth against mine. I didn't hesitate to kiss him back.

"I think I might have an even better idea," he said, excitement making his inner light shine through. "Are you busy tomorrow night?"

"I'm free, but isn't the whole point—" Before I could finish my thought, he'd pulled out his phone, dialed a saved number, and put it on the table with the speaker on.

It rang twice, then a familiar voice answered. "Hey, Mace. Um, what's up? Are you okay? I know we have movie night tomorrow, but I can come over today if you want." My heart went out to him. Mine and Mason's relationship obviously wasn't the only one that had taken a major hit. It was comforting to hear Jasper sound just as worried about Mason as I was.

"It's about movie night, actually." Mason darted an excited look at me, though I still had no clue where he was going with this.

"Oh. Did you... want to cancel?"

I wondered if Mason could hear the fear in his best friend's voice. Best guess said he didn't, especially given the confused frown now wrinkling his brow.

"What? No. I actually... How would you feel about me inviting Atticus?" Mason bit his bottom lip and glanced from the phone to me. I shrugged in acceptance of the silent question.

"When you say 'invite Atticus' is that because you're planning to get back together? Holy snap! Are you already back together?"

Mason's laughter chased away the last of the darkness that had taken up residence around my heart. I leaned forward with a grin, maintaining eye contact with Mason as I asked, "So, is that a yes?"

"Atticus? Atticus! Dang it, Mason, you're supposed to tell people when they're on speakerphone," Jasper griped unconvincingly.

Mason hunched his shoulders in an obvious display of chagrin. "Oops, sorry about that."

"You didn't answer the question," I prodded.

"Answer the..." Jasper sounded mildly confused, then remembered what I'd asked. "Heck yes, that's a yes! Obvi." There was an unnerving pause. "Oh no."

"What do you mean 'oh no'?" Mason and I asked together with the same inflection of panic.

"Nothing like that!" Jasper responded quickly. "I have to clean my apartment. And I only have one day," he added with a whine.

I threw my head back and laughed like I hadn't in weeks. Mason chuckled as well, but was ready with a solution. "We could just have movie night at my place."

"Mason, I love you. You know that... Or, I hope you know that. But your place is going to stink of makeup sex. I'm gonna have to take a hard pass."

Fuck, if I laughed any harder, I was probably going to pass out. Meanwhile, Mason's face was doing a damn good impression of a beet.

"Jasper," he hissed.

"What? Look, I'd better get started cleaning now if there's any chance of this place being presentable by tomorrow night. Oh, before I go. Atticus?" Jasper said tentatively.

"What's up?" I asked, shooting Mason a questioning look, though he didn't appear to have an answer.

"I'm really looking forward to meeting my best friend's boyfriend." Okay, yeah, I was fucking beaming. "Right. That's my quota of extra-sappy for the day. I'll see you two tomorrow at the usual time. And, Mason, don't forget—"

"The Chinese," Mason finished for him with a smirk. "I know the drill. I'm going to grab some mocktails too."

I was pretty sure they exchanged pleasantries and goodbyes, but I was too busy staring at Mason with so much joy in my heart it was a wonder it didn't burst. "I love you."

A light pink returned to his cheeks. "I love you too."

Before he could say anything else, I closed the distance to press our lips together again. The tender kiss went a long way toward soothing the bruises on my heart. His eyes were still closed and a soft smile graced his lips when I finally pulled away. He blinked them open after a moment, and his gaze caught on the sketch I'd been working on.

"This is really pretty. What is it?" He spun the sketchbook around to get an upright view of what turned out to be an intricate rain cloud with the sun peeking out behind it and a rainbow beneath it.

Suddenly, I knew what was wrong with my designs now. Somewhere along the way, I'd put Mason on a pedestal, which wasn't fair to either of us. Yes, he brought light to my life and was my "Sunshine" in every sense, but he also had darkness just like the rest of us. When I finally made the suncatcher I wanted for him, it'd be a balance of light and dark, with hope forever shining between them.

"It's a suncatcher. For you."

He looked at me in astonishment. "But—" I raised an eyebrow, and he altered whatever he was going to say. "I'm honored. Thank you." He paused, and a goofy smile split his face. "Hot damn! I'm going to have my very own Atticus Garner Original." We shared a laugh and wrapped each other once more in a tight embrace.

"Would now be a bad time to point out that I'm starving?" I asked a little abashed.

He checked the time, the grin never leaving his face. "If we hurry, we might could snag whatever pastries Kaleidoscope has left before they close up for the night."

"Fuck yes." I moaned in anticipation of the deliciousness. "And a coffee," I added as we made our way out of the hot shop hand-in-hand, our fingers intertwined. "I don't care if I'm awake half the night. I've missed that place."

Mason chuckled and kissed my cheek as we stepped onto the sidewalk in front of the Artists' Co-Op. "Now I know what I'm going to do to help make up for what I did. *Not* because I have to, but because I want to. Look at it this way, you'll be getting random gifts of coffee and pastries for the foreseeable future," he said with a grin.

I smiled back at him. "You have a real knack for finding the silver lining in just about anything. But you know what?"

"What?"

"You're the only bright side I need." I tugged him close for a quick kiss. "Now let's go stuff ourselves with pastries."

247

Chapter 29

"WE'RE REALLY DOING THIS." Yep, still couldn't quite believe it, though it was a little late to be doubting the reality. "Oh, here, let me help you with that, Mrs. Garner." I rushed over to help Atticus's mom with several suspiciously familiar dishes.

"Thank you, Mason. And how many times do I have to say? Call me Betty." She gave me a stern look, and I smiled. "It should be Harve helping with these, but I fear he's gotten to talking." She shook her head and leaned to the side for me to relieve her.

The moment I took the majority from her, my suspicions were confirmed—more casseroles. "Carmen?" I guessed, leading the way toward the kitchen, where veritable mountains of food littered the counters. The relationship Carmen had with her dad was pretty amazing. Sometimes the envy got to me, but I was working on it, and thanks to Dr. Evie, I was actually making progress.

"Not quite," Betty said in a sly tone that instantly got my attention.

I stopped halfway out of the kitchen and spun to face her. "Well, don't hold out on me now. You and Jace are my best sources of gossip."

"Hush you." She lightly smacked my arm in a show of rebuke, then promptly leaned close to whisper, "He seems rather taken with young Will Stevenson. Yes, he does. Keeps finding reasons to invite him over. So far they've repaired the back porch, talked hours upon hours of football, and rearranged no fewer than three rooms. Next, I'm expecting him to coerce Will into helping him refinish the floors. Will's been at the house more often than not since Atty moved out. Poor Carmen is at her wit's end with it." The concern might have been more believable if Betty hadn't also been grinning like a cartoon villain.

Suddenly, arms wrapped around my waist from behind, and a head popped over my shoulder. "Ooh, are we talking about how Dad is trying to play matchmaker with Carmen and Will?"

"Hey, love," I said just for Atticus and kissed his cheek. He briefly squeezed my waist, and I leaned against his solid chest.

"I feel like someone should tell him his helping is hurting," Atticus said, continuing from his earlier question.

Betty shrugged her shoulders and did probably the worst job I'd ever seen at trying to play innocent. "I don't know if I'd say that. Caught her looking up rentals in the area."

"That's fantastic! I was really hoping she'd stay." I glanced at Atticus. He and Carmen had gotten really close during her recovery, and I knew how much her staying would mean to him. Not that I was entirely unbiased. Carmen had easily become one of my best friends. Which wasn't a thought I'd have had even a month ago. Every now and again, the concept of having more than one best friend still blew my mind a bit.

"Oop, here they come now. Disperse. We look like a cluck of gossipy hens." Betty made shooing motions until she'd herded Atticus and me into the living room. Then she scampered off to talk with Maria.

"Can you believe it?" Atticus whispered in my ear.

I looked around the room, taking in the joy around me. There was Barry from the hot shop talking with Casey from Literary Lighthouse. Over by the half bath in the hallway, Denise looked like she was on the verge of worshiping Carmen, who was undoubtedly regaling the young woman with tales of her corporate exploits. In the area we planned to make a reading nook, Casey and Barry were having a heated debate, likely about the newly proposed county library. And walking toward us was my first ever best friend.

"Little late to be asking that," I said with a wink. Teasing each other about how wild it was to be moving into a new place together had become somewhat of a game. One I was fairly sure I was winning. But we could tally points later. *After* all our housewarming guests went back to their own homes.

It was more difficult than I cared to admit, waiting for Jasper to reach us. But I also knew it was important not to fall into old co-dependent behaviors. I wasn't sure if it was "thanks to therapy" or "no thanks to therapy" that I understood now how I'd—we'd—twisted our identities into each other. I'd always been convinced that *any* distance between me and Jasper would result in losing him, losing our friendship. Now I could see how unhealthy that was for both of us. The trick was remembering when it counted.

"Do you know if something happened between Jasper and Carmen?" Atticus asked.

I stepped back from my introspection to focus on why Atticus might think that. The closer Jasper got to us, the closer he also got to where Carmen was standing. I doubt I would have recognized anything out of the ordinary if Atticus hadn't pointed out Jasper's odd behavior. For some reason, he kept giving Carmen nervous glances, and he was giving her as wide a berth as the limited space in the hallway would allow.

"I thought things had gone well when we introduced them," Atticus commented when Jasper nearly took out another housewarming in his quest not to get too close to Carmen.

"Same here. Carmen can be intimidating for sure, but she seemed on her best behavior when we all hung out." Worry lapped at my insides. Then Atticus pulled me closer to him, his warmth and surety washing over me.

With a deep breath, I released what I could of the building fear that all of this was doomed. Leaping to worst-case scenarios was what had caused all the drama to start with. If something truly was wrong, I'd have to trust Carmen and Jasper to be honest with us. Until then, worrying myself into a tizzy wouldn't be helping anyone.

I glanced at Atticus with a soft smile. "You really are my rock. You know that?"

"At least I'm not as fragile as glass," he teased, adding a quick peck to my cheek as I laughed.

"What's so funny?" Jasper asked when he finally reached us.

I rolled my eyes dramatically and tried to pretend I didn't notice how awkward the atmosphere felt with all three of us together. "Someone is telling glass puns."

"It wasn't a glass pun. It was an observation," Atticus grumbled, prompting Jasper to snicker.

"Better to just embrace the puns." Jasper lifted his camera, which was hanging by a thick strap across his body. I wasn't surprised he'd brought it and was kind of grateful *someone* was taking pictures. He gestured for us to stand closer together. "Okay, you two, time for your closeup."

We rearranged ourselves as he asked. I hated how warm my face was as I settled into what I hoped appeared to be a casual pose.

"Got it," Jasper said, lowering the camera enough to grin at us.

I glanced at Atticus. That was weird. Normally, you could hear the shutter. Not that it was abnormally loud, just distinguishable. I shook my head and grinned. It never failed to amaze me how camera-shy I could be, considering my best friend was a photographer. Suddenly the shutter snapped several times. I gave Jasper a startled look.

"Candid is always better," he said with a wink.

I was on the verge of rolling my eyes again when I spotted a new addition to the guests. "Oh, look. Dustin was able to make it after all." I glanced at Jasper, who was now absorbed in reviewing the digital images on his camera, then gave Atticus a conspiratorial smile. "Do you think you could help him get situated?"

Jasper glanced up, looking mildly confused, before making the connection that I was talking to him. "Uh, yeah. I'll get him sorted. Though goodness help us if he brought food. I told Mom you didn't need anymore casseroles. Don't think this gets you two out of more pictures, though," he said in what sounded more like a threat than a promise.

We gave him a pair of nervous smiles and watched as he wove through the crowd. Dustin's face lit up with obvious relief when Jasper stepped up to him, and Atticus chuckled. I spun to face him, looping my arms around his neck.

"And what do you find so amusing, my love?"

He wrapped his arms around my waist and nodded toward the now happily chatting pair. "How long do you think it will take for him to realize?"

I glanced over my shoulder. Jasper was talking animatedly, and Dustin was listening with rapt attention, his cheeks a subtle pink. I snorted. "You mean when will he realize Dustin has a massive crush on him? Let's just say it will take a lot more than blinking neon lights for him to catch on. It's funny, really. Well, ironic."

"How so?"

"He's always so busy having crushes himself, he can never see when someone has one on him. Then again, I think he might be done with crushes for a while." I snuggled my face into Atticus's broad chest. Jasper would be okay without me by his side twenty-four-seven. I had to believe that, or neither of us would ever be able to live our lives.

"Hey." Atticus leaned back enough for me to lift my head and look at him. "You know there's nothing wrong with having a crush?"

I sighed. "I know, but—"

"*Nothing* wrong," he emphasized.

"You really are just the best man I've ever met," I said with the cheesiest of grins.

He gave me a sweet kiss that I counted on being a whole lot less chaste later. "And you, my dazzling Sunshine, are the brightest."

Sam Bolanos (she/they) is a genderqueer author and founder of Chaotic Neutral Press LLC. They believe in love, equality, and the Oxford comma. When not playing with her three dogs or spending time with her incredible husband, she's probably agonizing over edits or escaping into her latest fantasy.

NEWSLETTER: SUBSCRIBE
WEBSITE: SBOLANOS.COM
FACEBOOK: @SBOLANOS
READER GROUP: SAM'S SUNBEAMS
INSTAGRAM: @SBOLANOSBOOKS
TIKTOK: @SBOLANOSBOOKS